Melanie

WW Norton /50

THE BEST OF THE WEST 5

ALSO EDITED BY JAMES THOMAS

Flash Fiction *(with Denise Thomas and Tom Hazuka)*
The Best of the West, 1–4 *(with Denise Thomas)*
Sudden Fiction International *(with Robert Shapard)*
Sudden Fiction *(with Robert Shapard)*

ALSO BY JAMES THOMAS

Pictures, Moving *(Stories)*

INTRODUCTION BY

William
Kittredge

THE
BEST
OF THE
WEST

New
Stories
from the Wide Side of
the Missouri

5

EDITED BY

James Thomas and Denise Thomas

W. W. NORTON & COMPANY · NEW YORK · LONDON

The editors would like to thank Ted Cains for his invaluable assistance in putting together this year's volume, Carol Houck Smith for her unerring direction and outstanding literary acumen, and Nat Sobel for his steady nerves and keen sense of balance.

The Acknowledgments on page 295 are an extension of the copyright page.

Printed in the United States of America.
First Edition

The text of this book is composed in Goudy Old Style, with the display set in Century Bold Condensed. Composition and manufacturing by the Haddon Craftsmen, Inc.

LIBRARY OF CONGRESS CATALOGING-IN-PUBLICATION DATA
The Best of the West 5 : new stories from the wide side of the
  Missouri / edited by James Thomas and Denise Thomas; introduction by
  William Kittredge.
      p.   cm.
    1. Western stories. 2. Short stories, American—West (U.S.)
  3. American fiction—20th century.   4. West (U.S.)—Fiction.
  I. Thomas, James, 1946–   . II. Thomas, Denise, 1954–
  III. Title: Best of the West five.
  PS648.W4B474 1992
  813'.087408—dc20   92-5473

ISBN 0-393-03431-3 (CL)
ISBN 0-393-30962-2 (PA)
W.W. Norton & Company, Inc., 500 Fifth Avenue, New York, N.Y. 10110
W.W. Norton & Company Ltd., 10 Coptic Street, London WC1A 1PU

1   2   3   4   5   6   7   8   9   0

Again, and as always, for Jesse and Christopher

CONTENTS

EDITORS' NOTE

The Best of the West series was started in 1987 and attempts each autumn to celebrate between the covers of one book the best "western" stories published the year before (between November and November). We also list and honor "other notable western stories" we much admired but were unable to include: a list, we are happy to note, that continues to grow (this year forty-eight, up from last year's thirty-eight).

Indeed, we are pleased to report that for this fifth volume of the series we had the happy task of choosing from the very strongest field of contending stories we have yet seen. It was not only a bumper year for "western" stories, in terms of quantity, but also in terms of high literary quality, a pleasant phenomenon we will leave to others (including William Kittredge in his introduction here) to ponder and explicate; but *could it be*, as Nathanial Ames has said, that ". . . the progress of humane literature (like the sun) is from the East to the West . . ."?

We also find it important to note openly that the reason for a story's inclusion as "western" in each year's volume is as much subjective as it is technical, with geographical location of the story in the western United States only part of the selection process; what we look for besides the highest literary quality and readability is a sense of the western *experience*, whether contemporary or historical. The American West, it has often been noted, is as much a state of mind as it is a mindful set of states—a *sensibility*, it would seem, born out of both its perpetual newness and its stubborn oldness, out of both its celebrated hospitality and its ability to be suddenly and brutally hostile, of both its beauty and its rawness. As the series title is meant to suggest, the stories we're looking for are as much "of" the West as simply set "in" the West. Call it a geography of the heart, a geocultural survey of a very real West which is being constantly explored and settled—as well as literally and literarily reinvented—in this country's artistic imagination.

In recent years it has also been often noted that the "western," as a genre of fiction, has taken on new meanings, has "come of age," and has become part of the college of literature as much more than department or a "region." In order to expand this discussion, and to extend the commentary, we are pleased to continue the practice (which we began last year) of providing "guest" introductions to *The Best of the West*. We are particularly pleased that this year's introductory essay is by William Kittredge, well known for both his fiction (short and long) and for his literary nonfiction inspired and informed by the West. The selection of the stories lies with us, the editors, and we think that together they reflect the vitality of recent western storytelling; but we are sure you will find Kittredge's essay an interestingly informative account of the contemporary western literary "scene," a panoramic overview of where we are now.

The process of selecting stories for *The Best of the West* is continuous; we review all magazines that come to us. A list of those publications appears in the back of this volume. We invite editors of other magazines who would like to have their fiction considered for the series to include us on their complimentary subscription list. Send to James and Denise Thomas, *The Best of the West*, 802 Green Street, Yellow Springs, Ohio 45387.

INTRODUCTION

Renaissance in the New West

William Kittredge

In November 1978 Elliott Anderson, editor of the Chicago-based literary magazine *TriQuarterly*, suggested an issue of the magazine devoted to "Western Stories" and asked Steven Krauzer and me to help find new work by first-rate writers. There weren't as many good writers in the West then, but we ended up with a fine collection, which came out the spring of 1980. We didn't get anything from senior writers like Wallace Stegner or A.B. Guthrie or Norman Maclean or Wright Morris or John Graves. But we talked about them in our introduction, as members of the first generation of literary writers in the West—a genealogy that ran from Willa Cather (*My Antonia*, 1918) and Ole Rolevaag (*Giants in the Earth*, 1926) to Mari Sandoz (*Old Jules*, 1935), H. L. Davis (*Honey in the Horn*, 1935), and Walter Van Tilburg Clark (*The Ox-Bow Incident*, 1940) to Stegner (*The Big Rock Candy Mountain*, 1943) and Guthrie (*The Big Sky*, 1947).

And we did get a story ("Tom Fitch and the Sparrow Bride") from Dorothy Johnson, who was of their generation. In the late 1950s, she said, she'd sold it to *Collier's* magazine for $2,500, but *Collier's* folded before it was printed. "In those days, before TV wrecked the market," she said, "you could make a living with short stories." Indeed you could. Sell four or five to *Collier's* or *The Saturday Evening Post* every year, as she did, and you were home free. I don't recall exactly what we paid to print her story in *TriQuarterly*, but I think it was something like $250 (which was pretty good for a short story in a literary magazine).

We missed on a couple of younger writers we courted, John

Keeble *(Yellowfish)* and Ron Hansen *(Desperadoes)*, but we ended up with a strong body of work from a group who might be called mid-career or on the cusp or not exactly famous yet, although most of them became well known over the next decade, Edward Abbey and Thomas McGuane and Leslie Marmon Silko and Raymond Carver and Tobias Wolff and Richard Ford and John Sayles and John Nichols and Ivan Doig and Cyra McFadden and Cormac McCarthy—an excerpt from his astonishing master-piece, *Blood Meridian.*

And we found a genuine unknown, a young man who had come west from Cincinnati, David Quammen, who sent us a story that has been anthologized several times since ("Walking Out"). In Quammen we were in on the discovery of both a first-rate story and a man who soon proved to be an important writer.

Despite shortcomings—out of nineteen selections we printed only three by women (Dorothy Johnson, Leslie Marmon Silko, and Cyra McFadden) and one by a Native American (Silko), and none by a Hispanic—we felt that the project had been a success. Steven Krauzer and I said so in our introduction:

The current status of western writing is similar to that of southern American writing in the early 1930s when a major regional voice, in the persons of such authors as William Faulkner, Robert Penn Warren, Eudora Welty, Andrew Lytle, and Katherine Anne Porter, was beginning to be heard. Just as the old south was gone, the old west is gone. Free of the need to write either out of the mythology or against it, the writers of the new west, responding to the variety and quickness of life in their territory, are experiencing a period of enormous vitality.

On December 27, 1981, *The New York Times Magazine* published a smart piece of analysis by Russell Martin, called "Writers of the Purple Sage," complete with color photographs of

Thomas McGuane, N. Scott Momaday, Edward Abbey, and Wallace Stegner. In 1984 Martin and Marc Barasch published an anthology of the same name which included established writers we missed in *TriQuarterly*—among them N. Scott Momaday, James Welch, and Rudolfo Anaya—two Native Americans, and a Hispanic—and some new writers (two of them women) who were clearly around for the long haul: David Long, Rick DeMarinis, Gretel Ehrlich, and Elizabeth Tallent.

Which is the point of this recitation—the list of writers was expanding as we watched, starting to include more women and writers form outside the majority culture.

By February 1986, when I published an essay called "Doors to Our House" in *Northern Lights*, it was obvious to everybody that some more names needed to be added to the list—Ralph Beer for *The Blind Corral* (1986) and Patricia Henley for *Friday Night at the Silver Star* (1986). And we had two more books that I would call masterpieces—*Housekeeping* (1981) by Marilynne Robinson and Louise Erdrich's *Love Medicine* (1984). But the smart thing that I did, knowing I was still leaving a lot of people out of my listings, was to apologize for my ignorance.

Given what we understand as the western tradition of radical individualism amid wide open spaces, it was surprising to almost everybody when somebody noticed that our renaissance was often a communal enterprise. Writers tended to gather in the same towns, partly so that they could hang out with other people who read books, or have somebody to gossip with—about agents and divorces and the scandalous money somebody got from a movie deal, and how they pissed it away. Companionship—something like that. And partly they hung out together for a more serious reason, having to do with helping one another—I keep thinking of agricultural metaphors, like cross-fertilization.

My first contact with a community of writers (beyond graduate school) came in 1969. James Crumley had just published his first novel, *One to Count Cadence*, and quit his teaching job at the University of Montana. I was hired to replace him. In Missoula I found an enclave of good young writers centered on the poet Richard Hugo—people like the Native American poet, soon-to-be novelist James Welch. Crumley came back to town the next spring—and, as the years went by, others came and left, like Max Crawford and Sarah Vogan and Richard Ford, and others stayed, like essayist Bryan DiSalvatore and novelist Deirdre McNamer, and some left and came back, like the czar of Louisiana/Montana crime novels, James Lee Burke.

East across the Montana Rockies, in Livingston, there was another crowd centered on Thomas McGuane and William Hjortsburg (and maybe the spirit of Jim Harrison, who visited but never lived there). McGuane had come to Livingston, it was said, for the fishing. Before long they were joined by Tim Cahill and the late Richard Brautigan, and painter and writer and publisher (Clark City Press) Russell Chatham. In Missoula, in those days, we knew they were famous, and maybe rich. McGuane had written scripts for actual movies. They were a tough act to follow, and some of us thought of them as the competition. Now, as we age into some understanding of the foolishness of keeping count, we think of them as friends, in the same way we think of Quammen and Greg Keeler in Bozeman and David Long in Kalispell and Ralph Beer in Helena, and so many others, as part of our same community.

Other groups were forming in other places. Some of them, as in Missoula, centered on college writing programs; others, like the one in Livingston, were made up of writers who were looking for a good place to live while they got on with their work. The poet Richard Shelton has taught writing at the University of Arizona in Tucson for decades, sometimes with the late Edward Abbey and Native American writers Leslie Marmon Silko and N. Scott Momaday (whose *House Made of Dawn*, when it won the Pulitzer Prize in the late 1960s, was the first sure indication of the fine Native American work we were to see over the next decades). A community of writers, including Barbara King-solver, has formed in Tucson. And there's another group, in-cluding Ron Carlson and Alberto Rios, at Arizona State Univer-sity in Phoenix. In Salt Lake City, at the University of Utah, there are those who work and exchange work with David Kranes and Larry Levis. At the University of New Mexico it's Frederick Turner and Rudolfo Anaya.

Despite all the complaints about college writing programs, they are a phenomenon I applaud. As Dick Hugo once said, they may be the last place in America where you will find your life taken seriously (sometimes, of course, *too* seriously). I have never been able to define the so-called "workshop story"—I see everything imaginable in my classes. And besides, writing pro-grams are mostly excuses for getting people together in the same town. Not much actual learning takes place in classrooms. The important processes come on us by surprise, on fine spring after-noons while people lie on their backs in the grass and talk and study the clouds, or after midnight.

I recall a day in 1982 when Doug Peacock and Ed Abbey and I drove down from Tucson to visit William Eastlake at his place south of Bisbee. We whistled along with country music as we drove through the grassy highlands north of Patagonia, shot pool in Eastlake's family room overlooking the Mexican border, had us a meal in Bisbee, and spent some time lying to each other in a Tombstone tavern on the way home. I came out of that trip at least recognizing my moral obligation to speak my opinions, however unpopular. It was important in my education.

I met Scott Momaday for the first time at a barbeque in Peacock's backyard and spent the evening listening to big boys tell bear stories. For the first time I understood that tales in which the power of the hero is revealed in compassion for ani-mals can be seen as humility.

Another time at Peacock's I met Earth First! leader Dave

Foreman—a man I was uneasy with in the beginning. He acts on his ideas, I mostly write about mine; it's a difference I'm still trying to think through (or rationalize). Peacock grilled Mexican shrimp and Foreman and I talked about *Beyond Geography*, Frederick Turner's brilliant book, and agreed it had come to each of us at an important time, helping us ill-educated country boys to focus on ideas we had been trying to get clear for a long time. Turner articulated a version of history that allowed us to see our own personal histories. I began to understand how many children of the West, like Foreman and me, share the same deep-seated misgivings about our regional culture. We were playing, gossiping, helping educate one another.

In 1976 I went down to Sun Valley for a midsummer conference on Western movies. I came home (after four days of lectures and films and hangovers) trying to rethink the violence that lies so close at the heart of storytelling in my homeland—I kept going to the conferences Richard Hart staged at Sun Valley until they ran out in the early eighties. I got an education there, in history and the way ideas work on life, from many people, most powerfully Alvin Josephy and William Goetzmann.

Eventually I was invited to other writers' conferences, like the one held every June in Sitka where I met Alaskan naturalist-anthropologist Richard Nelson, whom I admire without reservation. I'm sorry I missed the next year, when Peter Nabokov and Barry Lopez were there with Nelson; they are still in touch, playing ideas off one another.

Such encounters are important in a territory so vast as the West. These days there are readings and workshops and conferences all over—in Driggs, Idaho, and Joseph, Oregon, and Park City, Utah, and Santa Fe and Billings and Rock Springs and Casper and Missoula and Aspen and Jackson Hole (sometimes we joke that cultural life in the West takes place in ski resorts trying to make their nut for the summer) and on and on. It's not that the readings or workshops are always so terrific—but writers and artists, particularly those getting started, need the support they get from one another.

It's my guess that the multicultural gatherings centered on the Guadelupe Institute in San Antonio, for instance, run by Ray Gonzales, will have a profound enfranchising effect on Chicano and Native American writers in the Southwest. A generation ago they quite justifiably felt left out of the national culture—no place to publish, no national reviews, no money—but now they are being taken very seriously. Not many writers from any culture work well in a vacuum. Defeat them enough, and all but the strongest or luckiest will give in to despair and quit. The loss is ours. Give them some support, and they get back to work.

This speculation can go on and on. I am attempting to detail some forces that have brought writing in the West to its present happy condition: that good western writers are literally everywhere—Rick Bass in the Yaak Valley of Montana, Dan O'Brien and Linda Hasselstrom on ranches in the Dakotas. There's an enclave of fine writers in Lewiston, Idaho, centered on Bob Wrigley and Mary Clearman Blew. There's Gretel Ehrlich in Shell, Wyoming, and Terry Tempest Williams in Salt Lake City, and Robert Bowswell and Antonya Nelson in Las Cruces, and Rick DeMarinis and Cormac McCarthy in El Paso, and Linda Hogan in Boulder. On the coast there's Ivan Doig and Victoria Jenkins in Seattle, and Craig Lesley and Tom Spanbauer and Molly Gloss in Portland.

There's Larry Woiwode in North Dakota, writing those wonderful Neumiller stories, and Jim Galvin from Tie Siding, Wyoming (his new book, *The Meadow*, is absolutely a masterpiece). And again, I apologize to the writers I've neglected to mention and to those I haven't heard of yet—writers in Minot and McCall and Sedona and Las Vegas and out in the sagebrush deserts of eastern Oregon.

Point is, they are getting to know one another and feeding ideas back and forth, pushing at one another; insights developed by one writer are turned in a new direction by another; great energy and intelligence is being focused on western issues; our regional life is being seriously reexamined and reevaluated, as are the complex ways in which we connect to life and history every- where.

Some of us believed the West would never have a literature until we had a great writer, our Faulkner, to pull our regional concerns together, giving them thematic coherence—but that was a kind of graduate school notion. Our Western thematic concerns are clear enough—we inhabit a place that looked to many people like a kind of paradise for the taking, and we are variously engaged in telling the story of what was done in the name of that taking (and is still being done), the ways it was done, the consequences, and what happened to the native people who already lived there.

Writers in the West don't need to have their themes defined. They just need to believe that they are doing important work, to be taken seriously.

It's been years since our *TriQuarterly* volume. Three of those writers—Ed Abbey, Ray Carver, and Dorothy Johnson—are dead and grievously missed, because we loved them, and because they did their work brilliantly, with great heart, and left us a history of honest writing which helps drive us to our own work.

Which gets us to the vivid, compelling stories chosen by James and Denise Thomas for this fine anthology—a part and continuation of that tradition. These stories are true hearted and smart, and they function as mirrors, in which we find ourselves reflected. In that they are as useful as money in the bank.

I'm proud to say that several of them were written by people I know. Dwight Yates is a friend from the early days in Missoula (I haven't seen him in twenty years); I taught with Ron Carlson a couple of years ago at Arizona State University; David Long was in my graduate classes at Montana in 1972 and 1973; Evan Williams was in a class I taught at Montana in the fall of 1990; Kent Nelson taught at Montana the following spring; Annick Smith has been my True Companion for fifteen years, through all sorts of adventure and long-distance travel.

I have a history of admiring their work. It's good that they are getting this mostly overdue recognition. But I should not be lobbying for the virtues of stories written by my friends. The world will take care of that, so I'll end on some words from "What Happened to Tully," by Tom McNeal, somebody I know nothing about, except that he sure knows how to get the telling done:

> These stories would always end with R.C.'s worries melting away like peppermints, at night while he slept, an idea Tully had gotten from a Willie Nelson song. Tully himself didn't care for peppermints, but whenever he was in Scottsbluff he stocked up from Woolworth's, so that the last thing each night, if Russell promised not to chew it, Tully could take a peppermint from a tin and lay it on his son's tongue before saying good night.

A story about the way stories (and Willie Nelson songs) can help us learn to care for and accommodate one another. The editors are to be congratulated for this collection. We're in good hands here.

WHERE WEST IS

Long before we were born
the people who lived in the world
had their way of finding west
without the use of delicate instruments.

One of them whose duty it was
to find west would begin to walk
in the direction of the setting sun
while chanting the tale of the world
in his head.

When he was finished
he would bend down and
draw a line in the dirt
with his finger.
Beyond this line
everything was west.

—THOM TAMMARO

THE   BEST   OF   THE   WEST   5

Tom McNeal

What Happened to Tully

Tully David Coates was a sleepy, smiley baby, "a child," said the Coateses' hired man a few years later, "who blinked open his eyes and believed at once in the good intentions of the world."

For Kansas, this was a pretty speech—Tully's folks needed a moment to respond. "A blessing," his mother decided, and his father, habitually unwilling to agree with her, said, "More likely a curse."

Their marriage was loud and wobbly, set loose in a farmhouse without close neighbors. Words were shouted, doors were slammed, locked, kicked open again. Tully brought out his coloring books. He hummed and colored, colored and hummed, waiting for his father to give up. Eventually his father would. He would withdraw to the barn, the tractor would pop and sputter, and once it had rumbled out of hearing, Tully's mother would suggest a horse ride into town or down to the creek, with Tully riding up front or, later on, hanging on to her belt loops from behind while his little brother, Marlen, rode forward. If the weather was bad, she might say, "Who's for cookies?" and they would bake a double batch with the radio on loud to oldies his mother would sometimes dance to, right there on the kitchen linoleum, twirling Tully along.

In Tully's fifth and sixth years the house grew quieter. His mother started getting headaches, not so bad during the day, but bad always at night. Tully's father began a course of peacemaking gestures. He took in his dishes from the table and on Sunday washed not just his but everyone else's too. When he went to town, he consented to buy groceries, and would throw in the makings for sundaes, which Tully's mother loved. And he bought her the mare she'd seen for sale in Hutchinson, a big gray horse who turned out to be just as fast and trainable as Tully's mother had said she'd be.

Still, the headaches kept up, got worse, and one morning when Tully was seven, his father, sitting unshaven at the breakfast table, told him and Marlen that their mother had gone to a hospital during the night. He gave as the reason a growth in her head. A few days later he left the boys for an afternoon, and when he came back, he said, "I was up to Hutch. It's done for good. She's buried."

Tully nodded but didn't believe what he'd heard. He expected the next telephone call to explain some terrible mistake, the next car up the dirt drive to carry his mother, damaged in some minor way—winged, maybe, in some kind of shootout. But all the cars ever brought was long-faced neighbors with food in covered dishes. Nothing was the same around the place, not his father, not his brother, not his mother's horse or garden or kitchen—they all took on the dull look of things left behind.

Tully decided that his mother had been called away on a secret mission by the government and couldn't get in touch with any of them even though she wanted to more than anything. He believed this was true even while telling himself that it was pretend.

In the spring Tully and Marlen stayed with a neighbor while their father drove through Wyoming and Nebraska, looking at land. Upon his return men began coming by the Coates place, writing checks and driving away with stock and equipment. Tully heard his father tell all these men the same thing. They were moving to an irrigated farm on the flats outside Goodnight, Nebraska.

Tully didn't know what flats were exactly, but he liked the sound of the town's name—it made him think of flannel sheets. He folded a note into a bread wrapper, went down to his mother's favorite sitting place by the creek, and tacked it to a tree. *If you can't find us we have gone to Goodnight Nebraska*, it said.

When they pulled away from that empty farmhouse outside Arlington, Kansas, the trunk and back seat and roof of the family Dodge were packed and strapped with all the Coateses' household goods. Three trucks fell in line behind them, each followed by a trailer, one of which carried the gray horse. Tully leaned far out the car window to look back and then held Marlen out for a view. "See?—it's like a circus moving!" he yelled, but Marlen pulled back and, hugging himself, began to whimper. Tully was glad when his father finally popped Marlen one and shut him up. There was no reason for whimpering. They were on an adventure, and at the end of it was going to be a new place to live. Tully poked his head out the window, stretched forward, began happily swallowing from the onrushing air. What he was feeling, though he didn't know yet what to call it, was the keen pleasure of leaving problems behind.

Time passed, months, years, and these lives took hold in the flats south of Goodnight. Tully's father farmed dutifully, cooked dutifully, accepted hail, drought, and flood without a word. Marlen grew plump and sullen, seemed always to expect the worst and believe he'd gotten it. But for Tully life was different. Things came easy to Tully. Pals came easy. School and sports came easy. Judging stock, fixing machinery, and bringing in crops came easy.

Girls also came easy.

"What's the big attraction?" April Reece asked him one night in The Spur, after watching him off and on for a couple of hours. Tully had come up beside her at the bar to order himself a beer between rounds of pool, and she'd started talking. April Reece was older than Tully and known for her flashy dressing and frankness. "No, really," she said, "it's beyond me," and Tully shrugged and turned up a palm as if to say that if it was true, it was beyond him, too. He was twenty-one, loose-limbed, hair the white-blond of cornsilk, pale green eyes in a smooth, unremarkable face. "Maybe it's that car you drive," April said, and drew a smile from Tully. He was interested in April—who wouldn't be?—but he made a point not to show it. He wandered off, played some cutthroat, gravitated back. She was wearing black—black sweater, black denims, black socks turned down over bright pink street shoes.

Tully covered the top of a dice cup, gave it a rattle, and with elaborate indifference said, "Wanna roll for a beer?" While they drank, she asked if he was still going out with the Smalley girl. "Ella and me're friends," he said agreeably, but it was less a statement of loyalty to Ella Smalley, though he had some of that, than it was a way of saying, Ask a question, get an answer. He thought of adding a truth, that Ella Smalley was *just* a friend, but he knew it would come out sounding puny. He signaled for two more beers. April liked a little tomato juice in hers. He himself couldn't stand red beer, but he liked pouring in the juice, which he did now, slowly, leaning forward to watch its color curl into the beer.

"Guess it doesn't take much to amuse you," April said, and Tully, letting his face open into a smile, said no, he guessed it didn't.

A month or so later, after sex on the warm, spacious hood of his old black Lincoln Continental, parked on a flat space over-looking the Niobrara, April pulled a blanket up around her and leaned on an elbow to regard him. "Well, I think the reason some girls go for you is that you've got this nice bland face, and in just the right light a girl can make it into anything she wants. It's a face that fits right into any of about six standard happy endings girls cook up for themselves."

Tully tugged the blanket back down, and she left them out there for observation, smooth floppy breasts with nipples the width of poker chips. Tully gave one breast a gentle lift with the back of his hand. "What six happy endings?"

April turned on her back, smiled, let her gaze float up into the night sky. "Can't remember."

Tully was amused that someone so reckless in public would be so careful with her secrets, but he didn't press. He rolled his pants into a pillow, set it between his back and the windshield, and sat up a little to bring into view the red beacon that topped a radio tower deep in the sandhills. He could also see it from his bedroom window at home; for years he had looked at it before going to sleep each night. It had been put up by the state patrol, but Tully always thought of it as something that belonged to him. It was a relay tower. By staring at it he could relay messages to anyone anywhere. To God or Abraham Lincoln or old Mr. Spence, the dog they left behind in Kansas. He told April how he used to really believe this.

A pleasant silence developed, and then April crooked a leg over his, gently took hold of his parts, and, after he'd come to life, said, "I love the way that works," which Tully figured for a lie, though a pleasing one just the same.

But April, her hand still at play, idly asked if his dating someone like Ella Smalley was a sign he meant to settle down.

Tully tried to think. "I don't know," he said finally, because he didn't. What threw him was the notion of what he *meant* to do. It suggested that planning out the next step was something people did, and the fact that he'd never given the line of his life any more thought than he might give to what crops to plant or where first to stalk his buck come fall made him feel suddenly deficient. So he was glad when April began kissing him again, sloppier even than before, but then, as things got interesting, April suddenly broke off a kiss and grabbed hold of his testicles so fiercely that Tully had to clench his teeth to keep from screaming. "Just one thing," she whispered into his ear, "and that is, if I hear of that Smalley girl or any other female for that matter winding up on this car hood with you, ever, I'm going to do something—don't ask me what—but something just to register my significant feelings about it, because this much of your life, Scout, is all mine." And Tully, in spite of his ferocious discomfort, mustered a laugh and said, "I'm paralyzed with fear," at which point April very slightly tightened her grip on him.

A month or so later, in June, Tully came in for supper and found the hood of his old Continental hanging from a cottonwood, where it had been rapped several hundred times with the ball peen hammer April still stood holding.

"Looks like it caught itself a meteor shower," Tully said. "Hoist it up there yourself?"

She nodded. "That was for Lori Hallick."

Tully worked up a smile. At least she wasn't mentioning Wendy Adams or Jill McIntyre. "Night has a thousand eyes," he said.

Ten days later April and her brother Ed drove the Continental, with its yellow replacement hood, into the open sandhills and used it for target practice. When she took Tully out to it that afternoon, she said, "Wendy Adams."

Tully circled the car, staring at the broken windows, tail-lights, and mirrors. April had let her temper take hold of her—something he believed he would never allow, a belief that produced in him now a kind of smugness he mistook for peace of mind. He grinned and said, well, the hood anyhow still looked usable. It was late afternoon, broad daylight, and April, glancing around, sliding out a grin, looked like someone who'd just caught the pleasant scent of mischief.

Ella Smalley was a different story. She was tall, skinny, and not especially attentive to her appearance. Her panty hose bagged and her eyebrows lay fuzzily against the grain, which made Tully want to lick a finger and smooth them down. Every now and then her wide, liquid brown eyes would take Tully by surprise, but by and alrge Ella was something Tully never gave much thought to. She was just there, was all, and always had been. She was quiet, she sneaked up on you like an orphan dog, always on the fringes of things, edging in with eyes down, looking up when it was safe. Ella Smalley saw a lot of things. She'd seen Mr. B. B. Holcomb, the town attorney, put a Sheaffer fountain pen, packet and all, into his inside coat pocket and leave Lloyd's Pharmacy, paying only for a Baby Ruth. She'd seen a fully dressed Indian man sitting below the crooked bridge alongside a woman wearing just a Human League T-shirt. One night through a cracked door she'd seen an aunt in horrible silent anger jab her uncle in the chest with her long hands, moving him backward across the bedroom until he sat down on the bed. Ella had wished her uncle would fight back, and then, when he didn't, decided he deserved it after all. She had been visiting. The next morning, when her aunt had served hot cakes and bacon in her usual manner, and her uncle had eaten hungrily and told a joke about hippopotamuses, Ella had gained a fuller view of adulthood. Usually she told Tully such things while they were cruising down the highway in the Continental. She liked riding along, to the Friday stock auction in Crawford, to the John Deere agency in Chadron, to Hollstein's Pack in Rushville—anywhere with a little distance to it. She would stare out the window and then, after a time, would turn to Tully and ask some little question. Did he think Mr. Shiff's wife was really his cousin? Did he know that Marlen, on a dare from the Heiting boys, had eaten six Mrs. Smith pies on the sidewalk in front of Frmka's IGA? Then a question that came sneaking closer, eyes down. Did his father ever laugh at *anything*? Her mother said that not being unhappy is a kind of happiness, but she didn't believe it—did he? So what had his mother been like, exactly, or did he remember?

Reckless popped into Tully's head, but that didn't sound like the right word to use for your mother. He said "glamorous" instead.

"Glamorous," Ella said carefully, as if trying to fit this piece into whatever picture she already had of Tully's mother.

Tully stared down the highway. "Well, afternoons, for example, she'd read magazines and drink peppermint schnapps while taking bubble baths that went on forever. And outside the house she always wore bright-red shoes, candy-apple red, even in church." He shook his head. "And, like on her horse. She wore these chaps, like she was living in Marlboro country or something, and she'd come flying toward you, pull up short, and toss down a look that made you feel almost privileged, like it came from a movie star or someone."

Ella nodded. Her mother had told her that a son's slant toward the mother predicted his slant toward the wife, so she let a mile or two pass and said, "What else?"

"Not much. Except when my mother died, that mare actually grieved. Wouldn't eat or look anybody in the eye for days. It was the same horse we have now. Jackie, after Jackie Kennedy. My mom was always big on famous people. Named my brother after Marlon Brando, except she misspelled it." He let out a snicker. "Just like my old man to let her."

"Name your brother that or misspell it?"

Tully laughed. "Either one, I guess."

And then Ella would be staring out the window again, letting things settle, until something else occurred to her to ask.

Tully never talked to Ella about other girlfriends, and she never asked. The closest they had come to arguing was over the car he bought to replace the shot-up Continental. It was a broad-hooded Buick LeSabre. It had over 100,000 miles on it, she pointed out. It took oil and guzzled gas. She had in mind a Plymouth Horizon they'd seen with only 60,000 on it. "That was four hundred dollars more, you seem to forget," he said mildly.

But Ella, her face flushed, said, "That doesn't matter a fraction of one little bit."

Tully thought Ella believed she had a duty to make him more wholesome. He thought his job was to make her less. So, to keep her from uttering another word about, say, the notion of charity, he might lean over and nibble at the slow white curve of her neck.

Ella was slender, didn't have much of a figure, and wouldn't let a hand under her undermost clothes, but she knew how to kiss. She kissed like there was no tomorrow. In fact, she kissed better than Lori Hallick or Wendy Adams or even April Reece when you got right down to it, if only kissing was all there was to it.

Behind the Coates place, on a platform mounted at the lower end of the barn roof, there stood an apparatus that had caught April's attention: a steel drum fitted with water piping and a shower head. The stall below was floored with a wooden pallet and enclosed on three sides. By midafternoon on summer days the water in the drum would have grown pleasantly warm, and on one such afternoon Tully's father happened to lead old Jackie around the corner of the barn while Tully stood under the stream of water with April's arms locked around his neck and legs around his waist. His hands were stirruped under her hips, moving her slowly, but he stopped when his eyes met his father's.

"What?" April said.

"My old man," he said, and April followed his gaze. Tully's father was walking the old mare off toward her stable. April forced a laugh. "Guess he got an eyeful."

He had, but he hadn't. He'd averted his eyes. He'd glanced at them, and then registered his chronic mournful look with Tully and kept walking. That was his way. He'd turned his eyes from every pretty girl Tully had ever brought around the place—every one, anyway, that Tully'd had doings with, which was something his father could always somehow detect.

As his father led the mare away, Tully out of stubbornness kept April around him, and they waddled as one into the barn, laughing, and finished up sitting on a saddle blanket still laughing and, toward the end, taking straw dust deep into their lungs. They had disengaged and stopped coughing and were listening to their own breathing when something chunked against the barn siding and then chunked again.

Tully crept over and peered through a window. His father was throwing rocks, *chunk*, pause, *chunk*, pause, *chunk*. "Work!" he yelled. "There is work to do, Tully David Coates!" He grubbed up more rocks over by the fence. "Work!" he yelled. "Work! Work! Work!" The word, repeated, seemed to slip free of its meaning—for a moment Tully thought he was listening to a foreign language.

"Jesus," April whispered, suddenly behind Tully, peeking out from behind him through the window. The rocks kept coming, and April, almost to herself, said, "Guess your dad's never going to like me now."

Tully looked past his father, stared out at the blank hills and white sky, and began to fill them in with greens, blues, an orange smiley sun.

His father kept shouting words and chucking rocks.

April said, "This is like a creepy movie."

"Just wait," Tully said. "Just wait."

He knew his father would eventually stop, and eventually his father did. He walked off, got into his pickup, and drove away, and the moment he was gone, Tully and April, as if by a spell, fell into their ease. April stood in a shaft of late sun. "Sure you got to get back to work?" she said, smiling at him there in the rich golden light.

Later in his life, if he stepped into the barn when the straw was dry and the angle of the sun just right, the feeling of this moment would come flooding back to Tully, and he would stand perfectly still so as not to lose the memory of those last simple kisses.

A few weeks later, while Tully's father and brother were off to a farm auction, a man came driving a late-model Chrysler up the long dirt drive of the Coates place. The plates said KANSAS. The man sat in the car with the windows rolled up, while his dust caught up with him and layered down over the car's shine. Then he got out and stood looking slowly around. Tully watched all this from the window of the Quonset shop where he was working on a pump shaft, honing down a new bushing for it from one too big. He switched off the grinder and walked out with a pipe wrench dangling from his hand.

"Over here!" he called out.

The man turned the wrong way. He was a big, wide-shouldered man with a stomach sloping evenly out from his chest. He looked maybe fifty. When, finally, he turned again, he seemed startled by Tully's appearance, and was looking at him in search of someone else, or so it seemed to Tully, who found himself doing the same thing with the man. Tully smiled but didn't offer his hand. "Do I know you?"

"Oh, I don't believe so," the man said. For a fat man he had delicate wrists and hands, and he had his white shirt sleeves rolled a couple of turns to show them off. From an interior pocket he withdrew a little brass case of business cards. *Mr. McC's Restaurant Supply*, they said. *Hays, Kansas. Mal McCreedy, Prop.* The man extended his hand. "McCreedy's my name."

"Tully Coates."

At these words the man's eyes laid back a little, seemed slightly less interested. He released Tully's hand and looked around.

Tully had seen this man somewhere, he was sure of it, but in some other form—in another getup, or maybe on the TV news. Tully was right-handed. The pipe wrench was in his left. He switched it and said, "Doubt if we'd have much need of restaurant supplies."

McCreedy turned and laughed drily. "Oh, no, I suppose not. Actually, I've been asked to look into the feasibility of a restaurant along Highway 20, either in Goodnight or Rushville. Using local-raised beef and chicken." He smiled. "Paying top dollar."

Tully nodded. He was no businessman, but the idea sounded half-baked.

McCreedy stared off toward the lambs and heifers. "You raise sheep and beef." He took a second look at the heifers.

"Charolais," Tully said. "We also raise some beefalo."

The man actually pressed his hands together. "Oh, perfect! Tourists would *love* ordering beefalo. How does it taste?"

"Above average," Tully said. He was wondering where these tourists would be coming from.

"*We?*" the man said, and when Tully looked confused, the man said, "I think you said, '*We* raise beefalo.' "

"Oh, yeah. My father, my brother, Marlen, and me. They're up to an auction lookng for a truck to buy."

McCreedy took this in carefully. Then, nodding, already moving, he said, "How about showing me your operation?"

Tully explained the cycle of backgrounding, summer pasture, and commercial feedlot, the average gain per day in each phase, but McCreedy didn't seem to be listening. He'd noticed the horse shed behind the barn. It was as if his whole mass tipped toward it. "You raise horses, too?"

"Just one," Tully said. Then, as they made for the shed, he said, "Thinking of serving horsemeat, too?"

The man didn't bother to laugh. He was walking faster. The mare was in her stall, poking her head out, curious. When McCreedy got to the fence, he slipped a hand into his pocket, brought it out cupped and empty, and made kissing noises. The mare ambled out, sniffed the empty hand, snorted into it. Then—and here a fat drop of sweat rolled coolly down Tully's ribs—the man cradled an arm around the mare's muzzle and let his fingers nibble at her nose and said in a crooning whisper, "Old Jackie, old Jackie, oh, old Jackie."

Tully became aware again of the pipe wrench in his hand. "Who are you?" he said, and the man, after just an instant, spun around wooden faced. Tully had two shocks of recognition. One was that he *had* seen the man before, only he'd looked taller then, and not fat. Tully had been maybe five. The man had come to their place in Kansas and argued with his mother a long time out on the mud porch. The other thing Tully understood was that the eyes behind this man's wide, masklike face were Marlen's eyes.

"I'm—"

"I don't care who you are," Tully said, and moving forward, he tapped the mare's muzzle lightly with the pipe wrench, to move her back and the man away.

McCreedy threw his hands up in mock surrender. Tully followed him back to his sedan at arm's length, all the while staring at the spot on the man's head where his pink, big-pored scalp showed. But McCreedy evidently had no inkling, because when he got into his car and lowered the window by pushing a button, he said, "Your mother went with me to California, but I wasn't enough for her either," and then had the big car in reverse by the time Tully, dumbfounded, trotting close to the backing car, grasped what McCreedy was saying and, before he could think what to do, was swinging the pipe wrench into the driver's side of the windshield, shooting fine cracks everywhere through the glass and crazing the image of the man sitting behind it.

The next few days Tully slept fitfully, ate poorly, mentioned McCreedy to no one. On Saturday night, when he saw April, they drove out to Walgren Lake, where he discovered that he was a lot less interested in fooling around than she was. When she asked how come, he just shrugged. "Well, this is a scream," April said. This was a new word of hers. Everything was a scream. At first Tully had thought she might've picked it up from an old movie, but now he figured she was getting this kind of thing from her new waitressing job in Alliance, thirty miles south. She'd also begun calling everybody Slick. "Thanks, Slick," she said, for example, to Teddy Hill, whose name she knew, when they stopped off later at McCarter's Mini-Mart for snacks. They parked at the overlook and drank beer, and April tried again to get Tully's interest, but finally gave up. Tully said he guessed he just didn't feel like it. April, without hiding her annoyance, said she'd take a rain check, and Tully went home to sleep the sleep of the dead. He didn't, though. He woke up at three and lay in bed until dawn thinking up flamboyant ways of killing McCreedy, usually after looking him in the eye and saying, "It's been a scream, Slick."

It seemed to Tully that all his feelings—about his mother, his father, his own sunny life—had been pulled inside out, and the ideas released kept running around in all directions. He blamed everybody for his mother's leaving. He blamed McCreedy for being sleazy, his father for being first loud and then wimpish, his brother for being pink and obese. He blamed his mother for being bored, the farm for being boring. And he blamed himself for being pesky, for never leaving her alone, for whining outside that locked bathroom door the whole time she took her afternoon bath.

Facing things head-on was not Tully's strong suit, but one day, while cultivating beans, he came across this hard little fact: What McCreedy had told him was not a revelation. It was a confirmation, a light turned on something he'd always sensed lurking off in the dark but never allowed himself to see. So this shifted things. He was not just his father's victim but his accomplice, too.

Tully began to work longer, harder; he was surprised how often barbs, thistles, and rusty metal tore at his arms. Sex, when resumed with April, was less frequent and took an angry turn. If she cried out, Tully would loosen his hold, but only just barely. At home he couldn't stop watching his father. He became resentfully aware of the way his father let Marlen or him make the lists of the day, the way he just read them and did what was written there. Tully began adding items. Ditch field three. Fence the river field. Weld the pipe trailer. His father did them all, and never said a word.

One day, at their noon meal, Tully's father was patiently cutting his pork chop into small neat pieces, cutting up his string beans, pouring a little milk on his potatoes, mashing them fine. So his wife left him, Tully thought. So what? So why didn't he just say she left and get on with it? Lots of people try to make a pissing post out of a person. That was bad. But it was worse when somebody swallowed it whole, made a life of it. Then it was pathetic.

Out of nowhere Marlen said, "Something gnawing on you?"

Tully started, turned. "Work," he thought to say. He made a grin. "More we do, more there is yet."

His father, still setting up his food, nodded without looking up. He was buttering bread now, making a project of evenness.

Marlen, with exaggerated surprise, said, "Do I hear Tully moaning about work? Our very own work-hard, play-hard, sleep-hard Tully?"

"Caught me at a tired moment, is all," Tully said.

Marlen took a bite of fatty meat and said in a joking voice, "What's the matter, your pecker getting all the sleep lately?"

"Fuck you, Slick," Tully said before he could catch himself, and a change came over the table. His father set his fork down, the radio weatherman talked about highs and lows within the growing zone, and the smile on Marlen's face, when it broke, was like a dawning.

In the next few weeks Marlen seemed to feed on Tully's brooding, to come slowly to life. He worked with barbells in the basement and cut down on sweets. He walked jauntily out to his tractor, whistled while pulling ticks from the dog, sang in the shower.

> It won't hurt
> When I fall down off this barstool . . .

Tully knew that whether brother or half-brother, he should've been happy about this change in Marlen, but he wasn't, not at all. All he heard in Marlen's voice was a McCreedylike cheeriness that just made him sourer.

"Your brother finally getting some?" April asked.

"Maybe in the ass," Tully said, and turned to April, who didn't laugh.

"You're really getting yourself an attitude," she said.

Ella put it another way. "For one full month now you've been like someone else," she said, and kept her arms folded against a little breeze. It was almost dusk. They stood near the last of her mother's garden, a few tomatoes, some soft squash.

Tully sucked his molar and stared off toward a field of bleached-out vines.

"Your dad don't get those beans in soon, they'll be blowing all over the county."

After a silence Ella said, "It's like all the time I'm with somebody that looks like Tully but isn't Tully at all."

He narrowed his eyes and turned on her. "Or maybe vice versa. Maybe this is the real thing." He stared not into her eyes but just above them, at the fuzzy eyebrows. "You want to know what's got hold of me?" He wanted to tell her about McCreedy, and thought he was going to, but when he opened his mouth, he heard himself telling her instead about his father catching him and April showering together—"showering" was his one concession to her feelings. Ella turned away, and when her shoulders began to tremble, he knew she was crying. He would see later that making her cry might've been his intention, but now he said, "Ella, for chrissakes, c'mon." She turned away when he tried to face her. "Hey, you knew April and me were like that."

Ella made for the house. She stopped, though. She came back. "I know what you do. I know what you and her do. I saw you once out by the river on top of your car, both of you thinking you were something unusually wonderful, even though it looked uncomfortable to me." She caught her breath. "So that's not it. But if what's been troubling you for a month is that your father caught you and her"—here Ella both lowered and tightened her voice—"*doing it*, then I don't want to hear about it, because you telling me something like this means you're thinking of me as your little friend, and the one thing I'm not, you . . . *birdbrain*, is your little *friend*." She must've sensed the unserious effect of "birdbrain," because for the first time her cheeks pinkened. She moved half-running toward the yard, and then her mother—what, Tully wondered, had she heard?—held open the back door, and Ella disappeared into the lighted opening of the house.

Tully saw April the next day, and again on Thursday. On Friday she was working a new shift, serving cocktails, in Alliance, and Tully was supposed to meet buddies at The Spur in Goodnight, but he didn't have the spirit for it. He tried phoning Ella, but Mrs. Smalley was screening the calls, which, he figured, was about what he deserved for going out with a girl still living at home.

Tully wandered out behind the barn, leaned against the fence, and listened to the crickets and the shush of the river on the bridge piles. He found his point of red light in the distance. He wanted to pass on his thoughts to somebody, but didn't know who. It was cool. From somewhere beyond the water came the smell of wood smoke, and all at once the season seemed to have turned without his noticing. Tully, to his surprise, was about to start crying, when off in the dark the old mare began nickering and fidgeting.

Tully turned. There, moving along the pens toward the mare, was the outline of his father. "Dessert!" he sang out in a soft voice and rattled a paper bag. "Didja think I'd forget?"

Tully sat quiet and watched his father dip bits of squash in a small jar of molasses and feed them one by one to the old mare. When they were gone, he carefully folded the sack flat, stroked the mare's nose, and returned to the house.

What Tully did then was nothing planned out. He just walked in, went over to where his father was reading the paper, and said, "A fat, pink-faced man named McCreedy came by about a month ago."

His father's face looked as if a window shade had suddenly snapped up, showing a version of him Tully was never meant to see, a softer, younger, scareder version. After a second or so he got the shade back down. He blinked and stared evenly at Tully. "So?"

"This McCreedy said our mother didn't die in Kansas. He said she ran off with him to California."

His father's eyes slid away. In a reciting-style voice he said, "That is a lie. Your mother is dead." He laid the open newspaper across himself like a lap robe. "What did you tell Marlen?"

"Nothing. Not for me to tell."

"Nothing *to* tell," his father said, and closed his eyes.

It was a bad winter. It went on and on and on. Snow began in early October, and by November the downstairs windows were darkened by drifts. Blizzards came once in January and twice in March, when several calves were lost. The last blizzard was the worst. Pheasants turned into the wind and died where they stood. "Imports," said Coates, Sr.—worth noting, because in the course of the winter he all but gave up speech. He meant the pheasants weren't indigenous, had been brought in from China, couldn't cope.

He'd installed a double-drum wood stove in the Quonset, and he spent long days there repairing everything on the place that needed repair, from machinery to old chairs. The routine was slow and steady, returning something fixed and hauling off to the Quonset something broken. He never showed off his work, never looked at who was in a room. "He's like a ghost," April said one day. "Ever notice how a door doesn't make a sound when he passes through it?" Tully noticed plenty. He watched his father wearing his greasy down jacket even in the house, moving slowly from room to room, looking straight ahead with half-alive eyes. His father began to smell. Tully wished his father were one or the other, dead or alive, which he supposed was how it could get with people you were obliged to love but didn't.

Tully saw April about once a week, depending. She'd rented a place in Alliance and taken a job doing some kind of dancing. Tully didn't ask for specifics, but he could guess at its nature. He didn't see Ella. She'd once come into the bar where April danced. "She was with some farmer," April said. "It was no

good, her being there. I couldn't dance at all like I like." Every
night that he could Marlen went into town, where, forty pounds
slimmer and in a new set of clothes, he for a time consistently
drew double takes. He went to dances, he went to bars. "Call me
a socializing fool," he said.

In late April the number-two and number-five alfalfa fields
took a hard freeze, the block on the old Case cabless cracked,
and the hydraulic on the flatbed truck began to work only sometimes. By this time Tully's father had entered a tidying phase,
cleaning out the basement, his desk, the kitchen cabinets. Like
Marlen, he didn't eat much, but while Marlen grew lean, Coates,
Sr., just got small. He kept punching new holes in his belt—the
end lolled down like the tongue of a tired dog.

April, who was driving a new Thunderbird, one night mentioned in passing that a Lebanese had married her, but strictly
for immigration reasons. His name was Essa; he worked for the
railroad, in management; they lived in the same house but separate rooms; and her marriage didn't mean anything needed to
change between her and Tully. One day in May he saw them
coming out of Gibson Discount in Alliance. Seeing her was like
seeing a high school friend dressed up as an adult in the junior
play. April was wearing a pantsuit. The Lebanese was in slacks
and a tie, his graying hair combed straight back, smoking a cigarette and pushing a new red rotary lawn mower across the asphalt parking lot. He looked forty. "Thirty-two," April told
Tully a few days later.

On the first warm day in June, Tully's father drove into town
and came back with sweets. He didn't eat his supper but afterward heated Hershey's fudge sauce and put out mountainous
sundaes for all three of them, ReddiWip, almonds, cherries, the
works. He ate slowly. When he finished his, he made himself
another, and when that bowl was empty, he began on the jar of
maraschino cherries. He ate them one by one. Finally the cherries were gone, and his father, running his finger into the syrup at

the bottom of the jar, said, "Where's the flatbed parked at?"

The next day his father rode the old mare out to work on the truck's hydraulics, rode out carrying a wooden toolbox with a wide leather strap tacked to it for a handle—like some old-fashioned country doctor, Tully imagined. When he hadn't come back by noon, Tully went out on the ATV and found him up at the river field, smashed between the frame and lift bed of the six-ton truck filled with alfalfa silage. He was unquestionably dead. The hydraulic worked when Tully tried it, but when the bed raised, all he saw was the way the scalp had moistly torn free and the way a bolt had made a neat hole in one of the broken parts of the skull. Tully lifted the body away and laid it down in the turn row and covered the smashed-in part of it with his shirt. He stood aside then and heaved, but nothing came up. He began to hear a sound. It was the old horse, tethered to the fence by a lunge line, tail-slapping her rump for flies.

That night, after they'd taken Coates, Sr., off on a gurney, after all the telephone calls, after two of the neighbors had come with casseroles, April ended a long silence by saying, "This'll probably sound bad, but it was almost like he was already dead. This just sort of makes it official."

Tully nodded. Her words seemed right, and yet they didn't account for how sudden the final part of the process felt. "You know," he said, "all that ice cream is probably still in him."

They were out at the porch stoop, April and Marlen sitting on it, Tully standing nearby. A mild westerly carried cottonwood fluff, the sound of buzzing electrical wires, the smell of fermenting silage. Tully could see the relay tower if he leaned a little. He wanted to pass on some word to his father, but he had the terrible feeling that he'd lost the right to believe in that sort of thing. He leaned back and closed his eyes. His resentment of his father had slipped away—he could hardly remember what it had felt like. That didn't seem funny to him. What seemed funny was how it had been converted to taking his father as is, and that *was* funny, in two different ways: one, that the minute you took a wider view of the way your father lived was the minute you realized he was a dead man, and two, that if you'd opened up to this view sooner instead of looking askance, he might've had enough room to make a decent life in. It was all pretty disappointing.

Out of the silence Marlen said, "This is the first time in my life where I can't even begin to think right," and in that moment a feeling unlike any other Tully had ever had for Marlen welled up suddenly inside him. He reached over and laid a hand on Marlen's shoulder, began to work gently at the muscle there, felt Marlen only just slightly give himself up to it.

After another little while April stood up and said she'd like to stay longer but she had told Essa she'd be home an hour ago. Marlen stirred himself and said yeah, maybe he'd take off too. Tully went to a knoll and watched their taillights part, the Thunderbird moving west toward Highway 87 and Alliance, Marlen's big Duster heading north toward Highway 20 and Goodnight.

He walked to the tack room and took the bridle down from where his father always hung it. When he came out of the barn, somebody was there, a tall dark form, over near the cottonwood.

"Hey," he said.

"Hey," Ella said.

Tully walked toward her, talking. "How long you been here?"

"Dunno." She ducked her head. "Not that long."

He looked around. "Where'd you park?"

"Up the way. I had a feeling she might be here."

"She married an A-rab," Tully said. "Talk about funny."

Ella nodded at the bridle. "Going somewhere?"

"For a ride, yeah." He stood staring at her. "Wanna come along?"

Ella said sure, and they were walking out toward the horse

shed when she stopped. "There's one thing I have to know. I have to know if your feelings for me have gone sour."

Tully gave a low laugh and said no, he didn't think they had.

The two of them headed out for the truck. They rode bare-back, the old horse rolling slowly beneath them. The moon was mostly hidden, and in the dark the rolled bales in the river field looked like sleeping sheep. "I like this," Ella said. "But how come we're doing it?"

Tully didn't answer. What he meant to do was retrace this just the way it had happened, get it straight in his mind.

When they got to the truck, Tully tied up the mare where his father had tied her. He started up the engine and tried the hydraulic. It went right up, the box tilting at forty-five degrees and holding. Tully stared at it a long time and then stepped forward to where his father had stood and, bending at the waist, leaned his head under the box. He stayed there and reached back with his left hand for the lever. It reached. It reached easy. Tully kept his hand tight around it for a second or two, thinking, and then stood up straight, stepped aside, and shot the lever back. The box slammed down fiercely, metal on metal, Tully let out a little grunt, and the truck jumped on its springs.

Tully had stood once in a circle of players up on the football field watching one of his buddies not come back to life. The silence then was like the silence now. It made loud the buzz of crickets and the blatting of a ewe. It made the world too mysterious for human beings.

Finally, Ella said, "That was horrible."

Tully kept staring at the truck. What his father had done wasn't right, he knew that, but at least it was something of his own, an act he had thought out and had completed and had taken responsibility for. His.

Ella and Tully rode back the way they came, but slower, looser-reined, the old mare with her smooth, rolling walk mostly finding her own way. When they got down along the river, Tully felt Ella behind him making some adjustment to her blouse. Then she rolled up his flannel shirt. He'd almost decided he'd misguessed her intent when he suddenly felt her bare skin against his back, and Tully was caught short at how fiercely he craved every single aspect of Ella Smalley, top to bottom, inside and out, A to Z.

Tully's firstborn was a boy. They named him Russell, after nobody. Russell Christopher Coates. When the boy was old enough, Tully would tell him bedside tales about a kid—a pistol—named R.C., who, come to think of it, looked a lot like Russell Christopher, except R.C. was left-handed, not right. This R.C. had a soapbox that took him to fairs, rodeos, and whatnot, and got its power from no one knew where; it would just keep taking him from one interesting place to another. "R.C." was a name his pals loved to call out, because it would get up in the air and carry from county to county and sometimes on cold nights from state to state, which, Tully said, would often scare the people in South Dakota. These stories would always end with R.C.'s worries melting away like peppermints, at night while he slept, an idea Tully had gotten from a Willie Nelson song. Tully himself didn't care for peppermints, but whenever he was in Scottsbluff he stocked up from Woolworths, so that last thing each night, if Russell promised not to chew it, Tully could take a peppermint from a tin and lay it on his son's tongue before saying good night.

Vince Passaro

Utah

Despite everything they told him, the boy continued to wander off alone, beyond the end of Spring Street, into the desert. His mother, who had theories about the men living out in the foothills, was particularly afraid. She remembered Horton Cashman, one of her own classmates, who had gotten into his father's car sixteen years ago and driven it straight out of town, across the sand, sunlight glinting off its blue roof. He had said he intended to meet up with the interstate, which back then hardly extended beyond Provo almost a hundred miles to the northeast. From there, he had said, he was going all the way to Chicago. There was no way he could have gotten that Chevrolet into those hills, everybody knew that, but he hadn't come back either. The Cashmans had pulled some people together and formed a search, but they never found him. Eventually they had resigned themselves.

And it had been almost five years later, a Saturday in early June, that the boy's mother had seen a group of men drive into town straight up Spring Street in what had to have been the Cashmans' old Chevrolet. It was weathered-looking, and beaten on, but the same model car plain as day. The appearance of those men in that car was too great a coincidence for the boy's mother to believe, but no one in town had said a word. She managed to hold her tongue for a week or so, until the following Sunday morning after services when she had walked up to the sheriff (her husband, Tom, trying to hold her back) and said, "How about that old chevy those boys were driving?"

The sheriff had blinked down on her slowly in the sunlight, his eyes through the bottoms of his wire-rimmed glasses looking round and wet as a dog's. "Seems to me they have the right to a working automobile, just like everybody else," he had finally said.

When they got home Tom had said that it wasn't certain at all that it was the same car, and if it was, why didn't the Cashmans do something? He didn't think it was right to meddle in any man's business and he hoped that when the time came he'd be treated the same.

And Horton Cashman wasn't the only one. She remembered each and every one of the others. There was Tony Lipco, only twelve years old, and Francis Barkman, whose grandparents had given him a pony one year and who, come springtime, had ridden it off into the desert, over Fool Creek, while the ocotillo and the primrose were all in bloom. That was the last anybody had heard of him. People thought there had been some kind of accident out there, probably a snake that had spooked the pony, but the boy's mother knew better. She believed there was only one kind of accident that happened to people in this part of the desert: the men in the hills. Every few years it came, usually to one of the young people, like a calling, where nothing would suit them but to be alone in that desert. Most of them came back, but a few didn't. The boy's mother found herself thinking more and more about those men now, and about the long collection of foothills that began a mile or so east of town, climbing steadily into the purple-black mountains that rose beyond them and looked down over them like an ancient threat. It wasn't just the townspeople anymore; there were strangers who had passed through on their way to settle out there. A flood, it seemed to her, but no one was saying much about it. Come late evenings, after darkness fell, she watched out her front window, looking east toward the mountains. Some nights she thought she could see flames burning, distant glimmers, flickerings of light. And in her mind she had formed a picture that kept repeating, like something big that happens on the news, over and over, a group of men huddled against the darkness, faces lit by fire.

His house had a way of settling into night that was as familiar to him as a voice, with creaks and shifts and a steady murmuring from his parents' room. The boy lay in bed and listened to it and to the sound of his pulse coming up at him through his pillow. He waited for his pulse to quiet and for the murmuring to die away and then he got up. He was still dressed. He slipped out his window onto the pale yellow pebbles of the yard. He dug each foot in softly as he walked, expert at muffling the sound of his steps on the stones. Until he hit the street he was all restraint. Then he took off.

First he ran and then he trotted and then he walked, taking Smith Street and Allen so that he didn't join up with Spring Street until out by Apple's junkyard, near where the sand had begun to crawl up over the asphalt and make its way toward town like a slow thief. Past the junkyard, about two hundred yards further down, there was a sign. "Road Ends," it said, and anybody who didn't notice it would find out soon enough, because another hundred yards or so and the pavement dropped off dead. A six-inch step down from nowhere to nowhere, old Apple liked to say, but the boy had come to think of it as something else.

The desert was coolest at night, and at night he could feel the things that were alive in it. It always seemed quiet at first, but gradually he could hear its noise, a soft hum like the way he imagined an insect's world to be, vibrations in a field of dark shapes. He walked out in it and let his eyes adjust to the light, his boots mashing the low brush and kicking the smaller stones. This darkness felt not so much natural as sacred, as if he were alone in a church lit by a few dim candles. He walked about a mile out, where there were three big rocks, like the ones that marked the beginning of the hill country but a little nearer to town than that, standing together and forming a small, open-sided hollow facing west. He sat down inside. The stone was pale white in the light. Sitting facing west he could see all the way back to the town, where the warning light at Spring and Elling flashed yellow at him, a distant voice. The stars spilled thickly across the sky and merged at the horizon into the few town lights still left burning. All of it shimmered as it came at him through the night-rising heat. A wind blew, warmed by that same heat, a feeling came over him of being alone but not quite alone, as if some presence of the desert had been stirred to come see who the stranger was. He listened for sounds, animals moving, but all he heard was the wind as it swept through the hollow of the three rocks. Then he slept, not aware of anything until dawn snuck over the hills behind him, streaking the gray-white desert with shadows of purple, red and blue.

The boy went to the county school, down the road toward Delta, the next town on. He did all right, because it wasn't very hard to do all right. In the sixth grade, a year before, they had tested his eyesight at twenty/ten. A pilot's eyes, the doctor had said, and since then he had wanted to be a pilot, in the Air Force. He was always the first to notice the small changes of color in the sky that meant new weather. Sometimes, looking out across that western desert, away from the hills, he thought about the ranges and the testing they had done out there. Older people in the town described what it had been like then, how they had prepared for test days as if they were going to see a parade, sitting in lawn chairs and wearing dark glasses in the yards of the westernmost houses. And he imagined it, what the land must have looked like, burnished in orange and black, under the mile-high tongues of fire.

Delicate sparrow-winged movements, hollow-boned, light as air. She was making breakfast. She put eggs on the plate and some fried beef and gravy. She was nervous, and because of her the boy was nervous, too.

"You were out this morning," she said, giving him the plate

"I woke up early," he said.

"Where were you?" she said.

"I went out to the junkyard," he said. He ate with his head down, moving the food in quickly. Normally she would have had him for it but today she didn't say anything. "I needed another tube for my bike," he said.

She was back at the sink, cleaning, all fluttery hands. "Where is it?" she said.

"Where's what?" he said.

"The tube you bought," she said.

"It's out back," he said. He scraped the gravy in from around the rim of the plate with his fork, making a stony, ringing sound.

"The one with all the patches?" she said.

"No, a new one. There's a few patches on it, though," he said. He tore a piece of bread and dipped it in the last of the red juice.

The boy's mother knew the usual stories. She had read about people who disappeared, people who took to the hills. Various groups, who knew what they believed? The men here, they could be eating coyote to survive, or growing plants for food, and marijuana, smoking the leaves, mashing the stalks into hemp. She didn't need anyone to tell her they were armed. There had been a man once who came from California, and he said they were part of a military group devoted to taking all the bank money back from the Jews.

But beyond the stories, she had what she knew, a knowledge of the men in the desert that came from an instinct dark and deep as a cave. She couldn't put a word on what to call them but she knew they were something besides revolutionaries or wild men. It reminded her of when she was a girl, just after she had come to Utah, and the monastery up in Huntsville had opened. She remembered the pictures from the paper, the men in dark robes, their faces lowered. They had looked like the usual kind of men that you might see on the street in one of the bigger towns, Ogden maybe. She remembered wondering if they had done something wrong, that they had to go to this place like a prison. Now she wondered whether the ones she had seen in the paper that many years ago were still alive. What did they do with the ones who died? Did they bury them on the place, or did they send them back to where they had come from, where they had lived before? It occurred to her that maybe they kept them in long stone hallways, like underground mausoleums, all rock and cool dampness.

Before dawn the boy rose and went out to a lonely place. He had long ago given up trying to understand his movement toward solitude, like the pull of rod to water. At home, at the school, in town, he felt like an imitation of himself, waiting to be discovered or made real. What had kept him from going before was fear, a vision he kept having of blackness and nothing. But the thing he had experienced on his secret nights wasn't enough. Now he would go and keep going, and who knew where he would land or when he would return? He was satisfied simply with the introduction into his life of a deepening mystery. He crossed Fool Creek in the first light and headed for the flats, past his three stones, walking fast in the coolness of morning until he was in the hills, where he had never been before, the rocks turning red in the sun-risen light, twisted and outcropping like figures from a different world.

There was water in the hills, that had been known since the miners' time, but the boy had never realized you could feel where water was, how the animals feel it and go. The air was different, the weight of it in his nose and mouth. Water weight. He could feel the weight of it too in the pair of canteens that bounced against his legs as he walked. Whenever he climbed they swung forward, banging against the rocks, the wide straps pulling his shoulders down.

He made it up to the first ridge and descended again, going more slowly as the heat came on. Between him and the next ridge there was a wavy field of stone. The miners had built a road into the hills about six miles farther north, near where the biggest of the old mines had been. They had been driven out there every day on the backs of flatbeds.

In the noonday heat he topped the second ridge. Beyond it, more rock. He felt a disappointment, he had expected something else. It wasn't all formed, what he thought would be here, a city or maybe just a clear path between the rocks, like a direction. Instead, the same nothing. He found a spot to sit and sat, out of the light. For the first time since leaving his house he took some water but after waiting so long he ended up drinking more than he had meant to. He couldn't believe how big the mountains were now, and how much darker. Two auto trips down south and into Colorado had proved it to him but it was hard to imagine that beyond these mountains were cities with trees and green grass lawns. He remembered the long drives, how they had stopped along the way and eaten in air-conditioned restaurants. Today he hadn't eaten and he hadn't brought any food and when he thought of his hunger something turned his mind away and closed his stomach like a clamp. Who had missed him? He knew it would be her first. Above him the birds were circling against the bleached sky. They wanted to know how dead he was.

The boy's mother sat at the dining room table, a half-pound of green beans laid out on brown paper in front of her. Her hands in her lap still held the knife she had been using to cut them. She knew he was in the desert. Past supper and he hadn't come. Tom was making a show of calling around, talking in a big cheery voice to people he hardly ever spoke to. He was on with the Rubys and then he held down the button and lifted it again to call John Singer, but she told him to stop, she was feeling sick. She couldn't stand to listen to him. He sat down next to her. As still as stone, hands folded, she stared past him through the living room and out the front window, where in the distance she could make out the mountains painted in strokes of dark purple and black. The foothills were just visible before them in the last of the light. "He's out in those hills there," she said to her husband, her boy's father. "You might as well leave the telephone alone."

A few minutes after eight that night they called the sheriff. He came over in the patrol car with Horace Green, one of his deputies, even though they had called him at home. In his civilian clothes, the boy's mother thought, he looked a little silly. She noticed that his blue slacks were similar to a pair Tom had. Horace, on duty, had his uniform on. The boy's mother sat in a chair in the living room, where she had been since giving Tom some supper, rarely looking away from the window, a rectangle of darkness on the eastern side of the room. She didn't offer the two men any coffee or beer or soda. She let Tom do the talking, except early on when she heard him saying, "He might have gone off into the desert toward the hills, across the creek at the stone bridge."

She interrupted him then. "He is already in that desert now, in the hills," she said. "The question is who is going to get him out, not where he is because that's where he is."

"She says he's been spending some time out there lately," Tom said to the sheriff.

"Ought to tell him not to go out there," Horace said. "It's pretty dangerous—"

"I'm sure they know that, Horace," the sheriff said, cutting in on him. "I'm sure the boy was told not to go hanging around in the desert by himself." He looked at the boy's mother. "Boys that age," he said, "they get ideas of their own."

He found a small space about twenty feet below the ridge line, a patch of sandy ground under an overhang, partly enclosed. He swept it out with his boots, watching along the base of the stone for cracks and holes that meant snakes. He sat himself back against the rock, near the front so he could look up onto the ridge. He waited. Dusk came on, the sky bands of blue and green. The mountains were scarred with black lines where shadows filled the ravines. The rocks were fire red, as if ignited by the last flames of the sunset, and later on when the paler light of the stars had taken over the sky these same rocks turned ash white, as if those flames had really burned them.

For a time after that he slept, he couldn't tell for how long. When he woke he was hungry. In the moonlight all the small stones reminded him of white cakes and bread loaves. There was a full canteen of water and another half. He sipped slowly on it. After sunrise he would have to find more.

The man standing by the stove had come all the way from Colorado. The boy's mother couldn't get it out of her head that he had come as far in a day to talk with Tom as her own people had come to settle here. He was built small and lean, like a whippet, and he had a silk bandana around his neck under his white shirt that he tied with a kind of city flair to it. His hair was long and he used something in it to comb it back. She noticed how he was completely unable to keep still, he had been all over the kitchen. He was leaning now in the corner where the stove met the countertop, smoking a cigarette, and he kept running his fingers along the smooth enamel in front of the burners. As he stroked the stovetop she watched his hand, the freckles on his brown skin, his gold ring and the cuff of his navy jacket where there was a small fray near the buttons.

"I believe as of right now we're in a cult situation," he was saying. He was talking about essentials. A helicopter, above all. Prior experience. Cult activity west of. Ramifications, hopes too high. Cult. Cult and. As well as the needless publicity. Then he was talking about the sheriff. He didn't want to say one thing or another about the sheriff. The sheriff. The sheriff has to think about the public. The sheriff's election. The sheriff has his reasons and some of them are good reasons as you know to play things down a little bit to keep everyone calm but let's not fool ourselves it's a difficult decision it's going to be difficult, difficult, cult, cult.

"We just want him back home safe," she heard Tom say. She was seated across from him at the table. There had been coffee and the coffee cups were pushed back against the wall to make way for a map that had been spread out across the Formica top. Tom kept running his big, padded hands over it, trying to smooth out the wrinkles. The boy's mother was sitting very straight, her own hands in her lap, unmoving. That word the man had used had set off a series of images and faces she couldn't quite put names on. Most of them were girls, from wealthy families. That was fine, she thought. They could expect that. Her kind of people were supposed to be left alone.

"Any rescue scenario you can think of is going to be touchy in those hills," the man from Colorado was saying. "The helicopter, the time, the things we'll need, they cost money."

"There's money," she heard Tom saying.

———

The bird on the ledge above him, its soft wings hung down. They were black at the tips and then dark silver and blue. It moved a few steps, was still, moved a few steps, was still again. The boy sat below, head bent back, taking in the feathers and the rock in the sunlight. When it moved its wings trembled and brushed the stone. Dust clung to them and sparkled, almost like drops of water. It was still for a while, then it let out a sudden shriek and flapped its wings twice, the sound of a paper bag roughly opened. It moved right and centered itself on the peak. The ledge came out like a V and the bird hung at the front of it, its wings curling down around the stone like two hands trying to reach each other.

The helicopter and the helicopter pilot came up from Las Vegas, not from Colorado as the boy's mother had expected. She began to believe that this man from Colorado had connections everywhere. He and the pilot were staying in the motel out on the state road, the whirlybird parked out behind it in the sand. People were saying that the pilot drank a lot, hung around in town until all hours. Twice a day, morning and evening, he and the man from Colorado flew into the hills.

Ten days went by, then twelve, then thirteen, and she felt herself getting weaker and weaker. On the day two weeks after the boy had gone off she didn't get up at all. The doctor came in and gave her something, she didn't listen to what it was. All she could notice was how he talked to her in that same chattery tone that Tom and everyone else had been using on her since the first night. She wondered whether people were planning to talk to her the rest of her life that way. After he gave her the shot she heard him with Tom, mumbling in the hall, they mumbled for a long time, mumble mumble mumble, I hope you die die die. She started to sing a song she remembered: There's a new day coming, a nice boy running, down the road. . . . She couldn't remember the rest but she knew she had sung it with her boy who was grown now. Her boy was grown and he'd gone off to work for the engineers. The creek was rising, instead of its usual trickle. By late summer it was over its banks and flooding the desert, and the Army had come in from the test ranges to build levees like they had done in Colorado the year of the bad flooding when she was nine. That's where her son was, he was out working in the desert with the engineers. He was working to hold the water back from sweeping across the last strip of desert and drowning everybody. They had built a dam and a new body of water had been formed, bigger than Salt Lake. She could see it, it went all the way from the edge of town to the mountains, the water glass smooth and silver-white, an immense mirror of the sky. It ran up an incline like the land and the tops of all the buttes in East Utah, everything running at that same incline up toward the highest peak of the mountains. Any day now that water would be loosed and it would start to roll down on them, because it was on an incline, gathering power with a mad rush and sweeping away everything, the silver mercury water. Her boy was out there and nobody to help him. Oh God oh God help my boy who is alone in the blazing desert light. Her head was filled with water, her mouth, her stomach, all water, then she was in it, on it, rolling over and rolling and rolling, caught in the crest of a giant silver wave.

A long plant, he sliced it and sucked it. He thought, forty days, forty nights, how to count? Without food. Not much water. He thought, hedgehog cactus, barrel cactus, threadplant, the purple nama, the night-blooming cereus. And the saguaro forests down in California. Not here, he thought. Here is the white-winged dove. He sliced long slices like strips of jerky and laid them coiled on a cloth. They were like the long yucca leaves or aloe, but not spiny. A juice inside. If poison fine he was already poisoned. Coiled and green like snakes. They were better dry. He chewed them.

The machine was coming again, he heard its noise. A distant rock-padded air-chopping chop. So rapid it almost buzzed. The noise came now every day in the daylight, he had heard it again and again, marking nothing. Now though it was louder than before, and it came and it came until he went under the ledge and stayed and it came and then his small space was filled with a chopping roar that shook him. It whipped the air. Its long shadow glided along the ground, smooth as a fish. Climbing past him it went up over the ridge and as it went he saw from under his stone its two sled blades sliding fast like greased skids over the high rocks. He knew what it was. Beyond the ridge its noise softened. Chopping the air in slices. He pulled together his canteens and the food he had prepared and he sheathed his knife and began walking. It went in so he went out. Against the sunlight he had his cap pulled low over his eyes, a bandana around his neck. He went fast, staying close to the rocks. He didn't feel the heat.

Alison Baker

How I Came West, and Why I Stayed

I t was a long, strange trip, over frozen plains and rivers and into the mountains, but when the going got really tough, I'd close my eyes, and I'd see them: Lisa, in camouflage pants, stalking bears; Debbi, in blaze orange, wheezing out mating calls until huge bull elk stampeded down the hills, ready to perform.

Now I stood outside the Silver Dollar Saloon, the wind whipping around my collar, my hands like two lumps of ice even in my Thinsulate-lined mittens. The sky was cluttered with stars, but I couldn't stand there staring at them all night. I took a deep breath and pushed my way through the swinging doors.

My glasses steamed up, but I could tell everyone was looking at me, because dead silence dropped over the room. I took off my glasses and wiped them clean on my neckerchief. Then I put them back on. I'd been right; every head in the bar was turned toward me, and the faces were sort of orange, and puffy-looking, in the light from the video games.

I cleared my throat. "I'm looking for cheerleaders," I said.

They looked at one another and then back at me.

"How's that?" said an old geezer at the bar.

"I said, I'm looking for cheerleaders," I said.

"That's what I thought you said," the old guy said. He guffawed, and suddenly the whole room erupted in laughter, people pounding one another on the back, slapping their thighs, rolling in the sawdust on the floor. I smiled, glad the ice was broken.

I walked over to the bar and sat down beside the old guy. He said I could call him Ol' Pete. "You cain't never find 'em, not in this weather," he said. The snow had stopped, but the night air was bitterly cold. The roads up the pass were closed, with drifts over twenty feet high.

"Haw!" Ol' Pete suddenly guffawed again, and the rest of the heads—hoary, bewhiskered, grizzled—turned back in my direction. "On'y a fool!" he said, and the others grinned and nodded, and chanted, "Fool, fool."

"Buy 'em a round," the bartender whispered, as she wiped off the bar in front of me.

"A round on me," I said, and an excited hum swept the room. After the third round the hum broke out into singing, and in the middle of ". . . deer and the antelope play . . ." someone sat down beside me.

"Why you want to go up there, anyway?" she said. I turned and looked her in the eye. She was dark, of indeterminate age, and she wore a buffalo-head helmet, complete with gleaming horns. "They wanted you up there, wouldn't they a' took you with 'em?"

I nodded. "I can't explain it," I said. "It's just something I have to do."

She nodded too. "I can understand that," she said. "It's big—bigger than you, maybe. What's your name, stranger?"

"Most folks call me Whitey," I said.

"It won't be easy, Whitey," my companion said. "I can coach you some, but it'll be hard work."

She said her name was Buffalo Gal, and that I could bunk with her. On one wall of her cabin she had a USGS map, all squiggles, with red-headed pins marking the cheerleader near-sightings. I stared at it but could find no pattern in the scattered red dots.

"They come and they go," Buffalo Gal said. "They might as well be bigfoots."

"Bigfeet," I said.

"Whatever," Buffalo Gal said.

She worked me hard. She never let up, never let me slack off. "Hit 'em again," she'd say, time after time. "Harder, harder." But she was generous in her praise, too. "Go, go, go!" she'd shout, as I telemarked through the aspens. I worked harder for Buffalo Gal than I'd ever worked before; something about her made you want to.

And then one evening, as we skied through a narrow canyon, Buffalo Gal stopped so fast that I crashed into her. "Listen," she said.

"Give me an *A!*" The voice came, faint as starlight, distant as the sigh of a bear in a snowbound cave. It was followed by a wailed response from a dozen throats: "*A!*" It echoed down the hills and canyons, and up under the trees around us.

"It's them," Buffalo Gal said.

Saturdays we made the long trek down to the Silver Dollar, just to be in contact with human beings, and to have a drink.

"Sure, I heard 'em," Ol' Pete said when I asked him. "Hear 'em all the time."

"Have you seen them?" I said.

"Hell," Ol' Pete said.

When he didn't say any more, I had to ask. "How can I find them, Pete?"

"Haw!" he guffawed, and nods and slow grins spread across the other faces in the room. "Where you from, Whitey?" he asked.

"Veedersburg, Indiana," I said.

"Well, then, I'll tell you," Ol' Pete said. "Them cheerleaders is like a poem. You don't go lookin' for a poem; it sort of comes to you, iffen yer in the right place, doin' the right thing." His rheumy eyes got rheumier, dripping a little, as he watched Lu, the bartender, wiping up some spilled milk. "You cain't predict. You can be out there for days, huntin', trackin' 'em across the range, countin' the buttercups, and you won't see hide nor hair. And then one day yer building a fire, or you just washed yer hair and yer mebbe smokin' some weed you saved up from yer last southern trip, and there she'll be, standin' afore you, smilin' down at you, her hand stretched out, whisperin' 'Score, Pete, score.'"

"Wow!" I said. "That happened to you?"

"Nope," he said.

Buffalo Gal and I skied home, heading back out of town and up the canyon through the moonlight. I looked around for shooting stars, and my nose twitched at the smells that skidded across the moonscape toward us: a last whiff of tobacco from the Silver Dollar, the sweet, flowery smell of someone's anti-static sheet from a dryer vent, the mucous-freezing smell of cold air rushing off the mountains. It was just the sort of time I might have seen them, if I'd only known.

In the mountains, in Montana, in winter, time loses its substance; it becomes meaningless. Night runs into day like the Ovaltine that Buffy stirred into our milk in the morning. I knew time had passed by the way the moon grew and shrank; I knew a week had gone by when we headed for the Silver Dollar on

Saturday night. But that's all I could tell you.

"That's how it is here," was all Buffalo Gal would say.

One day, up in Avery Pass, we came upon a single dainty foot-print, clear as day, left by a size-seven ripple-bottom gym shoe. I flung myself into the snow beside it. "How could she leave just one?" I cried, and when I put my face next to it, I sniffed the faintest of odors—rubber? Anti-fungal medication?

"You tell me," Buffalo Gal said. With her ice ax she chopped the footprint out of the frozen snow and laid it gently in her helmet. I pulled it along the ground behind me, the horns serving as runners across the snow. We flew down the mountain, down to the lower pass and back to the cabin, and the speed of our passage created a wind that freeze-dried the footprint, sucked the moisture right out of it. It was frozen so solid it would never melt.

We hung the footprint above the front door, hoping it would bring us luck.

I was beginning to understand how important the presence of the cheerleaders was to the local people. They were part of the mountain mythology, feral fauna as significant as the mountain lion, the grizzly, the Rocky Mountain bighorn sheep. And they were not a recent phenomenon, nor were they exotic visitors. The history of cheerleaders in Montana went back for many, many years: as far back as the reach of local memory.

Ol' Pete had given me a hint of what they meant. What the manatee is to the naturalist in the mangrove swamp, what the race car is to the Hoosier, what the tornado is to the Kansan— that is what the cheerleader is to the Montanan. Cheerleaders are Possibility, they are Chance, they are Fate; they are beauty, and grace, and poetry.

Many had learned the hard way that Ol' Pete was right: you couldn't find a cheerleader. You had to wait, and be ready. Many an expedition, hunters in their red flannel, stocking up their mules or their llamas or their ATVs with two or three weeks' worth of food, had set out determined—come what may!—to find the cheerleaders. They carried guns, too. "Hell," they'd say, if you asked why. Would they shoot a cheerleader? Would they hang a pink-cheeked, freckled face above the fireplace, among the furry heads of grizzlies and mule deer and moose, and the iridescent bodies of stuffed dead pheasants?

The truth was—the truth was that nobody really knew how he or she might react, if he or she actually found them.

And in all the years the cheerleaders had been in those parts, no one *had* found one. They'd found tracks, and signs: bits of pompon here and there, and of course my frozen footprint, and once an old, well-used megaphone, standing on its wide end under a spruce tree.

But many a hunter had returned cold, frostbitten, disappointed. And many a hunter had hung up her gun, and taken up, say, jogging, or t'ai chi—something that would get her outside, in the woods, on a hilltop—and in solitude, maybe whispering, she'd chant, "S-U-C-C-E-S-S." Just in case, someday, the cheerleaders came to *her*.

"Okay, B.G.," I said one evening, as we stretched like lazy cats before the glowing wood stove, each with her own bowl of popcorn—Buffy liked garlic powder on hers, but I stuck with melted butter. "What gives?"

"Ah," Buffalo Gal said. She smiled, and gazed dreamily at the stove. "Impetuous youth."

"Youth?" I said. "Buffy, I'm forty-two years old. I'm not exactly youth."

She shook her head and gave me a look I couldn't interpret. "Whitey," she said, "do you know how long I've been up here?"

"No," I said.

Buffalo Gal leaned over her popcorn bowl and put her face close to mine. "Neither do I," she said.

"But, Buffy," I said, "how do I find the cheerleaders?"

"How the hell do I know?" Buffy said. "I've been up here lo, these many moons, and I haven't found them yet."

When Buffalo Gal said that to me—when I realized that, by golly, she never had said she could help me find them—I had to ask. "Why are you up here, Buffalo Gal?" I said.

She smiled. "Whitey," she said, "I used to be a jock. I did every sport you can imagine—field hockey, tennis, jai alai. Seems like every time I turned around, there they were, supporting me all the way. Go! Go! Go! Yea, rah, Buffy!" She shook her head. "Guess I just didn't want to go on through life without 'em. Even if they're not cheering for me anymore, I just want to be near 'em, hear 'em, once in a while in the night. Just want to know they're there."

I nodded, and stood up. "I'm off," I said.

"See you around," she said.

That's the way it is in Montana. When the time comes to go, you go, and there are no hard feelings.

I don't know how far I skied that night, or how long. I was thinking as I went, and that's a dangerous thing to do. Thinking distracts you. You can get lost, thinking of something other than where you're going. You can ski right up the mountain and over the top, and get going so fast that, too late, you realize you've gone too far, that you have taken off into pure, crystal-clear Montana air. Every now and then in Montana you see someone who's done that, a skier, flying across the moon like a deformed Canada goose.

I don't know how far I skied, but when the trail ended, I was right where I knew I'd be: at the door of the Silver Dollar Saloon. I went inside, and when I'd wiped off my glasses, there was Buffy, nodding at me, and Ol' Pete lifting a finger from his glass in greeting.

I sat down at a little table and ordered a glass of milk. Then someone spoke. "What are you up to up there, anyway?" she said, across the crowded room.

I knew who it was: Renee, a lean, grim-faced ranch hand, not much older than I was. She'd ridden the rodeo circuit for a while and then come back to Montana to work Ephraim P. Williston's sheep ranch. Somewhere along the line she'd lost her left hand—caught in a lasso and squeezed right off when she was roping a steer—and most Saturday evenings she sat in the Silver Dollar with a chamois rag, rubbing and polishing her elk-antler hook until it gleamed. She was a tough customer, Renee; even the feral dogs stayed away from her flocks.

The bar was so still you could hear the chamois rubbing against her hook. She stared at me, her eyes in the shadow of the Stetson she never took off. Her hand, polishing, never stopped moving.

I swallowed the last of my milk. I put down the little glass, and then I looked up and across the room straight at where I figured her eyes were.

"Nothing," I said.

She took off her hat then, and I found myself looking into the hardest eyes I'd ever seen. They were as cold as ice, and dry ice at that; I had a tough time believing they'd ever cried, or looked at anything but bleak and windswept sagebrush desert.

I'd said the wrong thing.

"Sister," she said, "you just said the wrong thing. You come up here, from God knows where—"

"She's from Veedersburg, Indiana," Ol' Pete interrupted. "She never made no secret of that."

I threw him a grateful look, but Renee shook her head.

"From God knows where," she repeated. "You sit in here and drink with us; you follow Buffalo Gal around the woods like a goddamn puppy dog, sucking up everything she knows; you pry, and eavesdrop, and then you go out and harass our cheerleaders; and when I ask you, in a friendly, innocent manner, what you're doing, you say *Nothing?*"

The silence was so thick you could have cut it with a Bowie knife. I didn't know what to say. She was right about part of it: I did come in and drink with them, I did ask questions, I did follow Buffy around. But that part about harassing the cheerleaders was way off the mark.

How could I explain that I was doing this for *all* of us?

"All my life," I began, and I prayed my voice wouldn't shake, "I wanted nothing more than to be a cheerleader. All through my childhood my parents held up cheerleaders as role models for me. 'My dream,' my dad used to say, 'is that someday you'll be just like them.' We went to every game. And then when they started broadcasting games on TV—oh, I burned with the desire to be out there with them, leaping and bending and rolling on national television, and flinging my arms out to embrace the whole world!"

I paused for breath. I looked around the room, and I knew I'd struck a chord. No one was saying a word: all eyes either were on me or were dreamy, looking back to their own youthful aspirations, remembering the cheerleaders from all those little towns—Moab, Hammond, Rockland, Kennebunk. These ranch hands came from all over the country, and I suspected they'd come for much the same reason I had.

I took a deep breath. "I guess it's an old, old story," I went on. "For years I practiced, twirling my baton, getting in shape with tap lessons. I did so many splits that my legs would hardly stay closed. I memorized the chants, the yells, you name it."

They were nodding; they'd been there too.

"I never made the squad," I said quietly. "Not even the B squad. I just wasn't good enough."

A sigh rippled across the room; some of those dusty eyes were a little damp.

"You know," I said, "I wanted to be a cheerleader more than anything else in the world. I would have sold my soul." I laughed softly, sadly. "I guess it's still for sale."

"Hell," Ol' Pete said, "so's mine!"

71

"Whitey," Renee said, standing up and crossing the room to where I stood, "I misjudged you. I'm sorry." She did a forward lunge and stuck out her hand.

I took it. "Renee, Renee, Renee," I said. "You were right about so many things."

She punched me on the arm with her hook. "Howsabout a turn at the cards?" she said.

"Yeah! Yeah!" The crowd roared its approval, and Ol' Pete actually did a herkie. I grinned with pleasure; this was another Montana tradition. In many a saloon heated discussions came to an end when the cards were pulled out, and would-be pugilists resolved their differences with a hand or two of this traditional game of the Old West. It had saved the glassware and bar mirrors of a good many drinking and gaming establishments.

Eight of us sat down around a table, and Ol' Pete dealt the cards. Carol Ann, another shepherd from out at Williston's, held Renee's cards for her—she had trouble managing them with her hook.

The game wasn't a long one—these games never are—and one after another the players matched their last card and dropped out. Finally, as fate would have it, Renee and I were face to face. And, friendly as we now were, I was sweating.

I held two cards, and one of them was Her. Carol Ann was holding one card for Renee, and it was her draw. If she drew the matching card, she'd be out. But if she drew the Old Maid, I still had a chance.

Renee kept her eyes on my face and reached. Her hand hesitated above my cards; the tension—friendly tension—in the room was palpable. And then, as Renee's hand descended toward the Old Maid, she stopped. She lifted her head. "Listen," she said.

I'd heard it too. A rhythmic clapping, the soft patter of sneaker-shod feet. And then voices.

"H-O-W-D-Y! Hey-hey! We say hi!" And through the swinging door burst the first cheerleader the Silver Dollar had ever seen. She popped those doors back and bounced into the room, her hands rolling in front of her, her blond curls cascading over her shoulders. She bounded across the room, right over to our table, and dropped to one knee, one arm flung out to her side and the other straight over her head. "DeeDee!" she cried.

Another cheerleader leaped through the door and sprang over to kneel beside the first. Flinging her arms exactly the same way, she cried, "Kristi!"

And they kept on coming, the door swinging and banging against the wall, their little rubber-soled feet tap-tapping through the peanut shells that littered the Silver Dollar's floor. "Debbi! Suzi! Lori! Heather! Patti! Mindy! Lisa! Darlene!" They climbed on top of one another till their human pyramid reached the ceiling. They jumped up and landed in splits on the bar.

And in the dim light from the bar we saw that they had changed. Gone were their pleated skirts, the snowy white tennies, the matching panties. Their sweaters were black from the smoke of a thousand campfires and stiff with the arterial blood of dying elk. The dimpled knees were hidden in layers of wool, of heavy-duty twill, of camouflage-patterned neoprene. Their sneakers were gray, worn; their little socks showed through holes in the toes.

And their faces. No longer pink and shiny, their skin was rough from winter winds, wrinkled from the brutal western sun. Their blond hair was stringy and sort of greasy, unwashed for what must have been years.

But their teeth! One after another they smiled; again and again the gloom of the Silver Dollar was broken as their teeth flashed little reflections of the neon beer signs in the windows. Years of fluoridated water, decay-preventive dentifrices, and orthodontia had worked their magic. Whiter than new snow, more uniform than kernels of hybrid corn, brighter than Venus, Jupiter, and Mars in alignment, their teeth alone would have revealed them as the cheerleaders they were.

They stood, and knelt, and sat splayed before us in splendid formation, and then they windmilled their arms and all at once leaped into the air, spread-eagling their limbs toward the four corners of the world, and screamed, "Yea! Rah! Team!"

Something warm surged through my body; I looked at Renee, and she was smiling right into my eyes. She reached out and took the matching card.

I was the Old Maid.

The crowd went wild, and the cheerleaders bounced and hugged one another, tears rolling down their leathery cheeks, and they all clustered around Renee and wanted to pat her, and touch her, and have her sign their sneakers. It was Renee's moment of glory.

I might have felt really bad if something hadn't happened that warmed my heart all the way to the mitral valve. As everybody pushed over to the bar, the cheerleaders spontaneously stopped, and they all came back and stood around me, in a circle, and each one put her left hand on the right shoulder of the next cheerleader. And then they bent their knees, and they stuck out their right hands, and in unison they bobbed up and down, as if they were shaking my right hand, and they chanted, "YOU'RE OKAY. YOU'RE ALL RIGHT. YOU PUT UP A DARN GOOD FIGHT! Yea! Rah! Whitey!"

There wasn't a dry eye in the room. "A round on me!" I shouted. And they cheered me again.

In the days that followed, I knew something had changed. I had achieved a goal, a major one, and now—temporarily, anyway—I had nothing to strive for. I was happy, but I felt a little empty, too.

On about Wednesday, I was sitting listlessly in the sun, contemplating the bleak future that stretched ahead of me, when I heard someone coming. I looked around and saw that it was Buffalo Gal, and behind her was Renee.

Buffy got right to the point. "We've been huddling," she said. "We want you to stick around."

"I don't know," I said. "I'm not sure I can do this anymore."

"Not this," Renee said. "The Williston ranch has an opening for another shepherd. Carol Ann's getting hitched."

"I don't know anything about sheep," I said.

"You don't have to," Renee said. "They mill around, and you stand there. Or you sing to 'em, sometimes."

"Surely there's others more qualified," I said.

Renee gazed off at the horizon and rubbed her hook with her mitten. "The thing is, Whitey," she said, "most of us, we haven't seen a cheerleader since we've been here. It's what we came out here for, and we tried to do everything right, and we waited. But they never came until you got here. It's got us hoping again."

"Hoping?" I said.

Hard-bitten, rugged, dry-eyed as she was, she blushed. "We've started practicing again. It's all we really want, still. And we've realized that even if we'll never be varsity cheerleaders, we can still do the work, learn the new routines. And who knows? Someday they may need a substitute."

I looked at her. Something was in her face that I hadn't seen there before, but I recognized it. It was spirit: team spirit. It's something that's hard to find in the West, in Montana, in the wide-open spaces, where women spend most of their time alone. I thought, maybe that's it. It's not the adulation, the cheering, the popularity, that we want; it's team spirit.

"I guess I could learn," I said.

So I stayed. I'm still just an assistant shepherd—sort of on the B team—but I'll tell you something: sheep are the best pep club in the world to practice on. You can be out there in front of them walking on your hands, doing triple back flips, and they don't even look at you. They keep on munching the grass, ripping it out of the ground and chewing it up.

But it's in the nature of sheepherding, and of cheerleading, to stick with it, to keep on trying. You realize how hard the cheerleaders have worked to get where they are. That makes you work harder.

Sometimes, of a summer evening—oh, yes, summer finally came—I'll be out there on the range, practicing in front of my sheep. "Give me a P!" I'll shout, and the only response is from a border collie, who obliges on a nearby fence post. And then the warm summer wind picks up, just as the sun sets, and the sky is all red and purple and pink, and I hear, from miles away, "Two bits!" And maybe a distant figure cartwheels across a hilltop, silhouetted against the place where the sun just disappeared.

And then, from the east, where the sky is already dark, I hear "Four bits!" And I know it's Buffalo Gal, calling down from her lonely vigil on the mountain. And from up at the ranch house, where Renee is maybe loading supplies to bring out to us the next morning, comes "Six bits!" And I jump up and shout, "A dollar!"

And the next voice is so far away that the words aren't quite clear—it's up in high pastureland, where the sheep are chewing grass in the dark, and the little lambs are jumping around, or nursing on their moms, and the dogs are lying in the dust after a hard day, sleeping with one eye open, always on the lookout for coyotes. But we all know it's Ol' Pete, yelling, "If you got spirit, stand up and holler!"

And wherever we are, we leap into the sky and holler for all we're worth. Down in town they probably think it's thunder, but it's us, practicing, ready for when the snow flies in the fall and the cheerleaders come down from the high mountain passes. We'll be ready to go with them, hunting for the Big Game.

Lee K. Abbott

Getting Even

The ruckus started while I was on the phone to my fiancée, Mary Ellen Tillmon, trying to explain why I was in a room at the El Paso Airport Hilton Hotel instead of in her arms there in Denver.

"I got bumped," I told her. "Continental said they'd get me on tomorrow's flight. Promise."

"Oh, Walter," she said, "you just naturally find ways to foul up, don't you?"

That's when we heard it, the hooting and shrieking, and if I'd known then that out in the hall, that August of 1968, was a kid named Alton Corbett—"Buttermilk" to those in our fraternity who knew him better—then there'd be no good versus evil to tell you about and I'd be just another grown-up here in Deming, New Mexico, concerned only with the beef cattle I raise, the dues I owe the Mimbres Valley Country Club, and the bad rings that cause my Jeep to go *chuck-chucka-chug*.

"Get up, you sons-of-bitches," he was hollering, running from one door to another, banging and kicking and stomping. "Watch what's going on!"

"Who you got in there with you?" Mary Ellen said. "You're in the bar, aren't you?"

There was screeching that was neither jet planes nor the Clyde and Jim-Bob cowboy music from the lounge on the first floor.

"Wait a second," I told her, half-scared. I had nearly three thousand dollars on me that night, down payment on a shipment of yearling short horns my daddy had sold to Del Norte Packing, a feedlot outfit.

"Out of bed, out of bed, out of bed" is what I heard when I eased my door open, and what I saw, flying at me an arm and a leg at a time, was a young person, hair like a haystack, wearing Beach Boy swimming trunks and hurling himself against every closed door on his way.

"Turn on your TVs," he was ordering, smacking a wall a few paces from my own. "They're beating the shit out of us."

"Buttermilk?" I said, though not loud enough to be heard. A Senior, he'd been the pledge chairman when I rushed Lamda Chi as a Freshman, and back then he'd looked like my mother's idea of a bank teller—posture of the enviably erect kind and a toothy smile that involved the whole of his body.

"What is it?" Mary Ellen said.

I had switched on the TV—to what the next day's papers would describe as the "Overreaction" of the Chicago police department to the demonstrators, people more or less my own age, protesting at the Democratic party's national convention. "Ladies and gentlemen," an announcer was saying, "Ladies and gentlemen—"

"Walter, answer me," Mary Ellen was saying. "You still there?"

"Yes," I said. "I'm here," I said.

On the screen, people were being chased by Jeeps with barbed-wire barricades attached to their bumpers, and out in the hall, harsh and spooky and impossible as the images CBS was showing me, raged Buttermilk Corbett.

"I gotta go," I told Mary Ellen.

She was yapping about her own father, Harvey "Hootie" Tillmon, and what he expected from a son-in-law, which concerned a character upright and stubborn as a tree stump, when I heard Alton Corbett calling a West Texas hotel guest a retrograde, neo-bullshit, bullet-minded Fascist fuckface.

"Listen," I said, "I'll call you tomorrow."

"You don't get involved, Walter," she said. "You hear me?"

I had graduated from New Mexico State University in Las Cruces the previous May, but what I knew about Vietnam and foreign policy and LBJ or Hubert Horatio Humphrey and The Vietnam Day Committee was vastly inferior to what I knew about Natural Resources Economics, Agricultural Materials Processing Systems and Field Crop Breeding, the courses I'd taken so that I could inherit my father's ranch and thus be as carefree, raw-boned, tanned and well regarded as he. That's what I was thinking about when Alton Corbett slapped my door— what crop drying and soil conservation had to do with riot and turmoil and head-banging.

"I know you're in there," he was hollering, my door thudding. "Channel 4. It's happening, the revolution."

I'd been face to face with Alton exactly once: He'd stopped me outside Young House, the English building, snatched off my Derby Days hat, and told me to recite for him—backwards, for crying out loud—the Greek alphabet. "Now," he said, and that was all until, when I sputtered between Omicron and Tau, he shrugged and muttered, with more sympathy than malice, "Good God, what a geek."

Down the hall, in front of the room that turned out to be his, Alton was engaged in a dramatic finger-pointing and head-wagging conversation with a man built like a refrigerator, while across from me a woman in a poofy cocktail dress red enough to glow in the dark was saying, "Get him, Billy Puckett. Punch him in the nose."

"See?" Alton hollered. "This is what it's all about."

Up and down the corridor, folks, like bystanders at a car wreck, were peering out their doors, abashed and aghast, why-mouthed or huh-faced, and maybe—I'm not sure—I had the idea to shoo them away, or turn this off like the TV Alton had ordered us to watch.

"What're you looking at?" Alton was saying. "I'm an impassioned man, that's what. You people are weasels."

You couldn't hear much from Billy, the big man, except a kind of growling and, given the fury his size could be, the oddest, most inappropriate phrase, like cussing in church: "Pipe down, son. Put a lid on it."

Alton's head jerked up and down, hands waving. He shouted something about brutality and injustice and what would come around if it went around.

"Go ahead, clodhopper. See what happens."

"Aw, Jesus H. Christ," Billy was saying. "Why me?"

We'd come to a point where that hollering woman's boyfriend (I found out later that they'd known each other about five hours) had decided—with real reluctance, I believe—to coldcock my former frat brother.

"Son," Billy began, his fist up for everyone to see. This was less to hurt than to get Alton Corbett's much-divided attention. "Why don't you go back to your room now? You got everybody excited here."

"Go on, Billy," the woman shouted. "Mash that little bug. I hate them when they grin like that."

She had a cigarette going, her face as shiny as an eggplant, and

I thought how nice it would be to see her catch fire and disappear in a cloud of smoke; and then my attention went to Alton Corbett and how his own eyes had filled up with light and time and recognition.

"What say, geek?"

Something hot shot through me at that instant, I swear, and my instinct was to throw up my own hands and wave all of them—Alton, Billy, the woman, that man in his baggy PJs and that lady in her pink bathrobe—into Never-Never Land.

"What're we gonna do with this here proto-dipstick?" Alton said. "I recommend we give him kisses then turn him loose with a grin and a way to go."

Here it is, when I play these actions back in my mind, that what happened becomes less a movie than a slide show, each image sharp and surprising, violent as a nightstick: Sighing as if extremely tired, Billy punched; Alton Corbett collapsed; Billy said something intended to be the final word; Alton Corbett took exception and, from his knees this time, toppled over in a heap; and then, with Billy trudging back to his girlfriend—"I'm sorry, folks," he was saying, "I'm normally real peaceful myself"—three El Paso policemen appeared, and Alton Corbett, a welt on his cheek and his lip already swollen, arranged himself on the carpet, crossed his legs at the ankle and folded his skinny arms across his chest as if for a nap.

"Hey, Walter," he called. "This is what's called passive resistance. We go limp and think about being communists."

"Yes," I had said on the phone. "I am here," I had said.

"You know that shithead?" This was Billy's girlfriend again, her face a puzzle of pride and contempt, and I saw in her then what I eventually saw in Mary Ellen Tillmon when, over the next six and a half years, I screwed up.

"Outrage, repression, lies," Alton was saying, less his innermosts than an i-before-e-except-after-c recitation. "Shame on you bozos. This is a bourgeoisie insult."

In the woman's room before the door slammed shut, Billy was slouched at the foot of the bed. Behind me, my TV was going, the shouts and screams from it tinny and too cowboys-and-Indians to be real; and down the hall, a cop holding each wrist and the third grabbing his wriggling legs, Alton Corbett was being dragged toward the exit.

"Hey, Walter," he said. "Are you gonna help me or what?"

Then it was over, everybody else back indoors, nothing to indicate who'd done what or why. I felt cold, I remember, and took in the interesting way goose bumps came to my arms then went away. I could hear my own breathing, not ragged or quick, and wondered what hour it was, what day.

Something happened to me that night, I have concluded. Something as dire as death—or marriage or childbirth or bankruptcy—is for others, but as these events took place when I was twenty-one, smart only about what multiple-choice and fill-in-the-blanks can teach you, and stuffed with facts the value of which I couldn't have said in a million words, I didn't know what to think; or, having thought, what to do. Instead, feeling sneaky, I went to his open door, pushed it aside and stepped in: my conscience, which I imagined in the Hibbs and Hannon cowboy hat and Tony Lama boots my father wore, saying, "Walter, Jr., you dumb peckerwood."

Alton Corbett's empty room was the mess a whirlwind leaves behind. Plus it smelled like four dogs had been in there, stale and close and wet. The linen from the twin beds, mattresses shoved sidelong, was flung everywhere (I found a pillow in the bathtub), and the towels, soaked and knotted, were piled on a chair. This had been a place of panic and frenzy, as wrong as an umbrella blown inside out. What clothes he had—Levi's and socks and two button-down shirts like lawyers wear—were scattered on the floor, his Converse tennis shoes atop the TV, which was on but silent.

On the screen, crowds were running helter-skelter, the way

my cattle do when heat lightning strikes. A kid who looked like Wally Cleaver was dragging a sawhorse and pumping his fist, his mouth gulping air after air after air. In another scene, junk—ashtrays and trashcans and an easy chair—came hurtling down from the upper floors of a building that was itself a Hilton Hotel. The pictures kept coming, jagged and bouncy and tipped over. You heard not words, I was sure, but grunts and moans independent of thought, not from the brain but from other corners of the body.

Alton had a case of Coors beer in there, and I drank a can, the first mouthful tangy but still cold. Outside, it was quiet, eerily so, as if, were I to peek out the curtains, I would find myself upward toward heaven, my company the twinkly faraway stars children wish upon. "Alton Corbett," I said, not the last time I'd say his name to myself. I wondered how he'd gotten his foolish nickname and recalled that he came from Raton in the north near Colorado. He could flat-out outshine a shoe, I'd heard, and it's true he owned the first water bed in the frat house. His pals were named Squid and Univac and Rubberman, and his car—I don't know why I remembered this—was a Chevrolet Monza Spider, gold with wire rims, and then, at the moment I noticed his half-eaten room-service hamburger, next to his Longines wristwatch on the dresser, and observed a squad of blue-helmeted Chicago police charge willy-nilly into a line of boys and girls, I felt myself seize up inside, as if the engine of me had clicked and clanked and stalled, nothing in the world to start me going again.

"Aw, Christ," I muttered, my words like those Billy Puckett had used when he too realized he had unpleasant business to do.

Alton was being held at the Stanton Street precinct house, a cinder-block box that now is a Bob's Big Boy restaurant, the man I had to talk to at a counter in the booking room. Behind and above him hung TV screens showing what was going on in the cells: Alton was curled up on his cot, still barefooted but now in a too-small T-shirt.

"Been like that since we brought him in," the man said. "Did some singing for a while, then zonked out. Real polite."

I held up Alton's overnight bag.

"Could you see he gets this?" I asked. "Personal articles."

The man passed me a property sheet to fill out. A comb, I wrote down. A Norelco electric razor. I watched my hand on the page, noticed the pen I was using so badly. I was having trouble spelling, which I am usually expert at, and could not scribble my address down without getting the Star Route backwards. Overhead, like a ghost, Alton lay on his back, his dreams agreeable enough to make him smile.

"How much is bail?" I said, and this time the sergeant showed me another clipboard of papers, an arrest card smudged with Alton's fingerprints, plus information regarding hair color and date of birth. He was a flyweight, I read. He had brown eyes. He had a vaccination, smallpox, on his upper left arm.

"Let's see what we got here," the man said. It was a list of misdemeanors that seemed little related to what I'd seen hours before: disturbing the peace, public nuisance, interfering with something-or-other, assaulting an officer, fourth-degree vandalism, failure to do this and that, giving false witness—

"What's that for?" I wondered.

The sergeant smiled. He had forearms like Popeye and one tooth brown as saddle leather. "Claimed he was Fidel Castro."

Alton's had been the last room in the back of the frat house, over his door a hand-lettered sign: "Abandon hope all ye who enter here." It was Dante, he'd told everybody, a name laughable in my sophomore World Lit lecture for ideas of hell that didn't include sand and sun and wind, the elements we were familiar with.

"How much?" I asked, wondering why my head hurt.

"Almost two thousand. Which he forfeits if he doesn't show for court."

I was thinking of a course I'd aced, Principles of Animal Nutrition, and the joke-minded professor who'd taught it, then looked down to find my wallet in my hand. "What do you get when you cross a gorilla with a vulture?" we'd been asked once. And "What do you get when you play country-and-western music backwards?"

"You a relative?"

I shook my head. "Acquaintance."

This wasn't anything, I was telling myself. This was merely Walter Seivers Johnston, Jr., all six feet of him. This was but one person helping out another, much as strangers will do. This was only money and did not involve, like love or friendship, other things that can be given back and forth.

"You gotta sign," the sergeant said. "A receipt."

I made the *W* and *J* of me readable from across the room, and was almost out the door to the parking lot when the man asked if I was going to stay. "Be a half hour," he said. "More paperwork."

Omega, I thought, suddenly as Greek as Aristotle. Psi. Chi. Phi.

"You can pick him up around back," the man said. "Gonna be real difficult to get a taxi."

"No," I said, and, a dozen giant steps later, I was gone.

Almost six years would pass before I would indirectly hear about Alton Corbett again, during which time mine was a life that went from A to whatever B was, me as forward-looking as is a high-stepping and blindered horse. I married Mary Ellen Tillmon in 1969 and lived four entirely blissful years as the ramrod for the Double-H spread northeast of Colorado Springs. Every morning I showered in cold water, ate with a he-man's heartiness and hollered "how-do" to the outdoors before me. Then, in 1973, as my father in New Mexico was campaigning for the state senate, he had a heart attack and, according to my mother, after cursing himself and every derelict Democrat he knew, he died, which brought to the ranch me and Mary Ellen (then almost a mother herself to what is now the most helplessly beautiful girl in the Southwest). In the next year, notable in public affairs because of Patty Hearst and the resignation of President Nixon, my mother moved into town, a tidy Victorian house on Iron Street (where she still resides and from which she calls me nearly every day to learn how her wealth is doing).

I liked this life, I am telling you, was content doctoring spavin and founder and worms and wolf teeth in my wide-ranging livestock, and congratulated myself on knowing what grasses are edible, what not. I liked my foreman, a Jalisco wetback named Rojo; and my mostly good-humored roached mane cutting horse, Skeeter; and there was much pleasure to be found, in our Julys and Augusts, in just floating naked in a stock tank, my brain as uncluttered and calm as the horizon, any notion of Alton Corbett as far from me as the moon is from Miami.

"I'm an old cowhand," I'd sing, my warbling weak in the wind, "from the Rio Grande."

I liked, too, sitting in my office, an outbuilding I'd converted, where I studied graphs of the stocks I owned, seeing how, in a pattern heartening to behold, my BioGen and PolyTch had gone mainly up and up and up. I had my *Wall Street Journal*, rousing shoot-em-ups by Eric Ambler and the man who gave us James Bond, plus what reached me via the *Deming Headlight* and *Sports Illustrated*, and conceived of relations among folks to be as straight and true as a surveyor's section line. Hell, I was even pleased to learn—from KTSM, the only TV channel my antenna could pick up in those days—that Billy Puckett, the man who'd whacked Alton Corbett, was a coach with the University of Texas–El Paso Miners. I was pleased with all things close and far, and not until Mary Ellen, citing irreconcilable differences (which had to do, I think, with the seductions towns are and how shopping is at Dillard's or the malls in Albuquerque), moved out, taking our daughter, June Marie, with her—whereupon I went from stunned to baffled to very, very quiet. And Alton Corbett entered my life again.

It was a small item really, six lines in the "Transition" section of our alumni magazine—that page where we learn the bad luck that liver cancer is, or who married or what had become, say, of that chunky cheerleader who, on a dare, did the splits in Intro to Natural Philosophy. Alton Corbett, I read, was employed in Chicago, Illinois, as a financial analyst for the Arthur Andersen Company. He had married Bonnie Shaker, of Philadelphia, and they were living in Lake Forest (where, I have heard, the movie star Mr. T has a mansion).

"Well," I said, "isn't this a fine turn of events?"

I remember perusing that entry several times—the "married" and the "financial" and the "Chicago" parts—and then meandering into my kitchen to have a swallow of Jack Daniels. I was not jumpy, nor particularly smitten, as if I was no more connected to Alton than I was to the dozens of others on that page—that '71 graduate who now attended law school at UCLA, for example, or that woman who'd been appointed superintendent of the Belen Consolidated School District.

"Hang the Key on the Bunkhouse Door" was the song first in my mind, by Wilf Carter.

Like an ordinarily nosy person, I had "Who" questions, and "What" and "How." I wanted to know, in detail, how he'd gone from radical (if that's what he ever was) to Republican, what breakfast was like in jail and how, even, it was to wear a coat and tie. I could hear my house ticking and observed what plantlife I could see—brittlebrush and fireweed, monkey flower and beavertail—and then, while I stood at my sink, my jelly glass empty, I thought to make that long drive to the El Corral bar in Deming and, for the first time since Mary Ellen departed, raise some Pure-D, Grade-A, washed-behind-the-ears Cain.

That was the night I met Jean Furgeson and fell enough in love to be her steady companion for the next four years.

"It was just one of those things," I sang, plopping onto the bar stool next to her, "just one of those fabulous flings."

We'd known each other in high school, and she still looked as lively as she did in the Wildcat marching band she played trombone for—a woman whom the years had not robbed of her desire to toot, toot, toot.

"I know you, Slim?"

Hers was a suspicious face, to which, over the next few minutes, I aimed to bring a chuckle or a tee-hee-hee. On stage Uncle Roy and his Red Creek Wranglers were providing a twangy background, a potent mixture of slide guitar and yodeling that came at you like a truckful of turkeys.

"Would you like to dance?" I asked.

Her eyes shifted to and fro, and it occurred to me how life affirming it would be to breathe the mist or gel that made her hair so upswept and Spanish-like.

"Now, why would I want to do that?"

I managed a left-and-right with my rump that showed I wouldn't be coarse on the dance floor, bowed as a humble servant might, and at last opened my mouth to say I was filthy rich.

"Well, well," she remarked immediately and sashayed into my arms. "This is my lucky day, isn't it?"

I want to tell you now, without meaning evil by the contrast, that Miss Jean Furgeson was as different from my former wife as gunfire is from gargling. What's more, she had virtues too—not the cooking and sewing and small talk kind—some of which I understood while we moseyed round and round, as Uncle Roy crooned to us, and to the citizens who were our confederates that night, his hand-me-down sentiments about love and the losing of it.

"*Bueno*," I said, when she told me she'd been to Hollywood after high school, where, in a beach movie titled *Hanging Ten*, she'd played a coed especially photogenic at blood-curdling. "*Bueno*," I said when she told me about the bungalow she rented on Olive Street and how, cross her heart, she enjoyed her cashier's job at Meachum Chevrolet-Toyota near the Interstate. "Bueno" was my response to her sign, which was Scorpio, and to her secret ambition, interior design. *"Bueno,"* I said, us sliding back and forth, the balance of her well fit for my arms, her lips the real-life equivalent of moon-June-swoon lines you can read for yourself in old-time poetry.

And then her brow knit, and her eyes took on the telltale glimmer that is Oh-my-goodness itself.

"Why, you're Walt Johnston," she cried.

I was, I said. I truly was.

"Hell, nobody's seen you in a long time." She gripped me by the arms, like dry goods, twisting me this way and that, looking me over. "I heard you were in Montana—maybe Wyoming."

Well, I wasn't, I said. I truly was not.

"I like you semi-bald," she insisted, then poked me in the roll that is my stomach, and, strange to say, I felt compelled to speak about my personal life—the hollow it had lately been, its sockets and hinges, the quakes and boom-boom-boom it sometimes was.

"I like your moustache, too," she said, adding that I resembled Burt Reynolds, as large a compliment as it was a lie. "You look downright jaunty, Walter Johnston."

Here we stood, cheek to cheek, cowpokes and cowgirls spinning past us in a clip-clop that is one form of music too, and I said, from the deepest parts of me—the parts that had been too long lonely, and the parts, I ignorantly believed then, not linked to anything Alton Corbett meant to me—"Miss Jean, with all respect, why don't we go to your house and be sweet to each other?" Minutes later, separated by a squeaky brass bed and charming in our undies as we could be, she declared, "Walter, this is for pleasure only, see?" I was watching moonbeams pour off her body and thinking unmistakably glad thoughts about the world and what we're here for. "I've been married," she said, "to Buster Levisay, you remember him?" I did not: She could have been talking about a poinsettia. "Anyhow," she said, "I'm looking to kick up my heels for a time, just have some fun, okay?" I could grasp the wisdom in what she was saying and, in a paragraph, told her so.

"Good," she announced. "I knew you were a gentleman."

She stuck her hand out and it was no effort at all for me to lean forward to shake it.

"I'd like to do some kicking too," I said. "Maybe high as yours."

These are the years—before I heard directly from Alton Corbett—that whooshed by as swiftly as years can. For my birthday that April, my thirtieth, I hired a caterer from El Paso, over a hundred miles away, who erected a tent under which, for three noisy days and nights, cavorted and romped virtually everybody I knew in Deming. Even my mother drove out, escorted by our banker, Mr. Dillon Ripley. The Aggie Ramblers played for me, fast tunes and slow, and a thousand times I had to drink to my health or another piece of good fortune. We hunted jackrabbits at night and cooked up enough beef barbeque to feed most of Luna County. Miss Jean gave me golf clubs I had no innate talent to use and made a speech about my best point, which was honesty, and my next best point, which was—har-de-har-har—the singing voice of a chicken.

"Mister Johnston," she said to me later, "you're not very serious, are you?"

We were watching Buddy Merkins, the manager of the Ramada Inn, do a handstand on a picnic table, and from the scrub beyond my tack room we heard Bob Pettigrew yell about nitpicking he wouldn't any more put up with.

"What do you mean?" I asked.

"I mean, I'm trying to figure out what I've gotten myself into here."

I considered her and me and what there was yet to know in

the world, and I decided, I think now, to take my usual way out.

"Miss Jean," I said, "I'm just a college-educated shitkicker with a big bank account and an open mind."

In the next years, we bet the horse races at Sunland Park and tried snow skiing at Cloudcroft and twice drove over to Arizona to see the spring version of major league baseball in Tucson and Scottsdale. I introduced her to my daughter and was, in turn, introduced to her ex-husband Buster Levisay, a lineman for Southwestern Bell. We were together no more than three days a week and, as the Bible says we should, I endeavored to avoid the backward glance: she had her personal business, I mine. Still, I was happiest at sundown, when I stood on my patch of lawn, heedlessly whacking golf balls into the hinterlands—my swing a tragedy of flying elbows and wobbly knees—while behind me, on the porch, Miss Jean Furgeson, mirthful as fireworks, blasted out Beatle songs on her gleaming King trombone.

Then, as we'd begun, we ended.

"Riley Meachum has asked me to marry him," she said. "And I have accepted."

She drove up my dirt and gravel road, and from the moment her red pickup pulled off the Farm-to-Market highway almost a thousand yards north of my house, I'd felt a shift in me, slight but as definite as what tides make.

"Hey," I said, waving good-naturedly. "What're you hungry for?"

She was stopped near my front gate before it registered that the truck bed was full of boxes and, wobbling back and forth, the wicker rocker I'd given her.

"C'mon in," I hollered. The radio was going—yakety-yak about the Ayatollah, I think, and our embassy hostages—and I had nothing to fret about but fly rubs and the quality of steel T-posts.

"You stay right there for a second, okay?" she said. "I have to compose myself."

Here it was I had a thought, incomplete but already awful, and the desert, from parched hills that looked like bumps in the distance to crooked, scrawny mesquite bushes nearby, appeared remote and inhospitable—too far-fetched to be any place but a planet like Mars.

"I have your stuff," she said.

I could see that, I told her.

"I kept the coat, all right? Sentimental reasons."

She was referring to a fox stole, her Christmas gift, and I remembered the flip-flop my stomach did when she wore it at Sylvia and Marv Feldman's New Year's party.

"You should keep it all," I called. "I'm a generous guy."

In those boxes, which one by one she unloaded by herself, were other presents and necessities it had given me genuine satisfaction to buy her: stoneware and matching crockery from Sweden, the *Encyclopedia Brittanica*, porcelain figurines she'd oooohed over at the White House department store, a Mickey Mouse desk lamp, a Yamaha cassette player with buttons to satisfy every need related to the playing and recording of music, a portable RCA color TV so fancy it took me a Sunday to hook up—and now the whole of it, haphazardly piled and teetering, looked like what, in pictures I've seen, those pathetic dustbowl Okies used to tote toward wherever it was they ran out of gas.

"Don't get up, Walter," she ordered.

I had made a step forward and so, good at following orders, backed up to squat on my porch. I had two wishes: for a cigarette, which I'd given up, and a bourbon, which I hadn't.

"I'll be done in a few minutes," she said.

A name had occurred to me, Alton Corbett; and, in ways central to the explanation this story is, I felt only curiosity—not despair or fracture or anger—about what was to happen next or after that.

"You want something to drink?" I asked.

Riley Meachum, she said. Sober-minded Riley Polk Meachum. Who didn't pace at night. Or spill on himself. Or get crazy quiet. Riley Meachum, who was so chubby and whole-some it was impossible not to like him.

"This isn't strictly personal, Walter. I hope you see that. I got to be looking out for myself now, that's all."

I considered the far and near of my place—the tumbledown bunkhouse, the corrals there and there and there, one windmill yonder creaking round and round—and immediately I under-stood: there was a hole in me, she was saying, a fraction of me that was void as space itself. I was not a hundred percent any-thing, she said. Not lover or friend or daddy—not, leastways, like Riley Meachum, who was one hundred percent himself, which could be sad or gleeful or plain old humdrum, and conse-quently not unsettling whatsoever to be with.

"*Bueno*," I said, a word still meaningful between us.

My possessions were now tottering against the fence and she'd swung her truck around, its polished chrome the last of her I'd see.

"Maybe I could kiss you good-bye," I said.

She looked doubtful, then aglow with an insight.

"Let's shake hands," she said.

Up close, she did not appear riven or otherwise rent inside. This was the end, is all, and we had reached it.

"Maybe you ought to lose some weight, Walter."

A wind was whistling through the center of me, bitter as those in Alaska, and for a second I was saddened that she did not feel frozen too.

"*Adiós*, Miss Jean," I said, releasing her and standing aside so she could speed away.

Many, many months would pass before I'd hear from Alton Corbett, but I did not, gossip to the contrary, become addled or crumble to pieces. I was being prepared for something, I felt. I was waiting, alert like a sniper. In the meantime, dawn to dusk, I was your common *i*-dotter and *t*-crosser. By day, I herded cattle from one scrub-flecked range to another, their mooing and hoarse bawling as sensible as any phrase from my ranch hands. I paid for hay, fifty-pound blocks of iodized salt and the services of Dr. Weems, our vet; I rode fences and set traps for coyote. In need of shirts or pants, I marched into Anthony's Department Store on Zinc Street and afterwards treated myself to chicken-fried steak at Del Cruz's Triangle Drive-in. I talked on the phone to my mother, said "yes" and "no" as appropriate, and comported myself like a citizen with a serious private life.

"Alton Corbett," I said to myself. "Butter-goddam-milk."

By night, I played Atari Donkey Kong or watched movies like *Rambo* and anything featuring the Pink Panther. I forsook alcohol entirely, even beer. I took up reading, finding hours of delight in the crackpot vision of us offered by Sir Walter Raleigh, as well as what opinions a Dallas author named C. W. Smith had concerning good and bad. I was not shattered, I say, or in distress or modernistically dark-minded. Alton would phone. Or he would drive up my road. He would have a respectable haircut, shaved at the neck. And shined wingtip shoes to see yourself in. He would be softer, spongy in the belly the way we all are, and more mindful of authority. He would have his kids, Marvin and Roylene; his wife, Bonnie Shaker; his poodle dog, Fifi. He would tell me what he'd mumbled to Billy Puckett, the gent who'd clobbered him, and how fistfighting felt. He'd tell me what he'd been doing at the Hilton Hotel, specifically the circumstances that had sent him howling into the hallway. He would have words for me—dozens and dozens and dozens—and afterward the hole in me would be filled up and gone forever.

News of him reached me in March while I was scrubbing dishes and ruminating over such crossword clues as "lark or light preceder" (three letters, across) and "saturate" (six letters, down). I saw Cash Corrum, our mail carrier, park his Buick at my box next to the highway, heard him honk to signal he was done, and—saucepan there, coffee cup here—I did well to ignore the clatter and jangle and rattle that were my feelings.

"I'm an old cowhand," I sang, riding my Honda trail bike over three cattle guards to a stop beside blacktop that ran east and west into nothing.

I could smell rain, I remember, and noted the cloud work rumbling my way from California.

"Okay," I told myself, and opened my box to find what I knew would be there.

In letterhead fussy as that Miss Jean had bought to announce her nuptials almost two years before, it was an envelope from Dewey, Stone, Tyler & Howes, "Investment Counselors" on Montrose Street in Houston. An alarm had gone off in me, wicked and whiny, and I wondered naturally how Alton had gotten from Illinois to Texas. I thought about his wife, whom I imagined as tall and redheaded as Mr. Kissinger's Jill St. John, and the thousand-dollar smile she could turn on and off. I'd visited Houston and found it to have not one downtown but several, as though its people—those who needed counseling and not—were restive or too heat stricken to make up their minds.

Sitting by the roadway, my motorcycle making the putt-putt only an hour of tuning can accomplish, I regarded the other mail Cash Corrum had delivered: catalogues to thumb through (Sears, Monkey Wards, Horchow), bills to pay out of pocket money, a notice about who was appearing at the Thunderbird Lounge, and a rolled-up poster that said Rob Pettigrew's goods—his four-wheel-drive Ford, his portable troughs, his ranching-related etceteras—were up for auction (courtesy of Milton Wolf and Sons).

"Goddam," I said, the word from me that stood for, in six letters across or down, misery and silliness and time.

It was a check, nubby as braille, plus a sheet of stationery on which interest had been calculated.

"This is for your trouble," was the first sentence.

A face came to me from memory—not Alton's, but Mary

Ellen Tillmon's, my ex-wife, and I heard again what she'd called me when we divorced. "Lunkhead," she'd said. "Foolhardy," she'd said. And "supercilious," a word I had had to buy a dictionary to check on.

At the bottom of the page was his signature, more a doctor-like scrawl than penmanship you'd recognize as heartfelt.

This isn't about him, I was thinking. This is about me.

"We're even now," was his second, his last, sentence.

Inside me, crude and thick, valves opened and closed.

Astride my motorcycle, I sought to concentrate very hard; and, if it helps, you can imagine Walter Seivers Johnston as an Alfalfalike grade schooler faced with a three-page math problem and a half-hour time limit.

Alton Corbett was even with me now, yes. But I was not even with myself.

Like a starved dog to a soup bone, I went to Billy Puckett—who had, I am happy to say, risen over the years from coach of the UTEP Miner secondary to offensive coordinator and Associate Professor of Physical Education. The morning after I'd read Alton's letter, I filled my Jeep with gas and told my foreman, Rojo, that he was in charge. "This could take a day or two," I said. "Maybe longer." I was in a nearly singsong state of mind, joyous to see sunshine and inclined to honk "howdy" to those I-10 motorists who zipped past me in a hurry; and, hours later, light-footed and what-have-you in spirit, I presented myself to Mr. Puckett's secretary, in his field-house office, with the news that I was a reporter for the *Headlight* of Deming, New Mexico, eager to hear how his football team might fare the following fall.

"He's in a meeting," she said. "That man is a meeting fool."

I could believe that, I said.

"Would you like some coffee?" she asked. "We have Coke, too."

"That's very considerate of you," I said, scooting up a chair to talk nice to her.

Elaine Brittle, mother of two boys (though now separated from their tomcatting and guitar-banging father, Archie Lee) was just tickled as all get-out to be working for a man like Billy—who, by the by, preferred to be called that instead of his whole name which was William M-for-Murphy Puckett, II.

"Do tell?" I said, mine the other cheerful voice in that room. "That's just like him, I hear."

On the walls hung photographs of athletes past and present, the constant in each a smiling or serious-seeming Billy Puckett. Dressed in shorts or long pants, wearing a gimme-cap or head-phones, in hooded sweatshirt or orange pullover with UTEP stitched on the breast, he seemed as huge as I recalled, his a personality that boys and men alike wanted to stand next to, like a shade tree.

"You want some candy?" Mrs. Brittle asked me. It was a Valentine's gift, she said, from Billy, and the one I chewed into, though old, was as gooey as her point of view itself.

I was cool, my smile as disconnected from my inner organs as shit is from Shinola. Billy was another work of wonder to me, like magic to a kid. He had a wife, Maureen, and three children, the oldest of whom, Lilly, was a sophomore music education major and as show-biz on the piano as Van Cliburn or Liberace. He had a house in the north valley and a membership at the Coronado Country Club, El Paso's sagebrush Beverly Hills. He was Baptist—"though not the rednecky kind," Elaine whispered—and a Rotarian, not to mention a man who could read, well, Henry David Thoreau and tell you what was cockeyed about selfishness. I was collected, an ice cube inside, and mentally removed enough from myself to be in the other corner of the room, plotting; and by the time he walked in, as large in life as he was in time, and we were formally introduced, I knew his boot size, his allergies to the milk family of foods, and what year he'd received his Master's degree from Louisiana State University.

"We're gonna be miserable this season," he laughed, my hand thoroughly buried in his. "I got athletes out there with only one leg, or blind."

He had aged, yes, but not as remarkably as some I knew from back then; he had a face like a cupcake, plus the fine, square-cut hair you can find on a shoe brush.

"How's Harley Edwards?" he asked, referring to the editor I'd claimed to work for; and then, in Billy Puckett's office, him camped behind his desk and me in a chair next to a window that opened onto several basketball courts a couple of stories below, a look came to his eye—a glint as important, I think, as my own—and he said, "I know you, don't I?"

His was an office spacious enough to wrestle in, and I struggled to put in order all thoughts unique to my mission here.

"Names, I'm no good with," he said. "Where I know you from, son?"

So I told him—about Alton, about the Hilton, about that night and all that has descended from it, about the sour-minded woman he was with—

"Rita Bates," he said, his mood not a whit sparkly, as though she were a mistake he wasn't through paying for. "I wasn't married then, you understand? It was a matter of oat-sowing. A matter of bad judgment."

"Me, too," I said. "I was engaged."

He had put his feet up on the desk and was, with the deliberation of a traffic judge, studying what the ceiling could tell him. The air-conditioning had switched on, a frigid blast on my face, and I was waiting for some pops from my chest, something to say the cords in there had finally snapped.

"So what can I do for you?" he asked, which made it my turn to look up and down for inspiration.

"If it's all the same," I began, finding breathing easier than expected, "I'd like to slug you one."

We shared a moment then, fraught and time-filled, pointed as a stick: his feet slipped slowly to the floor, his chair groaned, his fingers went *tat-tat-tat* on his blotter, and there were, in the eye-to-eye we had, about ten thousand things to think about.

"Friend," he said, "your leg is shaking."

I grabbed my calf and, soon enough, brought my limb under control.

"This is important to you, I guess."

I admitted that, given the givens I was stuck with, it was.

"Holy moly," he said, not for a second speaking about God or righteous living. "Holy moly," he said about eight more times, and I could see his mind, as betrayed by his eyebrows and pursed lips, confront my proposal and race around it at a dozen speeds. He was bemused and taken aback and perplexed, as if I'd suggested he push a pile of peanuts across the room with his nose. I had learned from Elaine Brittle, his secretary, that he'd majored in sociology and that once he'd bench-pressed nearly four hundred pounds, and now these were facts as plain in the tilt of his head as the facts of how he slept at night and what he hollered in defeat.

"Lordy," he said, "I hate politics, don't you?"

I hastened to agree with him.

He had stood, his shirttails now tucked in, and moved his Rolodex to a spot by his phone, which was by his pencil holder, which was by his stopwatch. You could tell that, however peculiar, a decision had been reached.

"Is here okay?" he asked.

Modestly, I assured him it was.

"Hellfire." He laughed, "it's been ages since I had anything lunatic to talk about at the dinner table."

Alton Corbett wasn't with me when I hauled myself up: he was as meaningless to me as most science or what suffices for entertainment in Timbuktu. Instead, I was arguing with my knees, which seemed rusted stiff, and was tempted to apologize for the tight trousers I'd worn.

"You ever been in a fight before?" Coach Puckett said. "I mean, one with blood in it?"

I had not, so, patient as a preacher, he showed me how to make a fist, thumb outside the fingers.

"Thank you, sir," I said.

I felt like a player of his—or a former water boy, say—who had, unaccountably but profoundly, lost his obvious way in the world.

"Call me Billy," he said.

He arranged himself then, hands on his hips, his chin thrust out Palooka-style, eyes wide as if this were the Memorial Day pie toss, and I took a step back to wind up. There was only one more question to ask and, without hemming or hawing, I mustered the courage to ask it.

"You wouldn't want to get on your knees, would you?"

He tsked-tsked a bit, then looked inexpressibly sad. "They're all busted up, plus there's my dignity, you know."

I knew, indeed, and stepped back again to gather myself from the million places I'd been.

"Ready?" he said.

And, for the first time in umpteen umpteen years, I was.

Cathryn Alpert

Alamogordo

Three melons and a dwarf sat in the front seat of Marilee's '72 Dodge, but the cop seemed unamused. "I'd get rid of that bumper sticker, if I was you," he said. "Folks around here, they're proud of their history." Marilee's bumper sticker said, "One nuclear bomb can ruin your whole day." Wrong place, wrong time. This spot on the road crossing White Sands Missile Range was fifty miles southwest of Alamogordo.

"You two traveling together?" the cop asked.

"Might say," said Enoch.

The cop's lips drew together like a drawstring purse. It was midnight and he wore sunglasses. "I'd like to see your license," he said, shining his flashlight at the little man riding shotgun.

"No can do."

"You have any ID?"

"Nope."

"What's your name?"

"Enoch Swann."

"Where you from?"

"Des Moines."

The cop gave Enoch a hard look. Enoch stared back at the cop. Marilee dug her fingernail into a tear in the upholstery. Surely it was not against the law to share the front seat of a woman's car with two honeydews and a casaba.

"Those melons come with you from California?" the cop asked Marilee.

"Near Bowie. Little road stand," said Enoch.

Marilee's body stiffened. The cop had to know Enoch was lying. There had been nothing near Bowie, no road stand, and certainly not at night. Marilee wondered if they could be arrested for lying about fruit.

"Step out of the car," the cop ordered.

Enoch opened his door and lurched toward the rear of the automobile.

"You too, miss. Both of you stand over there," he said, aiming his flashlight into the space between the cars' bumpers.

Marilee did as she was asked, telling herself that none of this was happening.

"Put your hands on the trunk, spread your legs, and lean over. I'm going to search you."

The cop searched Enoch, then Marilee, patting them down from shoulders to feet. The patrol car's headlights shone up between their legs as they stood spread-eagled against the back of the Dart. "I'm going to search your car now."

For what? She wanted to ask him. On what grounds? For speeding? Was any of this legal? The cop climbed inside her car. "Is he going to find anything?" she whispered to Enoch.

"I'm not psychic."

"You shouldn't have said we bought the melons in Bowie. Don't you know it's against the law to take fruit across state borders? That's why they ask. You lied. You told him we bought it here in New Mexico."

"Bowie's in Arizona. If he knew his geography, he still could've nailed you. But he doesn't know jack. Look at him. He's an asshole."

The cop sat in the backseat of the Dodge, rifling through the contents of Marilee's purse. He flipped open her compact, ran his finger over the powder, sniffed, then tasted it.

"What's he doing?" she asked.

"Couple of lines," said Enoch.

What was it that had compelled her that afternoon to go back for the dwarf? Her mother had taught her never to pick up hitchhikers, a lesson she had not needed to learn. Always shy, she'd never had the inclination to extend herself to strangers, especially to someone as different as Enoch. Perhaps it was the look on his face as she drove by him the first time, a look which said he'd been standing on the road since dawn and hers was the first car that had slowed. Or perhaps it was the way he pulled his thumb in when he saw she was a woman alone. Or maybe it was nothing more than his obvious helplessness. Where he stood, alongside the interstate between Aztec and Sentinel, was nowhere; he'd been abandoned in the middle of the Arizona desert. As she passed him, the late-August sun reflected up off the asphalt so that his face seemed lit from all angles, open, devoid of shadow and threat. How dangerous, she asked herself, could a dwarf on crutches be?

At the first rest stop, Marilee turned the car around and drove back toward where she had seen the dwarf. She passed him again, on the other side of the highway. The dwarf followed her with his eyes as this time she drove west. It would be crazy to pick him up, she knew, but now she felt obligated since he'd seen her drive by twice. She couldn't pass him a third time.

Marilee crossed over the unpaved median and again headed east. She slowed as she approached him, tensing at the crunch of pebbles under her tires. Closer now, she studied his features. He was a clean dwarf. His brown hair was tidy; his face, newly shaven. He stood about four feet tall and carried a backpack. He wore cowboy boots, a red shirt, and jeans.

Marilee reached over to open the door as he hobbled toward the car. He tossed his backpack and both crutches into the back seat. They landed on her suitcase with a thud.

"Obliged," he said in a normal voice as she pulled back into the slow lane. Was it just midgets who sounded like Munchkins?

"Been out here long?" she asked.

"Not too."

So, she hadn't saved him from near death. No matter. She liked his voice and she liked his face—thick features and a nose which cocked slightly to one side. His skin was brown, his teeth clean, and when he raised his sunglasses to rub his eyes, she saw a glint of intelligence there.

"I'm Marilee."

"Enoch," he said, and held out his hand. She shook his fingers. They felt like a handful of Vienna sausages.

"Enoch's an unusual name." How typical, she thought. Dwarfs always have oddball names, like Eylif, or Egan, or Bror. A band of motorcyclists passed them in the oncoming lane. Enoch squirmed and put his feet up on the dashboard; his stubby legs extended fully. Marilee fixed her eyes on the road and pretended not to notice, determined neither to stare nor to appear intrigued. "So," she asked, "where you headed?"

"Same place you are."

She didn't like the way he said that. It sounded ominous, as if he saw their destinies about to overlap.

"Where are you from?"

"Kingman. Kingman, Arizona. Couple hundred miles north. Big fire few years back. That's when I split."

"Where you living now?"

"Here and there. In the desert."

Great, she thought. A weirdo.

"Take some melons," her mother had insisted, heaving three of them at her at once. "So in case the car breaks down, you'll have something to drink." It would never occur to her mother to take something direct, like a thermos. "And take this knife, too," she'd said. "You never know when you might need it." The kitchen knife lay hidden in the glove compartment. Marilee wondered if she would have the guts to use it, if necessary, and whether she'd be able to reach for it in time. Enoch shifted in the seat next to her. The honeydews rolled toward his thigh.

"My mother's idea," said Marilee, gathering the melons back into the space between them on the seat. "So if the car breaks down, I won't die of thirst. My mother's kind of out there, sometimes. Of course, if anything happened, I could always drink radiator water. I brought a knife, too, so if I had to I could hack up a cactus."

"Or a camel," said Enoch.

Definitely weird.

"So, where are we off to?" he asked. Again, her insides jumped. The highway stretched before them, a colorless slab dissolving into a blurred horizon. Except for the sun, the sky was empty. No clouds floated by. No birds flew. In other cars, people looked half sedated, as if hypnotized by the strobe of disappearing broken lines and the hum of tires on asphalt, the white noise of the open road. Marilee was glad to have gotten it in about the knife.

"Alamogordo," she replied. "To get married, but he doesn't know it yet. Well, he does and he doesn't. I mean, he asked me to marry him, but he doesn't know I'm on my way." Oh God, she thought, she shouldn't have told him that.

"Roll it down?" Enoch pointed to the window.

"Sure. It sticks sometimes. You have to really crank it."

The dwarf turned the handle but the window didn't stick. He then stood on the seat and reached for his backpack on top of her suitcase. What was he reaching for? A knife? A gun? Why in God's name had she picked him up?

A small bag of granola materialized from his backpack's zippered pocket. "Have some," he said.

Marilee considered her options. What if it was drugged? Was he going to eat some, too? She took a small handful. It tasted like a clump of dried weeds.

"What's his name?" asked Enoch.

"Who?"

"Mr. Wonderful."

"Oh. Larry. He's this guy I've been going with a long time. Since high school, really. Funny how you can end up with someone you knew back in high school. I mean, I don't know anyone I knew back in high school. Except him, of course." She was babbling.

"Larry what?"

Why did he want to know? "Larry Mitchell," she said, plugging in the first surname that came to mind.

"Boring," said Enoch. "Larry Mitchell. Mr. and Mrs. Larry Mitchell. Dull as dust."

Marilee studied the stretch of desert around her. Cactus. Tumbleweeds. Dirt for miles. A few rocks, not many. Probably insects under the rocks.

"What's he do, this guy, Larry?" He offered her another handful of granola, but she declined.

"He's in the military. Holloman Air Force Base."

"Does he fly jets?"

"He's a flight instructor."

"So," said Enoch, "you're going to roll into Alamogordo so you two can get hitched?"

"That's right."

"And he has no idea you're on your way?"

Heat rose off the pavement and warped vision, not unlike the aura of an impending migraine. "Well, he does, sort of. I mean he expects me. Soon. But he doesn't know when, exactly. I was going to surprise him."

"Sort of, 'Here I am. Let's find a church,' " said Enoch.

"Sort of."

"Sort of, 'Hi, I'm moving in. Hope you don't mind.' "

"No. Not like that at all. He's going to love it when I show up. He's been wanting this for a long time."

"And you?"

"I want it," she said. "I've thought about it. It makes sense that we get married."

"Why?"

"Look, are you hungry? I'm starving. I get bitchy when I don't eat. What's the next town?"

"Casa Grande."

"Let's look for a restaurant."

"YO! Casa Grande!" Enoch shouted, raising his fist in a power salute and stomping his feet on the dashboard. A toothbrush fell out of his pants cuff.

He was definitely one weird dwarf.

"Let's play a game," said Enoch, as soon as they had ordered. "I'll ask you a question, then you ask me. Whoever loses, pays."

"Okay," said Marilee, although she was not sure at all that it would be okay.

"Can an irresistible force encounter an immovable object?"

"Sure." She was glad his question had been nothing personal.

"Which one gives?"

Marilee thought about it for a moment. "Well, it's really just a matter of semantics."

"Not at all," said Enoch. Two middle-aged ladies in the next booth eyed them with curiosity. Enoch's chest was level with the edge of the table; Marilee was glad the waitress hadn't offered him a booster seat.

"Okay," she said. "I guess it's impossible to answer."

"Bingo. One to nothing. Your turn."

Marilee took her time. She turned down the corners of her paper place mat. She traced her spoon over the outline of a hobo eating pancakes. He looked a little like Enoch. She sipped coffee and stared out the window at the filling station next door. The attendant scratched himself when he must have thought no one was looking.

"All right, I've got one. Which came first, the chicken or the egg?"

"Impossible to know," said Enoch. "And a cliché."

"Think again." Two could play this game.

A group of teenagers erupted in laughter from across the room. They snuck occasional glances at Enoch. The dwarf's lips flushed purple.

"Impossible," he said again.

"The egg," said Marilee. "It's obvious. At some point there had to be a mutation. But by the time the egg is formed, it has all its genetic material intact. It's a potential chicken. So the responsible gene, the gene that made the critical difference, had to have mutated inside the hen, before it became part of the fertilized egg. And something had to pass on that altered gene. Something that was not quite a chicken, but gave rise to a mutant egg that was destined to become the first chicken."

Enoch's face brightened. "Yes, that's logical. Very good." Their waitress appeared with their dinners. She wore a ruffled skirt and an embroidered hat that said, "Doreen."

"I've got another."

"My turn," said Enoch, dipping a french fry in the Thousand Island dressing that ran out the side of his Hoboburger. "If

God is all-powerful, can He build an object too heavy for Him to move?"

"Another paradox."

"Are you certain?"

"Positive."

"I win," said Enoch. "If God is all-powerful, He can transcend paradox."

Marilee thought about this. "Interesting point," she conceded, forcing a smile; secretly, she was pissed. "Now it's my turn. A man is walking down a road. In order to take a step, he must first travel half that distance. A half step. Then, in order to take a half step, he must first travel a distance half the length of that. Will he ever reach his destination?" She bit into her club sandwich and hit a toothpick.

"Zeno's paradox. The answer is no."

"Wrong," said Marilee, with her mouth full. "Faulty premise. People don't move in half steps, do they?"

"Then again, some people don't move at all."

What was that supposed to mean? She pinched a blister from the end of her bacon and buried it under her carrot twist. "All right. How many angels can dance on the head of a pin?"

"Box step or hora?" said Enoch.

They ate the rest of their meal in silence. When Doreen brought their check, they agreed to split it. Marilee took the money to the cashier while Enoch went in search of a bathroom. She'd gone earlier, while the hostess was seating Enoch, because she didn't want to be seen walking through the restaurant with a dwarf.

She paid the bill and sat on the brown vinyl seat by the coffee shop's front door. Five minutes passed. Then ten. What was he doing in there? she wondered, then asked herself if she really wanted to know. And why, come to think of it, was she sitting there waiting? This was her chance. She'd never have to see him again.

Her keys jangled as she made her way swiftly through the parking lot. But as soon as she opened the car door, she saw that Enoch had left his backpack. Now what? She could leave it on the ground, but what if someone stole it? No, she'd have to take it into the restaurant and leave it for him there. She started the engine and steered the Dart toward the entrance. As she pulled up, an elderly woman held the door open for Enoch.

"That's nice," he said, resuming his seat next to the melons. "Bringing the car around. Thanks."

"Sure," she said. She knew what it felt like to steal from an invalid. Strike a child. Throw a kitten off a bridge.

"So," said Enoch, as soon as they were back on the highway. "What does this Larry guy do for kicks?"

Not again, thought Marilee. "Well, mainly he likes to jog, work out with weights, that sort of thing. He's into fitness. Poetry. Books about the Civil War."

"That's it?"

"Sometimes he has friends over and they rent movies."

"Porno flicks?"

"Oh, God no! He'd die." Marilee laughed. "I bet he's never even seen one."

"Have you?"

She looked over at the little man in her front seat cleaning his fingernails with the corner of a Hobo matchbook.

"So show me this guy," he said. "A picture. I want to see."

She rooted in her purse for her wallet, wondering at the same time if this was a good idea. Couldn't he just grab it out of her hand? That's silly, she thought. Where would he go? She opened her wallet with one hand and dug out a photo of a young man in camouflage fatigues. She handed it to Enoch. The man in the picture had blond hair and a weak chin. The badge over his pocket said "Johnston."

Enoch tossed the photo faceup on the dashboard. "So, you and this Larry guy plan to have kids?"

"Why do you keep asking me about Larry?"

"Fine. Let's talk about me."

Marilee wondered what she should ask him. She wanted to ask what it was like to be a dwarf, but the words stuck in her throat. "Okay. Tell me about the fire. In Kingston."

"Kingman," said Enoch. "Another time." A bug spattered against the windshield and left a yellow-green smear like the feathered tail of a comet. "I've got one," he said. "If a tree falls in the forest, and nobody's there to hear it, does it make a sound?"

"Talk about clichés."

"Yes, but does it?"

"It's a moot question. Without a witness, there's no way to know."

"I think it does," said Enoch.

"Based on what?"

"Track record. All trees that have ever fallen in the presence of people who can hear have made a sound. That means something."

"But one that falls in a deserted forest might fall silently. You can't prove that it doesn't. That's not logic."

"Then you rely on faith."

"What's faith got to do with it?"

"Where logic fails," said Enoch. "That's where faith steps in. Sometimes that's all you've got. You've got to have faith in the laws of physics and you've got to have faith in people. Remember that line?" he asked, turning to face her across the seat. "At the end of *Manhattan*, remember? Mariel Hemingway says that to Woody Allen. 'You've got to have faith in people.' Great line. Sums up the whole movie."

They continued east on Interstate 10, through Tucson, past Benson and Wilcox. The sign at the border said, "Welcome to New Mexico. Land of Enchantment." Enoch curled up on the seat next to the melons and fell asleep as darkness consumed the landscape. He slept through Marilee's stop for gas in Lordsburg. He slept through the convoy of trucks that rumbled by just east of Las Cruces. When he awoke, hours later, they were near White Sands Missile Range. Red and blue lights flashed in the rearview mirror.

Enoch stretched his legs and sat upright. What he said startled her. He said, "You're a woman and I'm a dwarf. Woody is neither. I've got to pee."

The cop crawled out of the back of Marilee's car. "We got a speed limit here, miss," he said. "Try and stay under it." He tore the ticket from his pad and handed it to her with a smile.

"Thanks," said Marilee.

"For what?" asked Enoch.

As the cop drove west, Enoch went in search of a bush. He didn't use his crutches and he wobbled as he walked. Marilee leaned against her front fender and stared off into the distant lights of Alamogordo. She hated getting tickets, hated cops almost as much as she hated herself for having been accommodating. She tried to think of a reason why this had been Enoch's fault, but couldn't. In a moment he returned.

When the interior light came on as Marilee opened her car door, she saw it down in her footwell. It was a pale scorpion, translucent almost, with two dark stripes running the length of its back. She drew back and motioned for Enoch to come over. How did it get there? How could it have crawled inside a car ten inches off the ground? Had the cop somehow brought it in? Or had it been hiding in some cranny of Enoch's backpack? Perhaps it had been there the whole time, down by her feet as she drove east from L.A.

"Get it out," she whispered.

"Easy," he cautioned. He reached down into the footwell and gently prodded the insect. It crawled onto his stubby fingers. Marilee froze. Was this guy crazy or just stupid? She wondered, for a moment, if he might try something funny like flinging it at her, or insisting she touch it. She took another step backward.

The insect crawled into Enoch's palm. He lifted it out of the footwell, but instead of tossing it into the desert, he just held it in his hand. Enoch looked at the scorpion. The scorpion looked back. Its legs seemed bulbous and awkwardly hinged, as if the result of some miscue of nature. It uncoiled its tail and raised up on its legs. Marilee felt she was going to throw up.

"Get rid of it," she whispered. A trickle of sweat ran down between her breasts.

"In a minute."

The scorpion's tail arched high over its head, its stinger suspended like a hooked needle, its pincers cocked, front and open. Standing in the light of the car's doorway, Enoch studied the insect, staring it down as if daring it to strike. A passing semi whipped dust in their faces, but neither of them flinched. Each stood poised for battle. Each bided his time, eyeing the other as if they shared some indelicate secret with which Marilee could presume no intimacy.

Finally, the scorpion lowered its tail. Enoch placed it in the dirt by the side of the road, where it crawled to safety beneath a broken styrofoam cup.

They continued east toward Alamogordo. In less than an hour they would be there and she would say good-bye to Enoch, dropping him off at the Y, perhaps, or maybe at a shelter. Then she would get out her map and find Larry's street. She would knock on his door in the middle of the night and he would open it and take her into his arms.

Marilee stepped down harder on the accelerator. Her muscles ached from driving; her lips tasted of salt. Brown dirt lodged in the cracks between her toes. "I could use a shower," she said, more to herself than to her companion.

"A pool!" said Enoch. "I know a place. On the road to El Paso. It's not far. I'll show you!"

A pool sounded wonderful. Clean water in which she could

bathe. Cool water in which she could float away under the stars. But it was out of the question. "I didn't bring a bathing suit."

"Swim naked."

Marilee felt a tightness grip her stomach. So this was it. This was where he'd jump her. Where he'd slip his little thing into her like a snake gliding into wet moss, and she'd end up with a little dwarf child she'd have to name Elwyn. And why not? Hadn't she picked him up off the side of some road? What jury would ever believe her. They'd say she'd asked for it, wanted it even.

Yet a pool sounded wonderful. It was after midnight. Her hair stuck to the back of her neck like a clump of seaweed. It would be a shame for Larry to see her like this. Besides, she was bigger than Enoch. Stronger, probably, too. A pool was just what she needed. She would swim in her underwear.

"So tell me about the fire," she said.

"No."

"You said you would. 'Later,' is what you said. I'd like to hear."

Marilee glanced across the seat at Enoch. His nose looked thicker in the darkness, and his face showed the first sings of stubble. "I told you about Larry."

"Fire!" shouted Enoch, so startling her she nearly swerved over the center line. "Burst of light! Fireball! Like a bomb going off! Butane. Storage tank. Erupted. Too much heat!" He was sitting on the edge of his seat, breathing hard and painting the fire with his hands. "Blowout! Exploded! Whole sky on fire!" His hand hit the rearview mirror. "Twelve people died. Twelve. Firemen," he said. "Too much heat."

Enoch stopped for a moment. He rubbed his eyes and scooted back on the seat so that his legs stuck straight out over the edge. "Rumors started," he continued, his voice lower now. "Children. You know how it is. Kids talk. Adults listen. Always the same. You're bound to be suspect if you're not like them. Grew up in that town. Guess they needed me."

Enoch stared silently at the oncoming headlights.

"I'm sorry," said Marilee.

"For what?"

"For what you went through. That's just awful. It's unfair."

"So who said life is fair?"

He had her there.

They drove the next twenty miles in silence. Then, Enoch spoke. He said, "Larry's not good enough for you."

It annoyed Marilee the way he said this, as if he'd been thinking about it for years. As if this dwarf had a corner on her dreams.

"VACA CY" said the sign above the Trinity Motel, a crumbling, one-story adobe which squatted upon the earth like a venerable Indian. The motel lay on the outskirts of Alamogordo, a few miles south of the city, near the base of the Sacramento Mountains. Trinity Site, according to Enoch, had actually been northwest.

They snuck into the motel courtyard through an unlocked wooden gate. The courtyard centered on the pool, a kidney bean with a slide in the middle. No lights were on in the rooms. The moon hadn't risen, but the stars shone so brightly Marilee could see Enoch clearly.

He propped his crutches against the back of a plastic chaise. Then, as if there were no one else around, he took off his clothes. Marilee could not tear her eyes away from his body. Deformed. Hunched. Contorted. One hip jutted out like a knot on a tree. His legs twisted at the knees. A concavity hollowed his chest as if he'd been punched in the sternum at birth. She'd had no idea. When he stripped off his shorts, she saw that his genitals were the size of a full-grown man's; they looked huge by comparison. How, she wondered, could a person live in such a body?

Yet Enoch seemed unbothered by his nakedness. He walked without crutches to the edge of the pool—wobbled really, heeling to the left with every other step. On crutches he'd appeared less awkward, more in control of his ungainly self. Marilee watched as he lowered his body into the water. There, he swam with ease, as if he were at home in his element.

Enoch did not look at Marilee as she disrobed. Or maybe he saw her out of the corner of his eye, she couldn't tell. She took off her jeans and cotton blouse and hung them over a chair. But starting for the pool, she hesitated at the sight of Enoch's twisted body floating on the water's surface. Open. Vulnerable. He looked more insect than human, with his large torso and dis-jointed limbs. A water bug. Easy prey. It seemed wrong, sud-denly, to feel self-conscious in the presence of someone like Enoch. She unhooked her bra and stepped out of her under-wear.

When she glanced up she saw that Enoch was watching her. This time he made no effort to turn away. She stood motionless by the edge of the pool and let him take in the sight of her. He stared shamelessly, as if he knew she wouldn't mind. As if he sensed this was exactly what she wanted. Her heart pounded. What would it be like, she wondered, to make love to a dwarf?

She shook out her hair and stepped down into the cool water. Enoch studied her every move. It felt strange and wonder-ful swimming nude, a freedom she had never known. She dove beneath the surface and let the water caress her skin, fan her hair, swirl all around her. She made waves in the water, turned somer-saults, rolled onto her back, spread her legs wide open.

What would Larry think if he could see her now? She laughed out loud at the thought of it: Larry in his loafers and button-down collar pacing at pool's edge, hissing through clenched teeth so as not to wake the occupants. Larry tossing her his jacket, remembering too late the wallet in its pocket. Larry swearing at Enoch, ordering him out of the pool, fists clenched and lip curled—a smoldering absurdity.

And Enoch—how might he respond? Slither out of the pool,

tail between his legs if he had a tail (which wouldn't much surprise her)? More likely tell Larry to go fuck himself. Splash water on his loafers. Thumb through his wallet. She smiled, a sad smile. Larry was only three miles north, in Alamogordo, yet he seemed farther from her now than the stars in the sky.

Marilee glanced over to where Enoch floated on his back. She swam to the deep end and floated next to him. What would he do with her body so close? Look at her? Reach out and touch her skin? She arched her back so her breasts broke through the water's surface. If he touched her now, would she push away or roll into his arms?

But he didn't touch her. Nor did he look at her breasts. Rather, he seemed content to float next to her and stare up into the night. The Milky Way cut a brilliant swath across the sky's blackness. She had never seen so many stars. Thousands of stars. Millions. Stars in number beyond her comprehension. Marilee listened to the faint drone of traffic from a distant highway. She felt light-years from anything familiar.

"I read a story once," said Enoch. "Science fiction, by Asimov. Called 'Nightfall.' About a planet with six suns, so there's always daylight. But every couple of thousand years, an eclipse throws the planet into total darkness. And when all those stars come out—stars nobody knew were there—all the people go insane."

Marilee gazed up into the desert night—so many stars it would take a lifetime to count. She felt Enoch's gnarled body bobbing close to hers in the water. So close, yet separate. Different, and alone. A strange silence took hold of her. Night silence. Water silence. Star silence. She threw her head back and let the water wash over her face, fill her eyes, stream out the corners of her mouth—liquid smooth as desert sand, liquid cool as starlight. She felt intoxicated by the water, the darkness, the explosion of stars. This is crazy, she thought.

Crazy, and real.

Ron Carlson

DeRay

One thing led to another. Liz and I started fixing up our place before the baby came. First the nursery and then wallpaper in the hall and new carpeting and then new linoleum and new cabinets in the kitchen and then a new small bay window for the kitchen; it was through this window that we would look out upon the lot and silently measure the progress of the weeds.

I was ready to use August to lean back and do a little reading, but you get a woman with an infant standing in a tidy little bay window, looking out at a thorny desert and seeing a grassy playground, and you get out the grid paper and sharpen the pencils and start making plans.

A dump truck unloaded nine yards of mountain topsoil. I took delivery of 18 railroad ties and 450 used bricks. I tiered the garden with three levels of ties and laid a brick walkway along the perimeter. I dug the postholes and stained the redwood before I assembled the fence, and then, when I nailed the boards in place—that's when my plan became apparent from the window. It would be a little world—safe, enclosed—where my daughter, when she got around to walking, would tumble in the thick green grass.

It was a dry summer and I'd wait until late in the day when the house could throw its shadow on the project and then I'd plunge out into the heat. Our pup, Burris, wouldn't even go out with me. I was only good for two hours, and then I'd stumble into the house, dehydrated, a crust of dirt on my forehead, my shirt soaked through. Burris would lift his head from the linoleum and then go back to sleep.

Evenings, while my strength held, I marched around the yard, pulling my old stepladder loaded with four cinder blocks, leveling the topsoil. I would drag it in slow figure eights through the thick dirt, with the rope cutting at my chest like a crude halter. And it was during this time, during my dray-horse days, that my neighbor DeRay would cruise in on his cycle and come to the fence and say, "Hey, good for you, Ace. I'd give you a hand, but I've already got a job. But you know where you can find a beer later."

So I started going over there when I'd feel the first dizziness from the heat. I'd drop the rope and pick my wet shirt away from my chest and walk next door and visit with DeRay.

If I told you that DeRay was a guy who was on parole and loved his motorcycle, it would be misleading, though he did have a big blue tattoo of a skull and a rose. He wore size-thirteen engineer boots and a biker's black cap, greasy as a living thing. In the evenings he arrived home, proud as a man on a horse, yanking the big Harley back onto its stand and throwing his right leg back over the bike purposefully to come to the ground and stand as a body utterly capable of trouble.

But the picture needs qualification. For instance: It wasn't actually parole. It was *like* parole. Once a month DeRay saw a guy at Social Services to state that he had not been in any bars. He could not go into a bar for another four months because he used to be in barroom fights. He would go to biker bars and when a fight would start, he would fight. It was his personality, they told him. He knew none of the people in the fights and the fights weren't about him in any way, but his personality—when it was exposed to a fight, especially indoors—dictated that he fight, too. So it wasn't parole. And he did have that tattoo on the inside of his right forearm, but unless he stopped to show it to you it was hard to tell there was a rose. It looked like a birth-mark.

He showed it to me one night on his front porch. Evenings were cool there and that is where he and Krystal sat on an old nappy couch and watched the traffic and drank beer. They drank exactly five six-packs every night, he told me, and, at first, thirty cans seemed a lot, and I worried that there might be a fight, but I came to see that DeRay generally slowed down over the evening, climbing off the porch in those big boots to move his Lawn Jet or to pack another six beers into the Igloo. Some nights he stood and talked to the traffic. If he started talking like that while I was around, I quietly left. It was his business.

The thing about DeRay that cannot be minimized was his love for his motorcycle. It was a large Harley-Davidson with a beautiful maroon gas tank and chrome fenders. The world was ten miles deep in the reflections. The way he listened to it when he first kicked the starter; the way he kept it running—silently— when he drove away in the morning, as if man and machine were being sucked into a vacuum, disappearing down the street; the way he dismounted with clear pleasure—these things showed his affection.

Once, Liz was out in front of our garage putting Allie in the stroller when DeRay came up and plucked the baby from her, saying, "Come on over here, baby, check these wheels." He put Allie on the seat of the huge motorcycle, and she broke into a real grin. She could see her face in a dozen shiny places. "See," DeRay said to Liz, "she loves it. It won't be long." He called to the porch: "Hey, Krystal, check this out!"

Krystal appeared and leaned over. "Oh, right, DeRay. She's a real mama. She's your new mama, all right."

I watched it all from our new kitchen window, and seeing DeRay there holding the baby on the Harley, I thought, There's the center—the two most loved things on the block.

Both DeRay and Krystal were somewhere in their forties. She was a lean woman who looked good in tight jeans. In the face she resembled Joan Baez, perhaps a little more worn—and her nose was larger, pretty and hawklike at the same time. Her long reddish hair was wired with some gray and she usually wore it all in a bandanna. She worked for the phone company and she told me she was one of four women in the entire state who were on line crews. She made it sound like a lot of fun. I'd sit on their porch, my head full of bubbles with yard fever, dirt and cold beer. One of my calves would start to tremble, and I imagined if I worked with Krystal she'd always be telling me what to do, like a mother, and I would do it. Her lean face seemed hard and affectionate. It had seen a lot of traffic, that was clear. From the corner of the porch, I could see my new kitchen window—Liz in there, moving around the high chair.

One night when I was at DeRay's, Krystal went inside, where we could hear her on the phone. "Her in-laws," DeRay told me. "Old Krystal's had herself a couple of cowboys."

Later, we were just talking when out of the blue he said, "What's the worst thing you ever did?"

I knew that he was going to make some confession—a theft or beating a woman, some threat he'd made stick. He looked hard that night, his face vaguely blue in the early-evening gloom.

"I don't know," I said. "Burn down the ROTC building." It

was an old joke. I was on the roof of the building the night it burned, but I was only peripherally involved in the crime.

"Oh, arson," DeRay mocked. "That's terrible."

I drank from my beer and went ahead: "What's the worst thing you ever did?"

"What you're doing now."

I sat up. "What am I doing?"

"Dragging dirt around. Putting in a yard."

"Oh," I said. "I hear that. It's torture."

"No, you don't. You don't even know," he said. "I've had three houses. How old do you think I am?"

"I don't know. Forty-five?"

"Forty-nine." He rocked forward and threw his beer can out with the others. "I've had three families, for chrissakes. And that doesn't even count this deal here." He gestured over his shoulder to where Krystal was on the phone. He snapped another beer open and grimaced over the first sip. "I mean, I put in some lawns."

"That's a lot of work," I said.

"Nah." He waved it off. "You can't even hear me. But listen, when you dig for the sprinklers, rent a trencher. You won't be sorry."

And DeRay was right. There is nothing better after an unbroken plain of manual labor than to introduce a little technology into the program. The trencher was beautiful. The large treaded tires measured the line exactly, and the entire mechanism crawled across my yard like a tortoise. The trench was carved as if with a knife, straight sides and a square bottom exactly eight inches from the surface. All the other feats of the past year—the room in the basement, the kitchen window, my straight fence—vanished before this, the first stage of my sprinkling system. That night, I worked way beyond my usual quitting time. When I finally looked up, I saw the yellow light in the kitchen; the world was dark.

This is when DeRay opened the gate and came up and took

the handlebars of the trencher out of my hands and conducted it to the end of the line. It was the last ditch. He surveyed the yard and switched the machine off. "Yeah, it's a good, simple machine," he said. "Load it up and come over for a beer."

I stayed at their place until almost eleven. I didn't count as I left, but I knew there were more than thirty empties on the lawn. DeRay receded from the conversation, and Krystal told me about her first husband, who was in a mental-health facility in Denver, a chronic schizophrenic. She filed to divorce him while he was in the hospital. "He was as crazy as you get to be," she said. "I still keep in touch with his mom and dad in Oklahoma City. He was a dear boy," Krystal said, "but he couldn't keep two things together, and his jealousy cost me three jobs."

When I went home, all the lights were off. I took my clothes off in the garage, as always, and padded in. Liz was in bed watching television. I could hear people laughing. I turned on the bathroom light and Liz said, "How're the Hell's Angels?"

"You've been watching too much *Letterman*." I came to the bedroom door.

"You've been outside this house since four o'clock. We had a lovely dinner."

"Oh, now we're going to fight about dinner?" I could feel the rough cuff of dirt around my neck and I hated standing there dirty and naked.

"We're going to fight about whatever I want to fight about."

"Look, Liz. Don't. I've been in the yard. We want the yard, right?" I felt the closeness of the rooms; it was suddenly strange to be inside. "I've got to take a shower," I said.

"Where are you?" she said before I could turn. It was a tough question, because I was right there full of beer, but she was onto something. It was August and I wasn't looking forward to school starting. I shrugged and showed her my brown arms. She looked at me and said, "Let it go, if you like. Just let the yard go."

———

I bought the controls for the sprinkling system. Opening the boxes on my lap and holding the timer compartment and the bank of valves was wonderful. The instruction booklet was well written: simple and illustrated. I took the whole thing over to DeRay and showed him.

"Yeah," he said, turning the valves over in his hand. "They've got this thing down to the bare minimum, and there's a two-week timer." I knew he was a union machinist for Hercules Powder Company, and in the four months he'd been my neighbor he told me that three different deals he'd worked up had gone into space on satellites. "You're going to be the king of irrigation with this thing."

Though Liz didn't like the idea, I put the control box on the guest-room wall downstairs. It took me two six-packs. She said it didn't look right, a sprinkler-system timer box on the guest-room wall. I said some things too, including that it was the only wall I could put it on. She just shrugged.

I finished that project at three o'clock in the morning. I went out in the garage and filled the spreader and spread the lawn seed all across the yard, first one way and then the other, in a complete checkerboard, just like it said on the package. It was quiet in the neighborhood and I tried to step lightly through the raked topsoil. There was no traffic on the streets, and the darkness was even and phosphorescent as I walked back and forth. It seemed like the time of night to spread your lawn seed.

The next morning, Liz woke me with a nudge from her foot. I was asleep on the floor in the nursery. "Who are you?" she said.

"We're all done," I said. "The yard's all done."

"Great," she said, carrying Allie into the kitchen. "Looks like we drank some beer last night. Did we have a good time? I think you've caught a little beer fever from your good buddy next door. This is being a hard summer on you."

Very late that night, Burris began barking and Allie woke and started crying. "What is it?" Liz said from her side of the bed.

"Nothing. It's okay," I said. There was a strange noise in the house, a low moan in the basement, that I understood immediately was the water pipes. I went to Allie and changed her diaper. She was awake by that time, so I carried her into the kitchen, where Burris was jumping at the window. I had set the system to start at four-thirty, which it now was, and outside the window the sprinklers, whispering powerfully, sprayed silver into the dark. I sat down, and Allie crawled up over my shoulder to watch the waterworks. Burris stood at the window on two legs, humming nervously. I swallowed and felt how tired I was, but there was something mesmerizing about the water darkening the soil in full circles. A moment later, the first bank of sprinklers went off and the second row sputtered and came on full, watering every inch I'd planned. It was a beautiful thing.

There were five banks, each set for twenty minutes, and when the last series—outside the fence—kicked on, I saw a problem. The heads were watering not only my strip of yard but the sidewalk and part of the street. Along the driveway, they were spraying well over my strip, and DeRay's motorcycle was dripping in the gray light.

I stood so sharply that Allie whimpered, and I took her quickly into Liz and laid her in the bed. I put on my robe and grabbed a towel, and I went outside. It was almost six and I wiped down the bike until the towel was sopping, and then I used the corner of my robe on the spokes and rims, and I was down on my knees when I heard voices, and two high-school girls in tennis clothes walked by, swinging their racquets. It was full light. I looked up and saw Liz in the kitchen window. Her face was clear to me. There was grit in my knees and my feet were cold.

"I'm going to have to adjust those last heads," I told her when I went inside.

"Why don't you make some coffee first," Liz said. She was sitting at the table. Allie was back in her crib, asleep.

"You want to talk about what's going on?" Liz said. I poured coffee into the filter and set it on the carafe.

"There's too much pressure this early," I said with my back to her. "We soaked DeRay's motorcycle."

"You're taking care of DeRay's motorcycle now?" she said. "You're going to get arrested, exposing yourself to school-girls."

After a long, tired moment of standing, staring at the drip-ping coffee, I poured a cup while it was still brewing and set it in front of my wife. "Look, Liz, everything's fine." I opened my hand to show the kitchen, the window, the yard. "And now the grass is going to grow."

That evening there was a knock at the kitchen door just after six. Liz answered it, and when she didn't come back to watch the news, I went out and found her talking to DeRay on the back porch. "Hello, Ace," he said to me.

"DeRay has invited us to . . ." Liz smiled. "What is it, DeRay?"

"They're testing one of our engines and I've got passes. We could make it a picnic."

Liz looked at me blankly, no clue, so I just said, "Let's do it. Sounds good. This is one of your engines?"

"We did some work on it. It's no big deal, but we can go up above the plant in the hills and get off the homestead for a while, right?"

"Right," I said, looking at Liz. "A picnic."

The Saturday of our picnic dawned gray—high clouds that mocked the end of summer. I offered to make the lunch, but Liz nudged me aside and made turkey sandwiches and put nectarines and iced tea and a six of Olympia in the cooler, along with a big bowl of her pasta salad. When I saw the beer I realized that she was going to do this right by the rules, and then when it turned into a tragedy or simple misery or some mistake, she would have her triumph. She had never bought a six-pack of Olympia in her life.

At eleven, we met DeRay and Krystal in our driveway. She was wearing a bright blue bandanna on her head. DeRay lifted his orange ice chest into the back of our Volvo and said, "Now follow us."

Before we were down the block, Liz said, "We're not driving like that."

"It's his right to change lanes," I said, moving left. "He's using his signals."

"We've got a baby in the car."

"Liz," I said, "I know we've got a baby in the car. And we're following DeRay out to Hercules Powder for a picnic. This is going to be a nice day."

As it turned out, Deray made the light at Thirteenth and we didn't. He disappeared ahead, the blue bandanna on Krystal's head dipping in front of two cars in the distance, and they were gone. We sat in silence. Allie was humming as if she had something to say and would say it next. There was no traffic on Thirteenth at all. How long is a traffic light? I've never known.

When the light turned green, Liz said, "Just let us out."

"Good," I said. "Where would I do that?"

"Right here," she said.

Without hesitation, instantly, I pulled against the curb. The sudden stop made Allie exhale with a high, sweet squeal. "Is this good?" I said.

Liz looked at me with a face I'd never seen. She unlocked her door and unbuckled her seat belt.

"Wait," I said. I knew I was out of control. "I'll drop you at Claire's. Shut your door."

She snapped her door closed but did not refasten her seat belt. I wheeled sharply back onto the street and dropped three blocks down to her sister's house. I jumped out and ran around to the baby's door and lifted her out. I kissed her and placed her in Liz's arms and went back around to my door. I didn't want any more talking. It was like the things I've done when I was drunk. Before I could measure anything, I was back on the access headed for West Valley.

I just thought about driving: how I would pass each car, dip right, reassume my lane and head out. When I entered the freeway, I hammered the Volvo to maximum speed. I hated this car. It had always been too heavy and too slow.

DeRay waited for me at the main gates of Hercules, the plant situated alone on the vast, gradual slope of the valley. There was a guard at the gate and DeRay waved me through, grinning, and then he and Krystal shot past me through the empty parking lot and under the red-checked water tower to the corner of the pavement, where they dropped onto a smooth dirt road that wound up the hill. Powdery dust lifted from their tires, and they led me up the lane and around into a small gravel parking area where there were already four blue government vans. Off to the side, about twenty people, half of them in military khaki, stood in the weeds. DeRay parked his bike and came over to where I was getting out of the Volvo.

"Where's the wife?" he said, looking in. "Is the baby here?"

"No, they decided to go to Liz's sister's."

"Oh, hell, that's too bad. This should be good."

We carried the coolers and a blanket to a high spot in the dry grass and spread out our gear. "Who are those guys?" I asked.

"The staff and some guys from Hill Air Force Base."

"Is it okay to have a beer?"

"That's why we brought it." He reached inside the orange Igloo for the cold cans and handed me a beer. Krystal wasn't drinking.

DeRay walked down a few yards to look at the bunker a half mile below. I had forgotten the view from out here. I could see the whole city against the Wasatch Range and each of the blue canyons: Little Cottonwood, Big Cottonwood, Mill Creek. On the hill, I could see the old white Ambassador Building, two blocks from my house, and I could imagine my yard, the fence.

Krystal was staring out over the valley. "Your wife didn't want to come to the country?" she said. I could tell that she knew all about it.

DeRay came back. "It's all set. In twenty minutes, you're going to hear some noise." He pointed to the bunker. "It'll fire south. They'll catch this on the university seismograph as a point two. What'd you bring to eat?"

We broke out the sandwiches and the salad. DeRay sat down on the blanket, Indian style, his big boots like furniture beneath him, and ate hungrily. "Hey, this is good," he said, pointing his fork at the pasta salad. "Nothing like a picnic." He drained his beer and tossed the can over his shoulder into the tall grass. "Just like home," he said. While we ate, DeRay waved at a couple of the guys by the vans, and later, when we were cleaning up the paper plates, one man walked up to us.

"How does it look?" DeRay asked him as they shook hands.

"Good, Ace. We've got a countdown."

DeRay introduced us to the man, Clint, and we all stood in a line facing the bunker. "In a minute you are going to see thirty seconds of the largest controlled explosion in the history of this state," DeRay said to me and winked. "We hope."

A moment later I saw the group near the vans all take a step backward, and then we saw the flash at the earthen mound become a huge white flare in a roar that seemed to flatten the grass around us. It was too bright to look at and hard to look away from, and the sound was ferocious, a pressure. I found myself turning my head to escape it, but there was no help. Clint wore sunglasses and was staring at the flash itself. He wasn't moving. Round balls of smoke rolled from the flame and began to tumble into the air, piling in a thick black column. Krystal watched with her head tilted. She was squinting and her mouth was open.

When it stopped, it stopped so suddenly it was as if someone had closed a door on it, and the roar was sucked out of the air and was replaced by a tinny buzzing that I realized was in my ears.

"Jesus Christ," Krystal said. She walked off a ways.

The people by the vans were kind of cheering and calling, and several of them turned and pointed at DeRay happily.

"Congratulations, Ace," Clint said and shook DeRay's hand again. "It was beautiful."

"Yeah, right," DeRay said. "Now on to phase four."

Clint walked down to where the group was boarding the vans, and two more guys came up and shook DeRay's hand, and then the four vans packed up and drove carefully down the dirt road, out of sight. I was watching the smoke cloud twist and roll silently in the sky, thick as oil. You could see this from our house. I wondered what Liz was doing, what she had told her sister. My ears simmered. With the vans gone this seemed a lonely place.

"That was your rocket?" I asked him.

"Fuel feed. I'm the fuel-feed guy."

I looked at him. "I thought you were a machinist."

"That's all it is, really." He pulled out another beer and sat on the cooler. "Just like this can. Same problem. You've got to keep the beer under pressure—two atmospheres. But you've got to cut the top here so I can open it with one finger. How deep do you score it? Figure that out and your problems are history." He lifted the tab and the beer hissed. He took a long swig and shrugged. "Oly's a good beer, right? We're having a fine picnic here. Am I right?"

Krystal walked toward us, arms folded.

DeRay said, "Hey, let's not head out yet." He stood. "Ace, you feel like riding the bike? I feel like a little ride." He turned to the woman. "You okay, Krystal, if we run up the hill for a minute? You can have some more of that great macaroni salad."

He started the Harley and I climbed on behind him. "Your wife is some cook. I'm sorry she missed this."

We cruised slowly down the road and through the lot. I was thinking about Liz and I felt bad and I could feel it getting worse. And it was funny, but I wanted it worse.

When we hit the highway, DeRay turned and said, "My second wife could cook," and he jammed the accelerator and we were lost in the wind, going seventy up the old road toward Copperton, slowing through Bingham and then hitting it hard again, winding up the canyon, using both sides of the road. It didn't matter. The air was at me like a hatchet, and I'd watch the yellow line drift under the bike, one side and then the other. At the top, the gate to the mine was closed. The mine had been closed for years.

DeRay pulled up to the gate, and I felt the dizzy pressure of stopping. "I come up here all the time," he said. "After work I just drive up. Push the gate." The chain was locked, but the gate opened three feet. He conducted the motorcycle easily under the chain. Near the pit, we sped up a paved incline and circled into the parking of the old visitors' center.

The structure was weathered. The back walls of the shelter held poster-sized framed photographs of the mining operations: a dynamite blast, the ore train in a tunnel, one of the giant trucks being filled by a mammoth loader. DeRay had gone to the overlook and was leaning on the rail, staring out at the vast rock amphitheater. The clouds above the copper mine were moving and shredding. The wind was chilly. "You want to bring the bike in?" I asked him. "We're going to get wet."

"Forget it," he said.

"I hope Krystal gets in the car."

"That woman knows what to do in the rain." He stood and pointed at four deer that walked along the uppermost level of the mine. "Check that."

"What are they looking for?" I said. The animals had made some kind of mistake.

DeRay leaned on the rail and said, "You know that Krystal's leaving."

"What?"

"Yeah, she has to go. Her crazy man is on leave. He's out. They weren't really divorced. You can't divorce someone who's crazy. Something. She's going out to his folks'."

"I didn't know. Hey, I'm sorry."

"Come on, what is it? She has to go," he said. DeRay rubbed his eyes with a thumb and a forefinger. His face in the dim light looked blue, the way it did some nights on his porch. When he looked up, he said, "Hey, look at you." I reached up and felt my hair standing up all over. "You're going to want to get a cap." DeRay lifted his and snugged it on my head. "Why don't you take it for a spin? Go ahead, down the road and back." He waved at the motorcycle and in the gloom his tattoo looked like a wound.

I said, "Krystal's a good woman."

"Oh, hell," he said. "They're all good women."

"Things happen," I said.

He turned to me. "No, they don't. I know all about this. Things don't *happen*. I'm an engineer. One thing leads to another. Listen. You're a nice kid, but that fence around your place won't stop a thing. What are you, thirty?"

We could smell the rain. It felt real late. It felt like October, November. When you have a baby, you have to put in a lawn. You're supposed to build a fence. There's no surprise in that. I am like every other man in that.

"That was some rocket," I said. I could taste trouble in my mouth and I felt kind of high, like a kid a long way from home. "I'm sorry Liz didn't see it. It won't be easy to describe."

DeRay pointed again at the deer and we watched as they tried to scramble up the steep mine slope. It was desperate, but so far away that we couldn't hear the gravel falling. They kept slipping. Finally, two made it and disappeared over the summit. The two left behind stood still. "Hey, don't listen to me," Deray said.

"I'm just squawking. We should have brought some beer."

I went out and mounted the Harley. It came back off the stand easier than I thought and started right up. I sat down in the seat and looked over at DeRay as the wheels crept forward. I could sense the ion charge before rain. We were definitely going to get wet. Just a little spin.

DeRay was right. He had been right about the trencher and he was right about one thing leading to another. I am not the kind of person who stays out in bad weather, but there I was. I lifted my feet from the pavement and felt it all happen. It was a big machine, more than I could handle, but I could just feel it wanting to balance. It began to drift. I'd never felt anything like it before. There were accidents in this thing. I would just take it down to the gate and right back up again.

Evan Williams

The Lake District

I n the eastern part of the state, in the high desert country, the traveler will come to the Lake District. Here the desert floor gives way to a layer of polished white granite as hard underfoot as swept marble tile. The granite forms smooth hills, undulating gently where the land has buckled from strain. Wherever the land dips down, water has pooled, creating lakes.

There are hundreds of these lakes scattered throughout the district. They range in size from tiny ponds to broad expanses of deep water. The largest lake features a rocky island favored by ducks passing through on their migrations.

This place, the Lake District, is singular in its interruption of the searing desert plain. It calls attention to itself, shimmering like a mirage. The traveler, his throat parched, can ill pass the Lake District by.

He will discover that the Lake District is beautiful, serenely so, a refuge nestled amidst the geologic turmoil. He could imagine a soothing smoothness to the rise and fall of the land. He could imagine quiet pools of water, undisturbed by the gentle western breeze that smells of cottonwoods and sage. He could sense in the Lake District the dimensions of recovery and renewal.

He will note that the Lake District conforms to an ordered, reassuring arrangement of the desert landscape, giving the impression of a pleasure garden, well tended and clean. Such propriety could hardly be an accident of nature, and suggests that the Lake District developed according to a deliberate plan.

He will be taken with the random, carefree placement of the lakes throughout the district; they lie scattered, here and there, across the high desert plain. That too would be part of the calculated effect: the lakes are like reflecting pools beside which the traveler can stroll, under no constraint to follow a regimented course. He could cover many miles, easily crossing the open terrain, visiting first one lake and then another.

It all sounds very quaint.

That, at least, is the general impression. The lack of reliable information on the Lake District allows for such unlimited, playful speculation. So little is known, the traveler can imagine the Lake District to be any kind of place he wants; the illusion will be sustained. The pleasure garden is merely the most obvious notion. It is as plausible as it is ludicrous, and impossible to challenge.

This much is certain: people stay out of the Lake District. Entering the Lake District will disconnect the traveler from the rest of the world, and he can never recover that distance.

The formation of the Lake District poses a geologic mystery. The rolling granite hills, the brilliant color of the stone, radically break from the surrounding desert, a barren plain of red clay that sifts through the traveler's fingers. The Lake District is out of place. Scientists cannot explain how it came to be there.

The origin of the water in the lakes is no easier to explain. Rain clouds hover teasingly above, dropping rain in misty curtains that never touch the ground. Scientists have yet to locate underground water deposits, rising in the form of springs, which might feed the lakes. Moreover, the lakes endure the heat of the desert with no evaporation, while there is no runoff in streams, no seepage into the ground. The lakes maintain a constant water level.

There exists no accurate map of the Lake District. A lone attempt by a government survey crew to map the area failed. Measurements taken one day proved skewed the next day when cross-checks were made. Never had the surveyors worked with such undependable data. Eventually they abandoned the project.

It has been suggested that the lakes may change position from day to day, the surface of the plain swelling and plunging like the open sea. This effect could account for the difficulty suffered trying to map the region. The surveyors were willing to take the suggestion seriously.

In the end the surveyors blamed their failure on the lack of a known reference point within the Lake District, a fixed standard from which to derive the rest of the map, to bring details into proper scale and juxtaposition. The surveyors had tried to design a chart out of nothing. They produced a map showing no detail, with no guide how to orient the map to match the physical landscape. The map was perfectly blank, and as accurate as it was useless.

The survey crew did find that exactly half of the lakes are poisonous. This small success is of no consolation to the traveler, for the surveyors neglected to label on their map which lakes are poisonous and which are safe. Nor could they say why some of the lakes should be poisonous, nor why it is so for exactly half. And since it is impossible to tell the difference just by looking, the traveler who dares to quench his thirst at the edge of a lake invites a grave uncertainty into his life.

It would be easy to find in the Lake District a parable on the limitations of the scientific method. Such accusation may be accurate and fair, but the issue goes deeper than that: the Lake District defies all inquiry. Nothing happens here. The water in the lakes lies perfectly still, makes no ripples in the strongest breeze. During most of the year the place is lifeless save for small creatures such as ants, and it is quiet save for the scattering sounds of tiny lizards, their tails whipping the rock as they dart away to capture one of the ants.

The wearisome strangeness of the Lake District centers on the lakes themselves. The lakes, after all, form the dominant feature of the district, and they have shown themselves to be the most bizarre. Even in their physical appearance the lakes resemble no other lakes in the world.

The water in the lakes is of exceptional clarity, so clear that the lakes are invisible. The whitewashed color of the granite produces this illusion; the bottoms of the lakes are so white that the sunlight glancing off the surface of the water generates no reflection. Enhancing the effect, the purity of the water assures that the lakes are free of contaminants which might stain the color of the rock or etch a distinct water line along the shore.

Lacking these visual indications, the lakes convey a sense of unreality. For example, at the largest lake, the one with the island, the ducks that float upon the surface seem to hover in mid-air. Beneath them the lake appears to be an empty pit. Intrigued, the traveler might descend into the pit to examine more closely the celestial ducks, only to thrash about in water he cannot see. Thus the traveler can discover the lakes only by accident, stumbling upon them, guided by the sensations of wetness and alarm.

It would be incorrect to suggest that the Lake District poses a danger, like a trap. The traveler could enter the district and pass through safely, meeting not a single lake along the way. The lakes naturally elude detection. But for the traveler who already finds himself at the edge of a lake, tracing the shoreline with his fingertips, the effect can only be deeply disturbing: he could not have anticipated this; what can he rely on anymore? Not surprisingly, human activity in the Lake District has been minimal. Nobody goes in there. The pattern began with the Indians of the high desert country, long before the white people came into the region. The Indians' orientation was practical: the water in the lakes was poisonous. The land supported no game, offered no nourishing plants, no forage for their horses. Of course they stayed away.

However, the Indians may have avoided the Lake District because it held spiritual significance for them. The Indians, seeing the pristine condition of the Lake District, may have revered the place as a remnant of the original landscape from an ancient spirit-time. The Lake District may have been a sacred origin place, and so was inviolable.

More than one legend tells of this original order to the world, and the Lake District plays a central role in those legends. The listener frequently hears described the spirit-people who dwelled at the bottoms of the lakes, an idea encouraged by the clarity of the lake water. The spirit-people never left the lake bottoms. They walked about, approached the shore at times, only to return to the bottom and sit awhile before walking about again. The eventual break from the spirit world came as a violent amputation, so perfectly disconnected as to lack any hint of a transition between them. Where at first there had been a spirit-world, there then emerged the world of the Indians, but no middle phase connected them.

For the Indians, then, to enter the Lake District meant to enter the impossible landscape, at once their origin place but also that place from which they were fundamentally alienated. It was an origin they could not recall. The feeling must have been unbearable. And so, at the close of the nineteenth century, when the approach of the army forced the Indians to flee across the Lake District, this exodus across sacred ground left the Indians wretched and in despair long before the army overtook them.

During the westward expansion of the mid-nineteenth century, the route of the emigrant wagon trains carefully circumvented the Lake District. The pioneers chose a wide detour to the south, across the open desert, and then worked north to regain their original course. To this day, both the railroad and the interstate highway follow this same route rather than cross the Lake District.

It would be easy to attribute this avoidance to the perceived worthlessness of the Lake District, a practical excuse, and one reinforced by the look of the region as you pass to the south along the highway: in the foreground, gnawing its sustenance from the dry hills, looms an automated cement factory, beyond which, across the hills, the Lake District cowers beneath the heavy clouded sky—as if anyone cared to glance in that direction anyway.

In the more recent past, attention focused on the Lake District— although only to contemplate its annihilation. A government agency concerned with matters of conservation and development issued an environmental-impact statement detailing a bleak scenario, in which the pristine ecology of the Lake District could not survive in light of the need for future development of the region. The Lake District, regrettably, would have to be sacrificed.

They did not say what the development would be. Perhaps someone planned to build a spa. Perhaps they merely referred to the soot that drifts from western cities and settles in dark stains upon the ground and taints the pristine water.

Perhaps their bureaucratic jargon veiled a deep anxiety that the structured human world excluded anomalies such as the Lake District, and henceforth it would be removed from memory and concern. By saying that the Lake District could not be saved, they were saying that it could not be allowed to exist because it could not possibly exist anyway.

The designers of the spa were careful to address ecological concerns early. They asked environmentalists to help with the design, and promised to incorporate their ideas into the plan. Together they formed a committee and worked on a design.

The joint committee reached a landmark decision. According to their plan, the largest lake in the district, the one with the island, would be removed before development began. The lake would be preserved more effectively than if it stayed in the wild, while development would go on unrestrained.

With elated conviction the project began. Funds were allocated. Engineers came in, this time armed with sophisticated equipment, advanced mathematical formulae, and a computer for data-entry and interpretation.

First they measured the dimensions of the lake, including depth soundings to determine the exact contours of the lake bottom. They fed the information into the computer and plotted the lake onto a three-dimensional graph. In this image, the ground that supported the lake seemed stripped away, and the lake appeared to float in a void, keeping its shape along the bottom and staying glassy smooth on top. The lake molded to the invisible press of earth without substance, for it had not been charted onto the graph, being of no interest to the engineers.

The image of the lake was then cross-sectioned into a mass of tiny cubes, the summation of which, by an effort of calculus and imagination, comprised the lake in abstract. Each section bore a set of graphic coordinates, reducing the lake to an elegant enciphered code.

The engineers then removed each unit of lake water, placing each in a glass box perhaps the size of a portable ice chest. On the side of each box the engineers labeled its coordinates. In this manner, box by box, the lake was removed, but carefully, so the engineers retained the data that would allow them to reconstruct the lake at a place out of harm's way.

A warehouse in the city awaited the lake. Inside, the engineers put the lake together again, matching the coordinates so as to place each box of water in its proper spot. Finally, using a minimum of discreet scaffolding and support wires, the lake appeared as it had on the computer design, suspended, floating. It was possible to walk beneath the lake, just as in the spirit world, and to imagine the lightness of the water, the beautiful crystalline shapes overhead. The glass boxes cast prisms of color onto the walls. Near the center of the room, where the island had been, a vaulting cavity filled with light. The light spilled onto the surface of the lake, scattered across, and diffracted over the edge to fall back down.

A stray mallard feather, balanced on its outer curve, lay unnoticed on the floor. It shuddered and glided away, yanked by the breeze as the men passed by. Then it stopped, poised in the darkness, as the men closed the door for the final time.

Several months later, a flock of ducks passed through the Lake District. The ducks expected the lake to be there. They saw no difference between the clear lake water and the empty void that had replaced it. As the ducks touched down on the water long since gone, they lost control, went into a free fall, and crashed into the rocks below. They broke their wings and thrashed in frantic circles on the ground. They made easy targets for coyote and fox in the area, who darted across the dusty lake bed to snatch them away. The rest of the ducks, watching from the now-defenseless island, left soon thereafter and were never seen again. When all the ducks had left, the area was quiet.

A sense of calm and normalcy quickly returned to the Lake District. The lake appeared as it always had, perfectly clear, perfectly invisible. The traveler familiar with the region noticed no change, save the absence of the ducks which, during certain seasons, was normal. The traveler who was new to the region found nothing to suggest that a lake had ever been there at all. To the delight of developers and environmentalists alike, the preservation had gone exactly according to plan, with the Lake District sustaining truly imperceptible impact. The engineers were applauded for their care and precision.

This atmosphere of congratulation soured when the developers visited the Lake District for the first time. They brought blueprints, a ribbon to slice, and a camera to photograph the ground-breaking ceremony. Upon arrival, the committee found the region unblemished, raising the suspicion that the lake was still there, that maybe the engineers had unwittingly carted off something entirely different, while the genuine lake remained behind, intact, unseen. They had wasted millions of dollars and accomplished nothing.

The developers were furious. They abandoned the project, and in their rage they cursed the Lake District. Then they went away. The Lake District had endured.

Or it had not endured, like a shadow when clouds pass overhead, and in the Lake District there are always clouds.

Susan M. Gaines

The Mouse

The mouse is tiny, even for a mouse—no bigger than a newborn baby's hand. He lives in a place of wide-open spaces and spectacular storms, of uplifted, rainbow-colored sediments and looming red cliffs carved into delicate, fantastical forms, an exalted place where the creative forces of the earth have surfaced and joined. But the mouse is too tiny to see this: he lives in a dull dry world of sand and sagebrush with a distant, perhaps nonexistent, sky.

It is by accident, not by design, that the mouse discovers the car. Hunted one night by an owl, a fluttering presence that he senses but cannot see, the mouse is dashing hysterically from bush to bush, when suddenly the owl is gone and he is under an

expansive stretch of cover, as if a sky has materialized above
him—a real sky that he can feel, almost see, a strange-smelling,
darker-than-night sky. Disoriented, the mouse freezes, nose
quivering to assess the strange scent. Then again he is propelled
into motion by a sound, more immediate than thunder, and a
light, more persistent than lightning, as if the night has been
overturned to day: the mouse, searching frantically for darkness,
is running upward toward his new sky and dipping, like a pool
ball, into the hole—a dark cavity, a hidden place. He stops.

Safe. It's a while before the mouse realizes how safe he is,
frozen there inside the frame of the car, but once he understands—that this is a whole universe of holes, of safe, tangible
skies and sweet, lovely darkness—he crawls deeper.

The man and woman who own the car awake in awe. The air is
clean and scented with sage, the place they have camped of such
sublime beauty—the sky so expansive and wild with wandering
clouds, the pastel colors and bizarre shapes of the cliffs so mag-
nificent, and the quiet so pure—that for the moment they forget
that the earth is no longer big, or powerful, or awe inspiring, that
such awe is outdated. It was dark when they set up camp the
night before, they had gone a long ways down this dirt road and
chosen this spot—this nameless spot somewhere in Utah—quite
at random. It is the beginning of the third day of what is to be an
extended vacation: they have spent the first two days driving,
escaping California.

In silence, they make their breakfast and pack up their tent.
They eat and drink their coffee standing up, turning in bewildered circles to admire the view. Then they rinse their dishes and
pack everything away in the car. When they have finished they
realize that, without thinking, they have prepared to leave, and
there is a brief discussion, that maybe they should stay, another
day, maybe two. But no, the man points out, they were planning
to go to the mountains, to the Grand Tetons, maybe Yellowstone, the car is full of backpacking gear and food. Well then,

maybe spend just half the day in the desert, up along that spectacular gorge they drove past the day before—maybe the man will be inspired and paint a picture, the woman can sit on a rock and write a poem. Anyway, says the woman as they drive off, they can always come back someday, stay awhile.

They haven't gone far down the dirt road, are nowhere near the gorge, when the mouse darts out from under the driver's seat. It runs across the man's foot, and when the foot moves— for the man jerks his foot and lets out a little yelp when he feels, looks down and sees, the mouse—it darts back under the seat.

"There's a mouse in here!" exclaims the man, glancing nervously at his feet as he pulls off the road.

"A mouse?" says the woman. "You're kidding."

"No—it just ran across my foot."

"Are you sure . . ."

"Yes I'm sure," says the man, climbing out of the car. He gets down on his knees and looks under the seat. "I don't see it."

The woman bends forward and looks as well. She gets out of the car and looks under her own seat. There is an umbrella there; she takes it and pokes the end under the seats, moves it about.

"Christ," says the man, standing back from the car. "If you wouldn't leave the doors open all the time when we camp—it probably crawled in last night."

"Well where could it be? Are you sure it was a mouse?"

"I saw it— Shit. I can't drive with a mouse running around my feet." He reaches across and takes a flashlight from the glove compartment. Laying his head on the floor, he shines the light under the seat. "You know, I think it's up in the foam." He gets up and starts pounding on the seat, sits on it and bounces up and down. No mouse. He gets out of the car and stands next to the open door, staring at the seat. "If we had some cigarettes we could smoke it out."

"I know!" The woman is smiling at him over the top of the car. "I have just the thing."

"What—" The man folds his arms across his chest, watching

her march round to the back of the car. He smiles when she isn't looking. She is thirty, and he is thirty-six. They have been living together for three years. Digging around in one of the bags, she finds what she's looking for and holds it up triumphantly. He laughs. "Mosquito coils?"

"Why not? Ought to work better than cigarettes—which we don't have, anyway."

"Yeah, I guess it's worth a try."

They light one of the coils and set it directly under the driver's seat. The woman sits in the passenger seat with the umbrella held at the ready, and the man watches outside the door on the driver's side.

They stay like that for a long time. The mouse doesn't appear.

"Shit, I don't believe this," says the man, slapping the seat twice.

The woman reaches under the seat and removes the mosquito coil. "Maybe it already left and we just didn't see it."

"Maybe." He sits down in the driver's seat and slides the key into the ignition, which sets off a buzzer because the doors are open. He is staring at the floor.

The mouse appears between the man's feet and disappears again more quickly than the man can move or speak.

"Like hell—" He lifts his feet off the floor. "Did you see it?"

"No . . ."

It is a very fast mouse. A desert mouse.

They get down with their heads on the floor and look under the seat again. "I think you're right," says the woman. "That it goes up in that foam."

"I'm gonna have to take the seat out—"

"Is that hard? Look, there're only four bolts."

The car is a little Mazda hatchback. Since the man keeps his tools in the compartment with the spare tire, under the floor in back, they have to take everything out of the car to get a wrench.

The man unscrews the four bolts, and together they lift the seat out and carry it away from the car. They turn it upside down and pry at the foam, but it is stapled into place with the upholstery—it cannot be removed without destroying the seat. Turning the seat over, they set it gently on the sand and back away, one on either side.

They are watching the seat intently, waiting for the mouse to come out, when a pickup comes down the dirt road. The truck slows as it nears them, but they keep their eyes fixed on the seat, and it doesn't stop. "Okay," says the woman, once the truck is out of sight. "Let's wait five more minutes." She giggles. "Come on, look at your watch."

The man looks at his watch and shakes his head. "I don't believe this."

Five minutes later they carry the seat back to the car.

"Were you watching really close when we took the seat out?" asks the man, tightening the bolts. "Maybe it got out then."

"I think I was watching—I don't know. If it's as fast as you say—I mean, I haven't seen it at all . . ."

"Let's try turning the engine on for a while. That's when it came out before, like it doesn't like the noise or the vibration or something."

This time the man sees the mouse clearly. It is peering out from behind the hinge of the open door. "Look, it's coming out," he whispers, stepping back to give the mouse plenty of room.

But the mouse is frightened by the man's movement: it slips back into the frame of the car.

"Damn, it was coming out, did you see it?"

"No—"

"It was right there behind the door . . . shit, that means it's inside the frame of the car, it can go anywhere." Leaning around the back of the driver's seat, he folds the carpet back. "Look, it wasn't in the seat at all, I bet it ran out from these holes in the floor."

The woman is laughing. "God, this is ridiculous. You're just going to have to drive with it, you know. We can't stay here forever."

"He was going to come out, if only I hadn't moved. He was just sitting there looking at me."

Perhaps, if the man had slammed the door quickly, he could have crushed the mouse.

The woman is putting the tools away, when she notices a pile of shredded insulation next to the spare tire. "What the . . ." She picks up the mess and hands it to the man.

"Christ, it's his nest! Here we are pounding on the seat like idiots, and he's been all over the car." He drops the insulation next to the tire and closes the compartment. They repack the car.

For the first two hours the man taps his clutch foot constantly; he says it's to keep the mouse from dashing out and startling him. The woman laughs, but she has her legs folded up under her on the seat. They drive past the gorge where they'd intended to stop without noticing.

The mouse has found its way back to its nest next to the spare tire and is quite comfortable. It quickly grows accustomed to the noise and vibration, and finds itself lulled to sleep.

In the first sizable town they come to, they find a Thrifty's and buy a package of two mousetraps.

"These aren't like the kind we used when I was a kid," says the man. He is having trouble setting the traps. "They're some kind of deluxe model." Finally he gets them set and puts one under the driver's seat. They take everything out of the car again and he puts the other next to the spare tire. The woman gathers up the shredded insulation and throws it away.

They drive to the mountains and camp in a campground

with plans to set out backpacking the next day. In the evening it gets cold enough that they need their down jackets.

During the night the mouse looks about for food. It finds the cheese under the front seat. Cheddar cheese. The mouse is so tiny that it can sit on the yellow plastic platform eating cheese without triggering the deluxe model mousetrap.

They have been hiking in silence for several hours. The woman is setting the pace. She stops abruptly and looks around her pack at the man. "What about water?" she says. It is beginning to rain. "There's no water in the car."

"Huh?"

She turns and continues up the trail. "The mouse can't survive without water."

"Oh, yeah, that's right—where's he gonna get water? Oh great, what if it dies inside the frame of the car somewhere and starts rotting. There's no way to even find it, let alone get it out."

"Or maybe he doesn't need much water—I mean, it's a desert mouse, can't they go for long periods without water? Don't they just survive on what they get from plants or something?"

"Probably. But I doubt our food has much water in it. Rice, nuts, dehydrated vegetables—Maybe he'll get so thirsty he'll find a way to escape. Remember the neighbor's dogs that time they got all frantic and dug their way out, because he accidently turned off the water on their Lick-It?"

"You think? But what's he going to do if he escapes here? It's a desert mouse, it won't know what to do in the mountains."

"What, are you worried?" The man laughs. "He'll have a lot better chance of surviving if he escapes than if he eats the cheese in those traps."

The woman doesn't say anything.

———

Each night the mouse crawls out of the wheel well, scampers down the wheel, and forages around the car. Each dawn it returns to safety. Other animals are intimidated by the car. They leave the mouse alone.

"Well, it doesn't smell like rotting mouse," says the woman, sticking her head into the car. They have returned to the campground after only three days in the mountains because it rained every day and they weren't being creative or even having fun. She pushes the food in one of the bags around. Before they left California she made up gourmet backpacking dinners and packaged each one in a separate plastic bag. There is a month's worth of food. "But it doesn't look like he's been into the food. Maybe he escaped after all."

"Shit, look at this," says the man holding up the trap that had been under the front seat. "He ate the cheese but the thing didn't go off."

The man adjusts the traps to the most sensitive setting; this time he uses white Gouda cheese as bait.

The thundershowers are not intermittent as they're supposed to be: it rains most of the time. They head north to Yellowstone and try another backpacking trip, but mosquitoes ruin that one. They decide to car-camp for a while, but the campgrounds in Yellowstone are so crowded and there are so many cars that they might as well have stayed in California. They head south to the desert, where there are no people, no mosquitoes, where the thunderstorms come and go in an hour.

They spend a lot of time driving. No pictures are painted, and the woman's little cloth-bound book is unopened; they chide each other that they are being unproductive. But still, they are having fun, they are seeing the lay of the land. They have plenty of time, the woman reminds the man, they are exploring. Every time they come upon a beautiful place, she proposes that they move there: California has gotten too crowded, too overrun by cars, she feels constricted. They spend a night in the beautiful place, but when they pack to leave in the morning the woman doesn't protest, because they are always headed somewhere else: somewhere that might be yet more beautiful, more inspirational, that might be perfect.

There has been no sign of the mouse for over a week. It hasn't touched the Gouda cheese. Perhaps it stayed in Wyoming. They have stopped talking about the mouse.

They are camping at a KOA. The woman complains—how can they stay in such an ugly, tacky place?—but they are desperate for showers and a place to do laundry. She spends twice as long as the man in her shower, and it is already dusk when she returns to their campsite. The man is squatting next to the car staring at the ground.

"What are you doing?"

"There's a mouse running around the car—"

"Where?" She squats down next to him.

"It just disappeared. I was just getting something out of the car and I look down and there's this mouse running around—"

"That's our mouse! It must have jumped out when you opened the door."

"Well, but I didn't see it jump out—"

"Come on, it's got to be our mouse." She shines her flashlight under the car.

"Wait, turn the light off. He doesn't like the light."

She turns the light off and they squat there in silence for a while, waiting.

"There he is!" says the man, pointing. There is just enough light for the woman to see the tiny shadow dash between the wheels.

"God it's so little!" she says.

They watch the mouse run up the wheel and disappear into the car. They have frightened it.

"I don't believe this," says the man, standing up. He glances at the woman. "That's probably how he got in to begin with."

"That's how he can get water—"

"God, it's weird—We scare him, and instead of running away he just goes back in the car."

"It's so incredibly tiny. I've never seen such a little mouse. Maybe it's a baby."

"No, I think that's just the way he is. He hasn't grown since I first saw him anyway."

They decide that the only way to get rid of the mouse is to wait until he's out of the car one night, and then move the car to where he can't find it. But, of course, the mouse is always too fast for that.

After a few nights they give up.

The woman, who was born in California, disdains campgrounds and takes pride in finding the most out-of-the-way places possible to camp. Tonight they have pulled off a back road in a national forest. The woman is a little nervous because they aren't far from a city, and their tent can be seen from the road, which is paved. She is afraid of the other people who might be camped in the forest. The man, who was born in New York City, is more afraid of being trampled by deer or pawed by a bear; the woman tells him that's ridiculous, though they might be trampled by cows. It takes them a long time to fall asleep.

They are awakened by the sound of hooves. Peering out the tent window, the woman sees a horse with a rider come toward them and stop. "Hello—" she calls out, but the rider doesn't answer, nor does he move.

"Where?" whispers the man. "I can't see a horse—"

"Right there—you see? The rider has a white shirt on."

The man still can't see them—the moon is just a sliver and it's very dark. But there is a commotion coming from the car, which is parked right next to the tent, and he can hear that. It sounds like everything is being pushed around inside the car.

"They've got us surrounded," whispers the woman. "And

one of them's going through the car. Didn't you hear the other horses?"

The man sticks his head out the door at the other end of the tent and shines the flashlight all around the car. "Nothing," he reports, zipping the tent closed. "No one in the car, no horses, no riders."

"Oh," says the woman. The noise in the car has stopped. "I guess it was just cows going by."

The man slides back into the sleeping bag. "Go to sleep."

"I'll just watch for a little longer," says the woman, still staring at the shadow that looks like a horse and rider.

The noise in the car starts up again, loud and unmistakable.

"Shit," says the man, lifting his head. "That's the mouse."

"Oh, God, you're right—Listen to it running around in there!" She slips down, turns on her side and stretches an arm across the man's chest. He twists onto his side as well, and she hugs his back. It's almost dawn, and they are very tired.

With a freedom and abandon never known before the car, the mouse explores his world. He has discovered caches of food beyond his wildest dreams, along with a myriad of strange, bizarre smells. He leaves the car now only to search for moisture, or sometimes out of simple curiosity, which is also new. He has found, however, the precise limits of this world, of the car's power of protection, and doesn't venture beyond them.

The woman is almost asleep when she is again jerked awake, this time by something scratching at the tent, right next to her ear.

It's just the mouse, she thinks, and turns over. We should go move the car now, she thinks, but doesn't say anything to the man, who has begun to snore.

They have used up a lot of food, and the woman is combining things and getting rid of half-empty bags, when she notices that the mouse has, indeed, been into the food. It has chewed the

corners on all the plastic bags, as if sampling each of their dinners and then moving on to the next. The woman puts as much
as she can fit into the cooler, which they never buy ice for anyway. The bag of gorp has sustained major damage: peanuts and
raisins spill all over when she picks up the bag. "I wonder if we
should throw out this gorp," she says to the man.

He examines the bag. "I don't know—this hole is big enough
that he could have actually gone inside."

"You think we could get some disease or something?"

"I'm just worried that maybe he pooped in there."

"Oh gross—" The woman starts picking through the bag,
but soon recognizes the improbability of finding an exception-
ally small mouse's droppings in a bag of raisins and nuts. She
pours the gorp into a new bag and puts it in the cooler: it's
expensive gorp, that she prepared herself, with cashews and Bra-
zil nuts and dried papaya.

The mouse hadn't needed to go inside the bag: it had chewed a
big hole in the plastic, and nuts and seeds and fruit had rained
down all around it.

The man is tired of their aimless wandering, of the nightly
searches for a campsite. The woman feels restless and cramped
from sitting in the car. They agree to spend a week in one place,
at a national park in the desert. It is far from the mouse's desert
and, though very beautiful, not as big. The woman writes two
poems while they are there. The man paints several pictures.
They go hiking every day. Then the week begins to drag, as if
they have been at this campsite forever. They decide to clean out
the car a little, then move on.

"Maybe we should check on the mouse while we're at it,"
says the man. The mouse has been with them for almost a month
now.

When they lift the panel covering the spare tire compartment, the mouse is sleeping on the ledge above the tire. It blinks at the sudden light and looks up at them lethargically.

Several seconds go by before anyone moves. Then the mouse leaps into its nest of chewed up insulation.

"Uhh," says the man. "A bag, get me a bag—" The woman hands him a paper bag, but before he can decide how to use it, the mouse darts out of its nest, runs up the side of the tire, and drops through the hole in the middle.

The man taps on the tire, and the mouse runs in circles.

"He can't get out of there, can he?" says the woman.

"I don't think so."

"Unless—" The mouse's nose has appeared at a slot in the hub of the wheel. The woman waves her hand, and it drops back out of sight.

"Maybe he can get out those side holes," says the man, "but not with us standing here. We've got him trapped."

"So now what."

"I don't know." The man finds his work gloves among the tools and puts them on.

"What if we block off all the side holes but one and cover that one with a bag. Then harass him inside the wheel until he runs into the bag—"

"I think he'll just run in circles . . . The thing is, we could just cover the wheel so he can't get out at all, and leave him there. There's no food, no water—"

"That's pretty awful—slow death—"

"Well Christ," the man says loudly. "I don't want to torture him either, I'm just trying to think of ways to get rid of him. You have any better ideas?"

The woman shakes her head.

"Let's clean some of this crap out of here," says the man.

They remove the tools, rags, plastic jug of antifreeze, tangle of rope, and mouse's nest from the compartment.

"Maybe if we block off this whole area and I lift the tire at one end you can drive him into the bag," says the man.

The woman shrugs. She tears the flaps off a box and they use them to block off any holes in the vicinity of the tire.

"Ready?" The man unscrews the bolt holding the spare tire down.

"Wait—" She arranges the paper bag on its side with the opening facing the side of the wheel, and tries to hold it flush with the bottom of the trunk. "Okay . . ."

The man tilts the wheel up; the mouse doesn't move. He tilts it more. "Damn it, come on—" The wheel is too heavy to hold like that for long. He lifts it a little more, and finally the mouse darts out on the side away from the bag. It scampers easily onto the ledge above the tire and disappears into a hole they haven't covered.

"Shit!" exclaims the woman, stomping her foot. "Damn." A lady at the next campsite is looking at them. "We're trying to catch this mouse that's been living in our car," explains the woman.

The lady smiles and looks away.

"I just hope we don't open up one day and find a whole bunch of baby mice," says the man.

The woman is driving. They have just crossed the border into California and the freeway seems to have filled instantly with traffic. She glances over at the man. "You think it's a female?" She looks down at the floor between her feet.

"How would I— Jesus will you watch the road!" A semi has cut in front of them while the woman is looking at the floor. She hits the brakes and they swerve slightly out of control, but avoid the semi.

"Pull over."

"It's okay."

"Pull over damn it, I want to drive."

The woman pulls over and switches to the passenger seat. After a while she says, "So even if the mouse is female where would she find a mate of her own species?"

"Maybe she was already pregnant."

"It's been over four weeks—I wonder how long a gestation period they have."

"Well, when we get home why don't you get a book about mice from the library."

The woman doesn't say anything. She doesn't want to think about getting home.

There is plenty of insulation in the back of the car; the mouse is busy chewing it up to replace its nest. It is a full-grown, male mouse.

When they get home the man cleans out the car. He waters the lawn and spends a day relaxing before going back to work. He mentions to the woman that the little house is really very comfortable, and that it's too bad they don't have the security of owning it. The woman quit her job to go on the trip. When the man goes back to work, she stays in the house and looks in the newspaper for another job. When she first moved in with the man she liked the house, which is surrounded by an old apricot orchard in a not-so-large town. But the not-so-large town is annexed by suburbs to a larger town, which is annexed by industrial parks to a city. The remnant of orchard really isn't very big and the neighbors' house is too close. There are cars everywhere. And the sky is oppressive: in the mornings it hangs heavy with fog, and even when the fog lifts the sky is too low, too close, not blue but off-white. When they have been back for a week, the woman tells the man that she wants to move.

"Where?" asks the man. He has just come in from work and is tired from the commute.

"Just somewhere else."

"We don't have any money." They have spent all their savings on gas.

The woman shrugs. "We can sell the car . . . Hitchhike—"

"Oh, Christ, this isn't 1968."

"Maybe we could go back to the desert—that one where the mouse lived."

The man laughs. "You're crazy. What are we going to do for jobs?"

"You can paint a lot of paintings and then we'll go to the city for a while and you can sell them. Maybe I can write something, you know, that I can sell, like travel stuff or something—"

"Oh yeah, dream on."

"I mean I can always get a job waitressing in some little town. And we wouldn't need much money—"

"Come on, you're thirty years old." Laughing again, he reaches out and pushes a strand of hair out of her face. "Speaking of the mouse, I think it's gone. I've been checking the back and there hasn't been a new nest in a week."

"I guess he finally got claustrophobia and left. I mean what kind of animal would want to live cooped up in the frame of a car anyway? He's probably out in the orchard somewhere—I wonder if he can mate with the field mice?"

"Actually, I think it was just getting all that food out of the car that did it—there's probably more to eat in the orchard."

The mouse from the Utah desert doesn't realize that the neighbors' cat is not intimidated by the car like other animals. It has only been in California for one day, when the cat bats it off the wheel with one paw. The neighbors' cat is a good hunter, she is always catching mice. She plays with them for a while before she eats them. Sometimes she doesn't eat them at all, but takes them into the house and leaves them on the kitchen floor. The mouse from the desert is the smallest mouse this cat has ever caught.

Christopher Tilghman

The Way People Run

Off the road, at least a hundred yards into the yellow scrub, Barry thinks he sees an animal, maybe an antelope, nuzzling the arid brush. He's surprised that it has wandered so far out into the open alone. About a mile ahead he sees the town, or what's left of it— a few blanched hackberry skeletons above a small gathering of houses centered on a two-story brick block. Even from this distance, he can tell that the wooden cornices and pediments of this building, the Commerce Building, are rotting. He has been seeing buildings like these and towns like this one for days; the only way he has of knowing that there are any people left is the sizzling rays of neon beer signs from one or two windows in an otherwise shuttered

façade. He glances at his speedometer, and then back at the antelope, but what he first saw as an animal in the brush has broken
apart, exploded limb by limb into children, six or seven of them
suddenly scattering from their clustered spot. They are all different sizes, and as they run one of the big ones tugs along the
littlest, a girl three or four years old, not much smaller than his
younger daughter, if the distance, and the shafts of morning light
through rain heads, and Barry's tired eyes can be trusted.

The café in town is still called the Virginian. Barry walks into
the darkness, not sure he should trust the floor. The place smells
of cigarettes and beer—not such a bad combination if left to age
on its own, but the air is heavy with air freshener. Lilac, maybe it
is, or Mountain Meadow. Someone is keeping a business going
in here, perhaps because the county road crew stops three times
a week, or because the motor-vehicle department keeps a branch
open every Tuesday. The tables around the edges of the room
are dull black squares rimmed with the semicircles of Windsor
chairs. The lamplight is bloodied by red shades at the tables and
the bar, but in the center of the room, dominating the territory
encompassed by its brilliant processed fluorescence, there is a
circular pie cabinet. It is steel and glass, and looks so new that
Barry wonders if it is for sale. On the third of six carrousel
shelves there is an apple pie, scarred by the removal of a single
triangle, revolving in solitary repetition.

Barry assumes that the Virginian survives partly on the
whims of strangers, but the waitress greets him with a surprised
look anyway. He looks for a name tag, or a hint that she might be
a relative of some sort. She's about his age, forties, sharp-jawed,
and very thin, so thin in her tight bluejeans that she looks almost
sexless. She shows him to a table and sets up the silverware in
front of him. He sees the pie revolving, watches it several times,
and then moves to face the wall. When the waitress comes back
with his menu she stares hard enough at his emptied place to
force him to explain.

"That pie thing," Barry says. "It's sort of distracting." It's possible that she will find this funny.

The waitress looks at him neutrally, which seems almost a favor. She's not going to knock the establishment; it's clear she's got the only job in town.

"Why is this place called the Virginian?" he asks, looking up from his menu. He has always wondered if the café was named after the book.

She shrugs. "Can't say. Is that where you're from?"

He shakes his head. He hopes she won't ask him "Where, then?" because the true answer is "New York." He hopes she won't ask "So what line are you in?" because these days he's not in any line at all, just sort of looking for work.

"Tourists don't stop in here much," she offers. She hands him this thought.

"Well, no. But . . ."

But what? Coming out West hadn't made a whole lot of sense from the beginning. Barry started this trip with interviews in Los Angeles—fund management, trading, stockbroking, anything with money—even though no one suggested there were any jobs there. He had a briefcase full of recommendations, résumés that came flooding out of copiers and laser printers by the ream in the last days of his firm on Wall Street. At first he called home every night to report. At each stop in California he kept hearing of the boom in Washington—Boeing and Microsoft—and he became part of a wave of suppliants heading north, pilgrims in business suits trying not to recognize each other. He began to want anything that wasn't his: someone's job, someone's car, someone's family. He hit bottom one night in a Seattle hotel that was shabbier than he ought to have risked, considering his mood. He cancelled his last interview and headed back over the Cascades toward home, but in the desert he began to lose his way. He was not entirely sure how many days he had been gone. The hundred-dollar bills that he had watched closely and had broken with anxiety suddenly seemed endless, sufficient forever. An obscure elation began to take the place of schedule and plan. And then, as if planted in his mind like a signpost, came the image of this town, and he turned south for it even as his wife, Polly, wailed on the telephone, as she demanded to know what this detour could possibly do to resolve their plight.

The waitress loses interest during this pause and backs off; she's not going to hazard any piece of herself with him, and there's no reason for her to. "What can I get you?" she asks.

Barry looks at his watch and tries to recall the last three or four times he has eaten, decides it's time for a full midday meal, and orders a strip steak. "Our mashed potatoes are real," says the menu. It has begun to seem almost miraculous that he can stop in these ruined Western towns and find food; it's been days since he's seen cattle, or fields of corn, or vegetable gardens; he doesn't even see delivery trucks on the road. He's been asking waitresses "Do you still have any bacon?" or "What have you got?" as if menus were just memories of the times before a civil war out there cut off supplies. He feels the same way about gas; he's begun to think that way about women.

Barry hears the voices of two men behind him—he saw them under their feed-store caps at the bar when he walked in—and suddenly he regrets turning his back to the room. Each time he overhears a conversation he feels he has made a connection; in the same way, it reassures him to read notices for upcoming county fairs and church events. The waitress is going to think he's crazy, he knows, but he moves to a third side of the table.

"Maybe I should put it here and wait for you to catch up to it," she says when she returns, holding his plate above the fourth place. She gives him a smile somewhere between exasperation and interest.

"No. I'm settled now," says Barry. He says this straight, unthinkingly, as part of this conversation, but the statement taken in his own slender context is ridiculous, so ridiculous that he finishes it with a kind of bleating laugh on the "now."

A little off, the waitress seems to decide; he's O.K. but just a little off. She puts down his plate and does not wait to ask him how everything is. He thinks it might be funny to ask her for fresh-ground pepper.

The food is quite good, and he relaxes as he eats. The café's rusting tin ceiling is high above him. Above that ceiling, on the second floor, there were once rooms to let, and in one of those rooms his mother spent a week or two just after the war. Barry can imagine the sounds from other rooms, lovemaking and the beribboned serenade of a Bakelite Motorola. The country was flooding then, filling with expectation, and she had gone to the plains to find her father, who had, so long ago, lost heart. The story of their meeting and the final hurt it had caused her had become over the years, for Barry and his sisters, the text for a sort of catechism: What is the nature of man? How does sin have power over us? What is meant by betrayal? Barry pictures his mother, her clothes neatly placed in the dresser, her pearls and her aspirin arranged on a stained white table furrowed with cigarette burns.

The waitress is sitting behind the cash register, reading a fashion magazine in the light of the pie cabinet. He beckons to her for another beer. She knows it's an Oly, and he feels recognized through it, and when she brings it she lingers for a second or two. The men at the bar have left.

"When I was coming in I thought I saw children out on the plain."

"I expect you did," she says. "Probably dropping cherry bombs down gopher holes."

"Isn't there a school here?" he asks thinking of Polly's checklist for evaluating a town: good schools, health care, Episcopal or Presbyterian church, pretty streets, Victorian houses, a Toyota dealership.

"In Rylla. But the bus has been broke for a couple of days." She picks up his plate and asks, "You want a piece of pie?"

Barry asks her for the check instead. He's ready to find out if she had known his grandfather, but the bartender gives her a call, and she leaves him with no apology. Back on the street he blinks in the sun; the clouds have passed, and now there's no color at all to the light, just illumination, just the searing pressure of day on these powdery buildings. He opens a road map on the hood of his car and then stares over it. There is a white church building with a yard bounded by rusty sheep fencing; the church had once been repainted up to about five feet high all around, and it looks as if it's sinking. Beside the church is a brown house trailer with two bicycles in front, and then a low green ranch with flowers in the yard, and finally an old gas station with an enigmatic hand-painted sign, running like bunting across the windows and door, saying "Welcome to Eleven-Mile Rodeo." The old man had been happy here; that was his chief offense, the irreparable rebuke carried home with his daughter, and the principal evidence of his madness.

"You lost?"

Barry looks up and sees the waitress blinking at him. He thinks for a moment that she is making a joke. "Which way to Broadway?" he asks.

"You ain't there," she says, but she doesn't laugh. Place, her place, isn't funny to her.

He thinks of the biggest city around and tells her that's where he's going.

"I go up there to the dentist," she says.

He folds up his map and he sees her noticing the pile of maps, maybe a hundred of them, which are spilled out onto the passenger seat of his car. This is how it has been lately: catching a glimpse of himself through other eyes. He can't help what they perceive, but he has been careful to shave regularly.

"You know," Barry says, "I've been wanting to ask you. I had some relatives who lived here once."

"Is that so?" She's at least somewhat interested in this unexpected fact, but not enough to ask who, as Barry thought she certainly would.

"Actually, it was my grandfather. Gordon Fox." Barry does not want to admit to her that he does not know when or how the old man died. Barry's mother must have killed her father off in a hundred different speculations, all of them deserved, asked for: drunken staggerings into danger, truculent exposures to the rage of others.

"You're kidding," the waitress says. She whistles. "Old Gordon!"

Barry looks at her carefully to gauge the reaction; claiming kinship with this maligned man could yield unpredictable results.

"Well, I'll be damned," she says, affectionately. She's smiling, at last, and it is quite a nice smile; it fills out her thin face and makes her softer. "He was a funny old prairie dog. He sort of collected cars. You ought to see his place." She gives him quick directions; out here, all directions are quick, even if the distances are long.

He shrugs as if this whole matter were actually not why he came, as if he had business to get on with, and she walks away. He watches her disappear around the church toward the edge of town. He gets in his car and backs out between a dusty Ford pickup and a Subaru; he thinks for a moment that they aren't real vehicles, just junkers without engines that have been left there by the owner of the Virginian to make the place seem popular. He gets back to the main road, and then turns in the direction she told him, back the way he came. He makes a few notations for his journal on the dashboard notepad. These days the journal is nothing but weather; he had recently kept pace with a front, going seventy to remain in the wind and black light, for hundreds of miles. It had left him breathless and exhilarated, as if he had been sailing in a gale.

Back on the prairie the children are one again; Barry imagines the pattern of their clusters and star-shaped explosions across the flats as fireworks. He keeps glancing over at them, and suddenly one of them breaks off and seems to be dancing madly around—a kind of Indian game, maybe. He looks again, and this time it seems that what is happening is that the child is waving at him, that they are all waving at him now. He stops the car and peers over; they are yelling at him. He gets out and begins walking toward them: the soil and the dry fuzz of undergrowth are brittle; his footsteps crunch like broken glass. A little way out he recognizes that he has underestimated the distance. It gets hot, and he slips off his shetland sweater.

When Barry begins to close on the children they turn back away from him, all looking at something at their feet. Now that he is drawing within several yards he realizes that it is a child on the ground. The boy has both his hands pressed white against his left eye socket. There is a little blood on his cheek and forehead and even some coming through his fingers. When Barry sees this he leaps forward. "What happened? What happened?" he says. "Is he all right?"

There are mumbles, but no one answers, not even the biggest, who must be at least sixteen. Instead, they just stare down at the damaged creature curled at their feet. There's a white dusting of soil on his hair and clothes. Barry kneels and says to the boy, "What's hurt? Are you O.K.?"

"My eye," the boy says, scared but not crying. The little girl, the one Barry noticed from the car, is whimpering, but the rest are silent.

"Jesus," says Barry. "Let me see." He reaches out and takes hold of one of the skinny wrists. The boy fights him, and Barry isn't sure what he's doing is right, because maybe the boy is really holding the eye in his head like this; maybe, all things considered, keeping pressure on it is best for the moment.

"What happened?" Barry says one more time, this time directing the question at the oldest.

"Firecracker must of lifted a rock or something. Didn't see it hit."

Barry looks at the firecrackers on the ground, and they seem big enough to be dynamite; they aren't what he would have called cherry bombs.

"Has someone gone to get help?" No one says anything; they are helpless and hopeless. Barry lets go of the boy's wrist, gently pressing his hand to tell him that he has changed his mind, that he doesn't want to see the wound, that it will be best to keep the pressure on. Barry steadies himself on his knees and then picks the boy up in his arms. The load is lighter than he expected, but they're a long way out; his car seems very distant. "Go ahead and tell someone to get a doctor," he shouts angrily at the others. They leave in a pack and head toward the town.

Barry is alone with the injured child. "What's your name?" he asks, trying not to sound winded.

The boy snuffles. Barry has to stop for a moment to take the weight off his arms by crouching over his knees. "You're hurting me," says the boy.

The boy smells musty, almost sour, nothing like the limpid fragrance of Barry's girls. The child's hair is coarse and spiky, and his twin cowlicks rub raw on Barry's bare arm; the boy's mouth is open, and Barry can see a gray spot of decay on one of the child's crooked teeth. The boy is becoming almost repellent to him, with these unexpressed needs and sullenly accepted favors, as if what the others knew was that this child deserved this missile in his eye, that it was his fault. He wishes the boy would cry or whimper or call out; this wounded silence, as if life and sight did not matter, is perhaps the worst of it.

"Just a little way to go now," says Barry. He's hoping that by the time he gets back to the road someone from the town will come; he doesn't want to get blood on Polly's Camry, though that's not going to keep him from doing the right thing. But no one is there, so he bats away the pile of maps on the passenger seat and lays the boy there. He goes out into the grasses and tries to rub some of the hardening blood off his hands.

Barry looks out for a car coming the other way, but there is nothing on the road; he's driving carefully to keep the boy from dropping his head onto the door upholstery. He has begun to fear that the boy and his dripping eye have been ceded to him for good, no take-backs. But there is, finally, some activity in town: a woman comes streaming out of the green ranch as he rounds the corner, and another woman and a younger man are climbing into a truck, a cherry-red Ford pickup with chrome pipes and reflective windows. The truck is so immaculate that Barry wonders how it got here; it's like an ocean liner on a lake. Barry expects to see the waitress; for some reason he has assumed all along that she will be the first person he greets, that the boy might even be hers.

"Wendall," yells the woman in the truck. She's a sight for this town—almost punk, with lots of makeup and a black leather jacket.

The boy still doesn't cry. What's wrong with him? Barry thinks.

The woman pulls the car door open and helps the boy out. "Can you see out of it, honey?"

"I dunno," the child says.

This single answer from the boy changes the woman's tone. "You know to stand clear," she says harshly, giving him a shake. She's treating him now as if he were a careless construction worker. "Get in the truck, and we'll take you to the doctor."

"No," the boy wails finally. It's the doctor and his waiting room, the smell of pain, maybe, and the glint of needles that set him off. Thank God, thinks Barry, the kid's human. In a few moments they are off, with not a word to Barry. He thinks suddenly—it comes with the visual force of hallucination—that this town is someone's miniature, exposed from above. He looks into the sky and half expects to see an enormous moon-eyed face blotting out the sun.

He's weaving on the sidewalk when this vision passes, and he looks up in surprise to see the little girl standing in front of him, her overalls straps loose on her tiny arms. She's dirt-streaked and is holding a filthy pink blanket with tattered strings of satin binding, but her hair is perfect under two purple barrettes.

"The boy's going to be all right," Barry calls out. "Wendall is going to be fine." He doesn't know why he says this, except that whenever something frightening or bad happens around Gay and Pattie, he tells them it will be all right. He tells them this even as he sinks into despair. Four children killed by stray bullets in a single night, his girls hear on the radio, and Dad says, "It's all right. They're in Heaven."

The girl asks, "Are you in the Army?"

"No," Barry says, not unfamiliar with the abruptness of a four-year-old's conversation.

"Will you play with me for these many minutes?" The girl holds up a sticky palm with all five digits spread.

"How many is that?" Barry asks encouragingly.

"Eight."

A voice comes from across the street just as Barry is ready to smile. "Winona! Don't talk to that man. Come here."

Barry figures the woman is just a little paranoid, and tries not to take it personally; he's a stranger, even if he did just save the life or eye or something of one of this town's sons. "That's right," he says to the girl. "Don't talk to strangers."

"Winona!"

The girl hesitates just long enough to exert a measure of independence. Barry gives a wave over toward the green ranch house: he thinks it's obvious that his wave means that he is a parent, too, that of course she shouldn't talk to him. But the mother takes his wave for a signal that she must act very quickly, and she runs over to swoop up the girl as if rescuing her from the path of a flood. It seems an overorchestrated gesture to Barry. The mother and girl reach the far side of the street, and the woman turns to defy him straight on, large breasts pushed out like musculature. When she's satisfied that Barry has been warned away sufficiently, she pulls the little girl back into the house. Barry sees then that what he took for flowers in her yard is actually litter: waxed cardboard from frozen-vegetable packs, tufts of white tissue, the orange spiral from a box of Tide.

Barry stands there flushed with anger. He cannot imagine how he could be treated as dangerous to small children. Everyone says he's great with kids. He cannot deny that he's a little uninvolved with his own daughters' daily experiences—Polly is a superb mother, really quite remarkable—but he's always figured he'll weigh in strongly when they're teen-agers or young adults. He's getting more and more indignant as he climbs back into his car: he's *from* this town, for God's sake. Sort of. He heads into the prairie. He thinks back to the directions the waitress gave him to his grandfather's spread—go west and go left. He likes the sound of it; he relaxes his anger and makes himself laugh heartily at the thought of these directions becoming some sort of credo for his grandfather, something for his family crest.

Barry's mother's campaign to eradicate her father's memory had been so meticulous and so persistent that there was virtually nothing about his flight that Barry did not know. It began in 1930 with an empty place at the head of the dinner table in Hartford, a setting of china and silver removed by the maid halfway through soup. Lobster bisque, if Barry recalled correctly. He had always been quite fond of his grandmother, a gutsy lady, and had suspected that she was happier to have her husband gone. But for years, dutifully, he had taken his mother's side in this matter, and even now, a pilgrim to the man's final place of rest, Barry can't imagine him being called affectionately "a funny old prairie dog."

He comes to a gravel road, about a mile beyond the point where he had found the children, and takes a left. The wheel tracks are deep as wagon trails, and the grass and brush bend under the car. He drives slowly, up over one rise and down into a deep basin. He seems not to be getting anywhere, for all this motion; the land just keeps rising and falling endlessly.

He drives on, and is finally aware of a different quality in the light behind the next rise, strands of luminescence. He reaches the crest and is immediately dazzled by a thousand shards of sun. Then, as his eyes adjust, he sees the source of all this confused display. He understands what the waitress meant when she said the old man collected cars. There are hundreds of them following the contours of this bowl, automobiles and vehicles of other sorts, things on wheels of every possible type. The sun finds the untarnished surfaces on all of them—chrome bumpers, headlamps and rearview mirrors, still-lustrous hoods and metallic-flaked fenders. The place is spotless and beautiful, as beautiful as anything he has seen on his trip through unrelieved decay and decline. Barry is stunned and uplifted by this dreadful vision. It could be nothing but a junk yard, but the man was clearly up to something, and whether or not he had thought of it this way, he had left behind a monument.

Barry gets out of his car and sits, watching the sun mark an hour or two on the face of this immense obsession. He tries hard, with as much concentration as he has put into anything in the past few months, to figure out what it means. He has not felt so refreshed in many days, has not sensed so many options since he was a teen-ager. There are invitations on the tip of each blade of grass, enticements everywhere.

After a while the rush passes. If there was a sign for him in this, he has not found it, or has not divined its meaning. He hasn't exactly decided what to do next, so he thinks he will return to the town. No doubt there will be someone who wants to thank him for bringing in the child. Perhaps the waitress will be on duty, and he can report back that he has visited Old Gordon's place.

There is no one in the Virginian. Barry grabs a newspaper—it's a few days old—and feels bold enough to go over to his table against the back wall and crack open the storm shutter. A shaft of white light cuts out a wedge of the greasy surface. He unfolds his paper and reads about the high-school sports, and then the social news. At one point a man comes in and walks straight to the bar to pour himself a draught beer with all the familiarity of someone getting water at his own kitchen sink; he stands for a moment, gives Barry a canine stare over the rim of his glass, finishes, and then slaps a handful of change on the bar before leaving. The bartender returns an hour or so later, sees the money, and drops it, coin by coin, into the separate bins of his cash register. It doesn't sound to Barry like much of a gross receipt for a long afternoon, and, in fact, the bartender glares at Barry, as if he damn well could have contributed something himself.

Barry goes back to his paper, and in a few more minutes the door opens and the waitress comes in. He is surprised by the strong nod of recognition he gets, and is flattered when she walks quickly to his table. She's wearing a name tag now, pinned to her gray sweatshirt—something more formal for supper, perhaps. Her name is May. "You brought Wendall Peters in. That was you."

Barry had forgotten, for these few moments, about the boy, and the modest surprise he shows is genuine. "Oh, that! Yes, I guess I did. Quite a thing."

"I can't believe it." She's very upset.

"How is he?" asks Barry.

"You don't know?"

"What?" he asks. How could he know anything? He could have been two hundred miles away by now.

"He's going to lose the eye. They're taking it out right now up to Good Shepherd." She turns to blow her nose.

Barry believes this; the boy was too still and didn't cry. Their pediatrician always made a joke about that: "The louder they cry . . ." He thinks of the boy's almost rancid odor. The feeling of the spiky hair against his arm comes back, and with it Barry's recognition that he had been *hoping* for something dramatic out of all this, something more than a few stitches in the boy's eyebrow. "It didn't seem that bad," Barry says, defending himself against his thoughts.

"I told them it was dangerous," says May.

Barry reflects that she had not sounded alarmed or nervous at lunch when she described to him what the children were doing. "Of course you did. One of my daughters is a hell-raiser," he adds, trying to remember whether he had told her before that he was a parent. He's been doing a good bit of lying out here—things like pretending he served in Vietnam, during Tet or in the Delta, or saying that he grew up in Arizona—harmless lies, just to ease his way among strangers.

May smiles, finally. "My boy, Everett, is so cautious he scares himself when he sneezes. He's six," she adds.

Wendall, Everett, Winona. What's with the names in this town? he wonders. "So he wasn't there?"

She seems slightly insulted by this deduction. "Well, sure he was there." She wrings a red dish towel that she has been holding the whole time. "It gives me shivers." She produces a real shiver, a trembling in her shoulders, and when it is done she asks, "Do you want a beer, an Olympia?"

Barry nods, suddenly feeling utterly at home. He has never had a regular eating place, or a regular bar, and has never felt like a patron of any establishment, except perhaps for the paper stand at the mouth of his subway stop. But in this one day he has started to act as if he owned this table, and the people who have been drifting into the bar seem to expect to see him sitting there. He begins to feel a permanence, as if the accidents of the day could not have occurred to a mere passerby. He likes May. Besides, he has been watching her thin-hipped body and is very turned on by her. He has never been unfaithful to Polly, but this could be different—physical and free. His saliva becomes electric at the hard-core images in his mind.

May brings him a beer and then recommends he order the pork chops. "Sure," he says.

Suddenly, the door of the Virginian bursts open, and Barry recognizes the man who had served himself at the bar earlier. He wavers in the doorway and then appears to remind himself to shout out hysterically, "They saved it! They think they saved the eye!"

There is a moment of reduced conversational hum. The man is obviously Wendall's father, quite a bit older than the wife who had claimed the boy earlier and driven off with a younger man. "That's good, Frank," says one male voice, but it is followed by a few snickers. It turns out that the medical report is the product of a drunk's extravagant, self-serving imagination. Frank weaves slightly but holds his place, as if he still expected to be mobbed at the door and carried aloft to the bar for a celebration. At last, May takes the man's hand and leads him over. The bartender shares a look with May, and then pours half a draught beer.

Barry himself is drinking more tonight than he has for weeks, months; he had lost the taste for it just about the time he hit the road. May brings his supper, and then checks back with him in the course of the evening, bringing him beers, giving him the quick line on the other customers, most of them men. There's not much else for her to do. One of the drunks yells at May to get her "skinny ass over here," and he makes a grab for her when she goes by. Barry knows he must accept the fact that she could not possibly have any interest in him. However this woman lives her life, it won't be him she's sleeping with tonight. He is beginning to crash, falling back on nothing but the foul breath of his night's drinking. He thinks about unrolling his sleeping bag and starts to look forward with dread to the morning's heavy dew.

"Where are you staying?" asks May. It's now just about closing time, and he's one of the last people left in the Virginian. The man who grabbed for her has gone. "Going to Rylla or something?"

Barry says, "Sure." Maybe that's it, a motel in Rylla.

"Well, you know," she says.

Barry reads May's hooded, apologetic eyes and slightly set lips, and is stunned to realize that all his unspoken prayers have been answered. She's going to ask him to stay—if not with her, then at least at her place. And she does.

"I've got a spare bedroom."

He accepts. She goes about her cleanup duties, and she makes no attempt at all to hide him; there is nothing furtive here, nothing to apologize for, as if everyone in the room would wish her well in finding a little unexpected companionship.

The air in May's house—one of two small bungalows behind the church—is stuffy with the chemical odors of carpeting. Most of the living room is taken up with a wooden-armed Colonial sofa, covered with a print of New England village scenes. The lamps and shades are part of the same set, and everything is very neat; the walls and ceiling are the same unfortunate light green. A man hasn't lived here in a long time—maybe never. There is a collection of china farm animals, and miniatures on a small hanging bookshelf. Barry pictures her adding to this collection, buying a new piece in Rylla and carrying it home in a box of cotton, taking it out and finding the best place for it on the shelf beside the other knickknacks, the woolly lamb, and the tea set for six. He sits on the sofa, following her with his ears as she wakes her boy, carries him to the toilet so he can pee, returns him to bed, and then begins to make coffee in the kitchen. There seems to have been no baby sitter. Barry tries to figure out where the spare bedroom must be.

May talks to him from the kitchen—a confident intimacy, as if he had always been where she expects him to be and always would be. "You know, I'm still real skittish about that accident."

Barry yells back, "Yeah. There's something really frightening about an eye injury. Eyes seem so vulnerable, anyway."

She is obviously so struck by the aptness of this comment that she leans her head around the door to answer. "That's a real interesting point."

Barry is quite amazed that he is doing so well; it really has been some time since he's tried to converse. "Eyes are so important," he yells back, now that she has returned to the stove. There is a clinking of cups and the rattle of a burner grate on a cheap range.

Barry scouts around the room, looking at the tabletops and the shallow window wells; except for a telephone book, there isn't a single printed word in the house, as far as he can tell. He finds that comforting. "This is very kind of you." He yells again. "This is a very nice home." He's learned in his travels to use the word "home" and not "house," to say "sack" for "paper bag," and to pump his own gas without paying first.

She comes in with coffee, looks around the room, and it's clear that she, too, is comforted by what she sees. "I like things to be nice," she says. She's relaxed in her private space; he thinks of Polly. He is upset, but then relieved to find that he can't really recall her face.

May shakes him out of his thoughts; he must have been quiet for a beat too long.

"I guess at noontime when you drove in you never thought you'd get involved in something like this," she says.

He isn't sure what she means by "this": her or the town. "You never know."

"It's not always exciting around here." She begins this statement quite straight, but realizes halfway through that it's funny.

"How can you stand it?" says Barry, and they both laugh. He hasn't used irony in weeks; at home, everything that everyone—his friends, people at work, Polly—says is indirect. May eyes him as if she had just realized that he's been holding out on her, that he's been playing possum behind all his Eastern reserve. He can tell the idea of making love to him is in her mind.

"Have you ever thought of leaving here?" he asks.

She's already told him she grew up on the other side of the Commerce Building, in a house that burned down. She shakes her head and shrugs at the same time. "It ain't the bright lights," she says, suddenly undreamy and unchildlike and very defensive, "but it's home."

Barry is busy slamming on the brakes. "Sure. You don't understand. I love it here."

"Mom?" It's Everett. His voice is just as fearful and squeaky as May made him sound in the café.

"Sh-h-h," says May to Barry, and crouches as if she were ducking the snare in her son's call.

"Mom? Who's there?"

She gives up. "No one, honey. Go to sleep."

The boy starts to cry—not an entirely convincing cry, to Barry's trained ear. "I had a nightmare. I dreamed grachity was letting go and we all started to float."

May looks at Barry apologetically and leaves him. When she comes back, after a longer interval than Barry anticipated, she is holding clean, folded sheets, a pillow, and a towel—not a good sign. His heart sinks. But she sits down again beside him and puts her foot up on the sofa cushion between them, close enough to touch him, and after a few silent moments he drops his hand onto her calf. They talk, and then lean forward and kiss. Her saliva has a slightly odd taste and her mouth feels very different from Polly's; her back is hard and taut to his touch, but maybe she's just tense. They move to her bedroom, which is arranged just like a motel room, with a low dresser with a mirror above it along the wall opposite the bed. They start to unbutton and unzip each other's clothes, with a few nervous laughs, and then she pulls herself away to the bathroom in disarray. Barry catches sight of his reflection for a moment and tells himself, in a disbelieving and wildly thrilled way, that in a very few minutes it will be happening: he will plunge over one of the edges of his life with Polly. He wonders what it would be like to think of it as his "former" life. May comes back in a pink terry-cloth bathrobe, and it opens, at one point, right up to her waist. She turns out the light and slows things down, making him hold her in his arms for a few minutes in the darkness. Barry is startled by how good this feels—the pressure and heated silk of another's flesh. He has not had sex—or "made love" or whatever he should call this—in some weeks, and his stomach churns with desire; his ears seem to ring when, finally, her hand brushes him. She has almost no bottom, and her stomach is as flat as a teen-ager's. He finds soft-ness here and there on her body. When he enters her she feels athletic, wiry as a runner, and she moves in pleasure. It makes him think of Polly's fuller, more cushioned body, inertly receiv-ing, but it ends with a long, almost sweet, chirping from May, and his own surprised thank-yous.

Barry wakes up in the spare bedroom and looks out the window at the early morning. He's looking directly into a cemetery, close enough to read the names on many of the stones, to see the carved image of Calvary etched in the pink granite of the most recent gravestone. Beyond the barbed boundaries of this slightly green plot the yellow plains stretch out to a bare, purple rise. The events of the preceding day run quickly past his eyes—the first sight of town, meeting May, the boy's eye, his grandfather's cars: as recent as they are, Barry has the sensation that these random events have been awaiting him for many years. He looks at a life-size statue of Jesus in the center of the graveyard. It stands on a pedestal of rust-colored concrete marked with the phrase "I Am the Life" arranged in a triangle of letters, a word to a line.

He dresses with as little sound as possible, not because he wants to slip out but because he hears the boy out there. Soon there is the bustle of a child's being sent to school, and a door closing—presumably the bus is working again. Barry comes out at last. May is still in her bathrobe, and any embarrassment in this meeting is dispelled in a second. The kitchen's aluminum-legged table is set with two chairs, May's and Everett's. On the cramped counter behind her is a large school picture of the boy—he's nice-looking, with a very slender face—and Barry is relieved at not recognizing him from the roadside.

"You seem real rested," May says. It's clear she thinks it's her—and it is, in some part.

"Best I've felt in weeks."

"I slept pretty well myself," she says. She reaches back to rub her neck languidly.

"I like it here a lot," he says. He's sitting in Everett's seat. "I mean the land around here."

"Not much like home," she offers, although Barry doesn't remember telling her where home is. She assumes a position in front of the stove, waiting for his breakfast request.

"I can't explain it, but I feel there are answers here, on your plains. Do you know what I mean?"

She doesn't, really. She has turned her back to the stove.

"It may be a kind of unique place," he says.

Her expression darkens slightly as he tells her that the statue in the cemetery reminded him that Christ went out into the wilderness. "Forty days and forty nights," he hums, trying to get the melody of an old hymn.

"I wouldn't know," she says. "I'm not up on my Bible."

"Neither am I," he admits.

May is a little unnerved by this conversation; Barry sees this. She says, "When you're back with your wife and working at your new job you'll think of us. And Old Gordon's cars."

"I guess," he says, "that I think I'm going to stick around a little longer." Maybe it's time for him to admit—to himself, anyway—that he has left Polly and the girls for good, that he is never going back.

May rewraps her terry-cloth bathrobe tightly across her front and tightens the cord. "Here?"

"Well, I don't mean freeloading off you."

"Hey," she says, "I like it. You just make it sound a little permanent."

"I just mean I'd like to look around. Maybe see what's up in real estate."

"Here?" she asks again.

"Pretty crazy, isn't it?"

"I just don't understand. You mean *move* here? Why would anyone *do* that?"

Barry is losing clarity somewhat. "I'm married," he says. "I have children." He doesn't know why he is telling her this again, after the night before, but it *is* a reason. Isn't it? "Hell," says Barry. He means—and she clearly understands him to mean—that anything is possible in this world, that anything could make sense. "I'm looking for investment possibilities."

"Not here," May says. "Not in my town. I didn't invite you here because I'm looking for new neighbors."

"I can't ask you to understand."

"We had a nice time, a really nice time, but shouldn't you go home? There's nothing for you here."

"Maybe you have to come from the outside."

"Well," she says. She shrugs. "This whole damn county, this whole state, is going down the tubes. You'd have to be nuts . . ." Her thought trails off. Barry can't debate with her. In fact, he's starting to feel quite pushed and frustrated by what she is saying: his chest tightens, which is exactly what happens when he's on the phone with Polly. Being alone, after all, means you can think your own thoughts without interference.

She goes to the sink to do dishes; he never even got a cup of coffee. He thinks of her body inside the bathrobe and wishes they could make love again. It could still happen; if he shows up at her door at ten tonight, she may tell him she's so glad he hasn't left yet, that she hopes he'll stay a while longer. Or maybe during the day she'll think vaguely that he'll come back, but she'll be here in the evening and he'll be hundreds of miles away.

This morning, the time for them is past, though, that's for sure. He's said or done something a little weird—not that he knows exactly what it is. Now that everything is settled, now that she believes she'll never see him again, she's cheerful. "You going to see your granddad's place again on your way out? You sure seemed impressed."

He remembers that he carried on a bit about it after they were done with lovemaking. He doesn't answer, wondering if he should be angry about any of this, about May's sleeping with him and then throwing him out, about his grandfather's having left no message or sign for him but a field of junked cars, about Polly, a thin reed at the end of a telephone line, charting his decline like a stockbroker hoping to find his fifty-two-week low.

"Quite a place," says May. She is referring to his grandfather's.

Still in her bathrobe, May sees him out the door. A reddish sun is rising over a very cold morning. Barry walks down the dusty path by the church and comes out facing the middle of the Commerce Building. He can see a sign, an incongruously cute rebus, in one of the empty storefronts, "Fred and Alice's Used -4 Store." Quite a place, he thinks as he throws his toilet kit into the trunk of his car. He fishes for a map, not one for a specific state but the one he rarely uses: the western half of the country, from the Mississippi to the Pacific. It spreads out across the dashboard and fills the entire windshield. Thousands of shattered, ruined towns—pulses of light in his own darkened sky.

He turns, finally, for Rylla. It's west, and the sun pushes down on him. Two or three miles out of town he makes out a large shape on the side of the road. It's the school bus, the town's bus, and he assumes it has broken down again: the front door, the emergency exit, and the hood are all open. But as he draws close he sees no sign of the children; it's a little spooky, as if the bus had been waylaid. He gets out of his car and calls, but there is no answer. He pokes his head in the doorway of the bus and calls again. The key is in the ignition, and on an impulse he tries it, but the engine doesn't catch. He knows perfectly well that none of this is his business, and he is about to turn his back when he notices an end of a pink blanket peeping out into the aisle of haze-gray seats. He walks back and picks it up, recognizing it as the beloved and trusted friend of that little girl, Winona. For a moment his mind floods with images: ankle socks, size-six T-shirts, dolls, and vinyl purses shiny with sequins. He quickly drops the blanket back on the seat, and backs out the door into the prairie, and stands there surveying the bounds of this vast, ownerless domain, wondering if this is really the way these things happen, the way people run.

Frances Stokes Hoekstra

One-Eyed Jacks

I sat on the top rail of the corral fence and considered one more time what Hutch had said about my mother. From the top rail I could see nearly all the ranch buildings. Everyone but me was in the ranch house, having lunch. Nearly hidden in the aspens back by the stream was the cabin I shared with Mother and my little brother, Charlie. At the hitching post my horse, Mouse, was sleeping upright in the noon sun. Beyond the hitching post a dirt road ran past the fenced pastures and out into the open range.

Mother, Charlie, and I had been in Wyoming almost a month. Mother loved the West. She'd taken a six-week pack trip in Jackson Hole when she was seventeen and said she'd been waiting ever since, until Charlie was old enough, to take us both out here. I'd never known Mother to go anywhere without Dad, but this ranch belonged to a classmate of hers from school, and Mother was so crazy about Wyoming I guess she hadn't wanted to wait any longer. "You're going to love the West, Jenny," she said.

The train trip took three days. All the way out, she talked to us about how sage smelled, and she gave me Struthers Burt's *The Diary of a Dude Wrangler* to read. Mother's classmate Sue and her husband, Dan, were the first grown-ups Charlie and I were allowed to call by their first names. Dan and Sue took a few families from back East as guests each summer in order to make the ranch pay. We were the only family there at present.

I wished I wasn't a dude. I wished Dad had wanted to start life over in Wyoming like Dan, but Mother said there were usually complicated reasons for doing something like that. Sue and Mother were both thirty-nine, which was hard to believe, because Sue's hair had gray streaks all through it and her face was weather-beaten. Sue's son, Larry, who was fifteen, thought my mother was beautiful. "My mom could have looked like yours," he'd said to me a few nights ago, "if she hadn't had to work so hard out here."

I saw Charlie walking down to the corral from the ranch house. He waved his camera at me. Dad had given Charlie a camera for his tenth birthday in May, and Mouse and I were his favorite subjects. But Mouse had ears that went out sideways like a sheep's, unless he was very excited, so whenever Charlie took a picture of us I'd stand by Mouse's head and prop his ears up and forward with my right hand. I climbed down from the corral fence and went over to the hitching post to fake Mouse's alert look. I leaned into the warmth of his dusty, fuzzy neck and remembered how Hutch had pulled his hat down over his eyes as he watched my mother walk away from the corral. "That's my kind of woman," he'd said under his breath.

What she'd done earlier that morning was help to save a horse's life. The chestnut gelding had come in off the range with the other horses before breakfast, but sometime during the night he'd gotten into barbed wire and it had torn a hole on the inside of one hip. The blood pulsed out bright red; as fast as water comes out of an open faucet. He stood with his head hanging low by the small stream that cut through the corral, and Hutch knelt in the muck and mud beside him and pressed his thumbs up into the wound to halt the bleeding. He kept calling for someone to bring him the arterial clamps from the barn, but Charlie and I might as well have been glued to the top rail of the corral fence. Larry was there, too, but Larry looked green as if he might faint. The horse swayed on his three good legs. The other animals milled about, curious, and there was blood trickling through the stream as it went under the fence. I don't know where Mother came from, but suddenly she was kneeling in the mud beside Hutch. "Show me where to put my thumbs, Jim," she said, "and you go get the clamps." Hutch's real name was Jim Hutchins, and he was the head wrangler.

By the time the two of them had finished working on the gelding, Mother's bluejeans were caked with mud and manure and the blood had run over her shirt and down her arms. But her eyes were soft and alive and you could see how happy she was. "Well, thanks, Caroline," Hutch said. Mother wiped her forehead with her hand and there was a red streak where her fingers had been. "I'm going to clean myself up," she said lightly. There was a little electric charge of excitement in her. You had the sense she was dancing inside.

I waited until before dinner to tell Charlie what Hutch had said. We were alone in the cabin, and I knocked on the door of Charlie's room. Charlie and I were very close, and up until a year ago we went in and out of each other's rooms without thinking. But I was thirteen and Charlie couldn't do that anymore. Most of the time I knocked on his door just to be fair. I knew he wouldn't mind if I came barging in. Charlie looked up to me.

"Hutch said Mother was his kind of woman," I told him. "He said that right after she left the corral this morning."

"I thought that horse was going to keel over dead," said Charlie. "And Larry looked as if he was going to puke." Charlie was concentrating on trying to light the kerosene lamp on his bureau. Charlie was afraid of fire. Mother had taken him to see *Bambi* when he was five, and the forest fire at the end of the movie had given him nightmares for months. Charlie wouldn't strike matches, though you could tell he wanted to. He practiced each evening on the lamp.

"Nothing's going to happen, Charlie," I said. "Just strike it."

"I can't," said Charlie. Charlie looks a lot like Mother around the eyes. He looks a lot like Mother, period, which I don't think is fair since he's a boy. I look more like Dad. It's funny how those things get reversed.

I took the matches from him, lit the kerosene lamp, and turned the wick up high. The flame leapt around inside the glass and Charlie backed away a little. I looked at the two of us reflected in the mirror above the bureau. Our faces were gold in the lamplight. I had knotted a red polka-dot bandanna around my throat. I hadn't worn a bandanna before. I thought it made me look dramatically older.

After Mother saved the gelding's life, she was different. She stopped napping, for one thing. At home Mother always napped after lunch. She'd lie down on the top of her bed under an afghan, read a few pages of a novel, and drift off to sleep. Now, after lunch, she wanted to teach me and Charlie how to play poker. Larry asked to join us, but Mother didn't let him because he thought poker was boring if there weren't wild cards.

"Wild cards," said Mother softly, shuffling the thumbed and dirty deck Dan had lent her, "are absolutely out. They destroy the odds. If one-eyed jacks are wild, how can you judge the value of a king-high pair?"

"Where'd you learn to play poker?" I asked her.

"The cowboys taught me when I was seventeen," she said. I glanced over at the chaps hanging on a nail by the door. Mother had bought a pair of bat-wing leather chaps that first summer she was in Wyoming, and her favorite cowboys had carved their initials into the wide belt. I called them *chaps* at first but she said, "No, Jenny, *shaps*; it's from the Mexican word "chaparreras." The chaps fastened low on her hips with a large Indian silver buckle.

Mother was very good at poker. At least she always won the penny-ante, nickel-limit games we played on the porch of our cabin in the slow hour after lunch when the ranch drew its breath so quietly you could hear the cicadas hum in the grass. She could shuffle and deal like lightning. I was clumsier. Often when I dealt the cards, one would flip faceup and we'd have to start over.

"Oh, Mom," Charlie protested. "It was only a seven of hearts."

"This isn't a child's game, Charlie." She swept in the dealt cards, reshuffled, and handed the pack to me once again. "And when you pick up your hand this time, Jenny, chest your cards."

We played cold hands, five-card stud, five-card draw, seven-card stud high/low. Charlie liked seven-card stud high/low because he could bet so many times, but Mother said five-card draw was the game to master. "That's where bluffing comes in," she told us. Bluffing, she said, was like putting in golf. It was where fortunes were won or lost. "I'm a very good bluffer," she warned us, unnecessarily. She cleaned me and Charlie out almost every afternoon, whether she had the good cards or not. "You have to hide what you're thinking. I can read your face like a flash, Jenny."

"Why do you take our money?" Charlie asked. "We could play for matches." He had a stockpile of matches in his sock drawer.

"You have to judge the risks," Mother said. "In poker the stakes are high." She lit a cigarette. She turned her head to the side and blew the smoke away from us. After every few puffs she stuck out the tip of her tongue and pinched off the tiny flecks of tobacco.

"Hutch rolls his own cigarettes," I said.

"They go out on him a lot," said Charlie. "And the shape is lumpy."

"I can roll my own, too," said Mother. No doubt the cowboys had taught her how to do that when she was seventeen.

You might think Mother and I were getting along especially well, given my sudden interest in her as a femme fatale, but the truth was I was happier when she wasn't around. There were times those first weeks when I thought I might suffocate with happiness. The way the mountains rose up from the floor of the desert made me feel as if the entire Mormon Tabernacle Choir was inside me, singing. I'd never been in such limitless space before. I tried to breathe it in, and my chest felt tight with the amount of air and how sharp it was. Larry had stopped teasing me. Hutch said one day that Larry was sweet on me and what was I going to do about it? I said, "Nothing," in a sulky tone of voice, because Larry wasn't very interesting. He wasn't at all a Son of the West. He didn't have the leanness of Hutch, or his chiseled features. He looked like a studious boy from back East, which was where he went to school nine months of the year. It was hard to think of Larry as being from Wyoming. He had no mystique.

Sometimes in the early morning I woke up to the sound of the bells on the lead horses as they came in from the open range. Hutch left at five-thirty each morning to wrangle them in before breakfast. I'd lie in bed under a pile of blankets in the cool gray first light and think of how it would be to ride out with him when the shadows cast on the trails still came from the stars and the moon. I knew it was hard riding, at a constant trot, and Mouse had a trot that sent my backbone up into my teeth, but I thought he might let me come along. I asked Mother what she thought my chances were.

"Oh, Jenny," she said, "I've wanted to go wrangling, too. Maybe we could go together. I'll see what Jim says." It was late afternoon, and Mother was toweling her hair dry after a shower. We washed our hair every day because of the dust. She was in her underwear, and I saw she had the same weird sunburn pattern I did, darkly tanned on her face and forearms, smooth white skin everywhere else.

When Mother changed for dinner at the ranch she wore clean jeans and sweaters like me, but at home when she and Dad went out she was silky and shimmered and smelled of Chanel No. 5. I remember once when I was eight or nine, she came in to say good night to us, dressed for a ball. She wore a green chiffon evening gown. Charlie and I were on our stomachs reading comics on the floor. The first thing I saw was Mother's feet in gold slippers and these little waves of green chiffon kissing her ankles. She leaned down to say good night and I saw the swell of her breasts above the strapless bodice. When I was eight I thought Mother had huge breasts. But she didn't. It was her legs she was vain about. I was almost as tall as she now, and when she said she'd ask Hutch if she could come wrangling, I felt a lump in my throat as if I'd swallowed wrong. I wanted to tell her to go back where she belonged, which was at the door of our house waiting for me to come home from school, or on her bed in the afternoons napping because she had nothing much to do.

"Go by yourself if you want to so much," I said. My voice was rude, but Mother acted as if she hadn't noticed.

"Come on, Jenny. We'll have fun."

"You go," I grumbled. "I've changed my mind anyway. I like to sleep late." Mother put on a fresh shirt. It was a Western shirt with snaps instead of buttons. She played with the snaps at her throat. "Go alone," I repeated.

Mother turned away from me. "I can't," she said. She reminded me of Charlie trying to light the kerosene lamp.

That night I asked Hutch if I could go wrangling with him the next morning. He said yes. It was the best hour and a half of my life. When I was younger, I used to play a game with Charlie whenever we went on long drives in the car with our parents. We'd spot horses and dogs out the window and yell "Zit" for horses and "Zat" for dogs. You got two points for a dog and five points for each horse. One hundred points won the game, but the drives didn't usually last that long, so we decided you could win the game immediately if you were the first to see two stallions fighting on the edge of a cliff. Wrangling the horses in at daybreak with Hutch was impossibly wonderful, like winning the game because you saw the stallions. At the very end, he made me gallop on ahead and open the corral gate. I swung the gate open just seconds before the whole herd thundered through. Hutch dismounted, and we shut the gate together. He rolled himself a cigarette. Hutch smoked his cigarettes right down to the butt. I sometimes wondered why his moustache didn't smoulder. The air was cold on my cheeks, but we'd ridden so hard I could feel the sweat as it dried on the back of my neck.

"That was terrific," I said.

Hutch put his hand on my shoulder. "You did real good, Jenny—your mother teach you how to ride?"

I was feeling so fine I didn't mind that he'd brought Mother into the conversation. I thought of her sleeping, or maybe lying awake with the sound of the bells in her thoughts. "She saw to it we had riding lessons," I said. "She's teaching us poker, now, though. Charlie and me and Mom, we play almost every afternoon."

"She any good?" Hutch asked. We walked up to the ranch house. The sun had risen above the ridges and canyons behind the ranch, and streaks of it darted like wildfire across the tips of the grasses. Already it was warm enough for me to take off my wool jacket. "She's very good," I said. "We play for money, and she wins all the time." Hutch chuckled. "We'll have to get up a game, then." He said, "I'll speak to Dan about it."

They set the game for the next Saturday night. Dan invited two other ranchers, and Hutch asked a few cowboys over from Jackson. Charlie and I were allowed to watch since we promised to keep our mouths shut. Sue cooked up vats of popcorn. I went down to the ranch house early to help her set up. Sue was a comfortable person to be around. She taught school in Jackson during the winter, and she treated me with the friendly interest teachers always take in good pupils.

Sue and I stood by the enormous cast-iron stove, stirring the pans of exploding corn. Sue's face was red with the heat. Dan put six-packs of beer in a bucket full of ice. Larry set out the three decks of cards on the round wooden table in the living room.

"Are you going to play?" I asked Larry.

"Only if the one-eyed jacks are wild."

"That's poker for kids," I said. "I bet that's how you play at school."

"We are kids, Jenny," Larry said.

Mother was the only woman invited. When she walked into the living room I almost laughed because she had dressed to look fragile in a white silk blouse and full pleated Indian cotton skirt. She smiled and shook her head imperceptibly to tell me not to give her away. I was proud of the way she looked gentle and delicate when I knew she was going to play tough, like a man. Hutch came in and tipped his hat to her. She shook hands with the other ranchers and the cowboys from Jackson. Hutch offered her one of his cigarettes, and she smoothed it between her fingers awhile, spreading out the tobacco rolled inside. I watched how she lifted up her throat a little as she drew in the smoke, and a few seconds later I saw her tongue flick across her lips.

Hutch grinned at me. "Jenny," he said, "what're you wearing that bandanny for? Cut your throat?" I whipped off the bandanna and stuffed it in my back jeans pocket.

"You don't have to take it off just because he said that,"
Larry hissed in my ear.

Charlie called from the porch, "Jenny, Larry, come out here
quick. There's shooting stars, zillions of them."

I ran out to the porch. The Milky Way marched across the
August night like the Star-Spangled Banner unfurling. I'd maybe
seen one shooting star in my life before, but that night they
careened toward the earth every few seconds. We tried to count,
but there were too many. Sue came out on the porch with us.
"It's a meteor shower," she said quietly. She put her arm around
me because I was trembling. Someone had put on the record
player in the living room. Ezio Pinza was singing "Some En-
chanted Evening." "I'm not cold," I said. "I'm perfectly happy.
If I was to die tonight it'd be all right."

When we went back in, the game had begun. We watched
for a while, but then Larry invited Charlie into his room to see
the new flies he'd tied for trout fishing, and I lay down on the
sofa and looked into the fire Dan had built. Mother was holding
her own. I looked into the flames, and the whole world disappeared except for the sounds of the cards being shuffled, the
murmur of voices, and the memory of stars hurtling through the
sky. Sue went to bed around eleven. Charlie came out of Larry's
room and fell asleep on the rug in front of the fire, like a puppy.
Larry got whiskey for the cowboys. There was a haze of blue
smoke above the table. Dan lost his stake and quit. A little later
the two ranchers stood up, cashed in their chips, and left.
Mother, Hutch, and the cowboys from Jackson took a break.

I offered everyone more popcorn. "I can't eat that junk,"
Hutch said. "I have a trick stomach. It's always going back on
me."

"So does Mother's," I said. "She throws up at any little
thing." Mother frowned. Hutch leaned against the chimney. "If
you want to compare stomachs, Caroline, I'll put mine up
against yours anytime." I jumped, and Mother sent him one of

those freezing looks she turns on me when I get out of line.
Hutch smiled. Suddenly I wanted Mother to beat him at poker. I
wasn't sleepy any longer, and when the card playing resumed I
paced around in back of the players. They didn't like it much,
me looking into their hands, but I was quiet and they stopped
paying attention to me after a while. Mother and Hutch were
even. She'd win a pot, then he would. Or he'd fold before risking
much. Or she would. I'd never seen Mother keep so still. When
she dealt the cards, only her wrists moved.

"Last hand," said one of the cowboys. He and his friends
were hanging on to the edges of the game. Hutch and Mother
had most of the chips between them. It was five-card draw. I
stood behind Mother. She had two pairs and an odd club. She
bid on that round as if she had three of a kind already, and when
it was her turn to draw she said "one," going for the full house.
She didn't get it. Her pairs were queens and tens, which wasn't
spectacular. I slipped around behind Hutch, who held three
nines. Mother bet a mess of chips, and Hutch raised her. The
cowboys folded. I stood behind Mother again, knowing Hutch
had her beat. She saw him and raised the ante again. He did the
same. There was a three-limit raise to each hand. Mother never
flicked an eyelash. She pushed all her chips into the center. I
drew in my breath. It made a little hissing sound.

Hutch looked across at me and stroked one end of his moustache with two fingers. "Jenny, gal," he said very softly, "growed
men have been shot for less." He borrowed some chips from the
bank, added them to his own, and called her.

Mother got really angry. "For God's sake, Jenny. Take
Charlie and go home, will you. You spoiled the evening for me."

I felt tears sting in my eyes. I hadn't meant to make a sound.

"Just go home, Jenny." Mother rubbed the back of her neck.
"Larry'll walk you and Charlie back to the cabin. I'll be along in
a few minutes." I looked at Hutch. Save me, I told him silently.
Walk me home.

Larry nudged Charlie awake and stood up. "Come on, you two."

"You stay where you are," I said. "Charlie and I can get home fine by ourselves."

"Don't turn down good offers, darlin'," said Hutch. "You can never tell about bears."

"Bears," I said scornfully. My heart was racing. "Who're you kidding? Walk *her* home, why don't you"—I jerked my head at Mother—"if you're so concerned about bears."

I grabbed Charlie by the hand and left the ranch house. We looked up at the sky, but the stars stood still.

"Did Mother win?" Charlie asked.

"No," I said. "She tried to bluff and lost." When we got back to the cabin, I waited until Charlie had undressed and crawled into bed. Then I went out on the porch. I sat down on one of the chairs and tilted it back against the wall of the cabin. I felt old. I sat there in the dark of the porch, waiting.

The moon and stars were so bright you could see them coming from quite a distance down the path. They walked side by side, not touching. About fifty feet from the porch, they stopped. He put his hand on her shoulder, the way he had with me when we'd shut the gate on the horses.

I thought the kiss would be no different from the kisses I'd seen in the movies. I thought I'd watch and cough or something right in the middle of the clinch. But Mother went into him like she had no bones of her own, and he put his hands in her hair and then ran them up inside the back of her jacket. I remembered she was wearing a white silk shirt. I had to look away. It wasn't like in the movies. It wasn't something to be watched. After a while I looked up again. Hutch wasn't there any longer. Mother stood in the path in the moonlight with one hand on her lips. Then she walked up to the cabin and onto the porch. It looked more like swimming than walking.

"Hello, Mother," I said, when she reached the top step.

"Jenny." She put her hand on the railing. "What're you doing out here?"

"Bears," I said, and my voice was really hard. "Oh sure."

"You should be in bed, Jenny."

"So should you."

"Jenny," she said again.

"That's my name."

"Please," she said.

It was very dark on the porch. Mother had to go past me to get into the cabin, and I knew she didn't want to do that. I tipped back again against the wall and felt hot and cold. We'd woken Charlie up. His room was right by the front door. "Who's out there?" he called, "Jenny, Mom?"

Neither one of us moved. We could hear Charlie stumbling around in his room. Then a light blossomed in the doorway. Charlie came to the door in the red-gold warmth of the kerosene lamp. His hair was standing straight up and his pajama top was on backwards.

"Oh gosh, I did it. I struck the match. Nothing happened, Jen, just like you said." He swung the lamp back and forth and the light went from my face to hers.

Mother used the interruption to scoot past me. "Charlie, that's wonderful." She took the lamp from him, set it on the table and hugged him hard. "You're freezing, go back to bed."

I thumped the back of the chair against the wall once or twice more. Mother's face, caught for that instant in the sweep of light from Charlie's lamp, had been unprotected. But I was her daughter. I didn't have to understand.

Mary Morris

Around the World

I'd never seen him at the laundromat before. If I had, I would've remembered because Blue Mesa where we live is a small town and not that many newcomers use the laundromat, even though it's a nice place to do your clothes. Lots of big cream-colored machines that go around, bright neon lights overhead. I like this laundromat because it has big wire baskets where you can stick your clothes as you move them from washing machine to dryer and because they've got big tables where you can fold. I love to fold. I love to take hot towels or even Scott's jeans and wrap my arms in them and smell how clean they are and let the warmth rush over me while I fold.

He was blond and taut and stood just outside the door smoking when I came back in after talking to Patti on the phone. Patti is my girlhood friend. I drop my kids off at Patti's or she drops hers off at my place when we've got things to do, but usually once we get somewhere we just call each other on the phone so it seems silly to go anyplace since we could just sit at the kitchen table and talk at home. From the laundromat phone, that's right beside the gas pump, I talked to Patti for a while about Ross, her husband, who was coming home later and later, and when I got off the phone, the blond man was standing there, smoking.

I probably wouldn't have even noticed him if I hadn't come back and seen that the wash in my dryer wasn't mine. I knew it wasn't mine the minute I looked in and saw. Because I never mix my whites with my colors, not even to dry. I always keep them nice and separate so the dark lint doesn't get on the baby's things or mix in with Scott's shirts. Not that Scott would care. He hardly ever wears a white shirt unless it's a Sunday and maybe we go to church, if he's up in time. But it's a point of pride with me, to do my wash this way.

But that day I looked in and saw how a green sock was floating with white underwear, the jockey, not the boxer kind, and jeans mixed in with white T-shirts, and so I knew that wash was not mine. At first I thought mine had been stolen, which happens sometimes with drifters coming through, but then I saw it piled in one of the wire baskets. Scott's jeans weren't even dry. I picked them up and pressed them to my cheek. They still had that wet feel along the seams that Scott would notice right away if he put them on.

Scott's jeans always took so long to wash. There was all that horse hair and stench. Always a bad smell I couldn't quite get out. But everything seemed to smell that way to me. Sometimes I'd lie in bed at night and just smell the rooms around me. The smell of children, of talc and urine, of excrement and sweat, the smells of the dogs and cats who wandered in and out of rooms, the smell of clover and wheat, of horse and hay, the sweet, stale smell that got into all Scott's clothes, into his hair, into his nails, that got into my body when he made love to me. And when he lay on top of me, after making love, I could smell the horses as if they were right there in the room.

When I saw that the clothes in the dryer weren't mine and mine were sitting still damp in a wire basket, that was when I looked at him. It was the first I saw him really and he was looking at me and so I said, "Excuse me, but did you take my wash out of the dryer?"

"It had stopped," he said, looking at me with very sharp eyes like a weasel.

"It wasn't dry."

"It was just sitting there," he said, taking a drag.

I fumbled through my things, starting to sort them. I would have put them back in, but all the dryers were full. "I'm missing a red sock," I said, holding up a mateless one. The blond man looked at me dumbly. "I said I'm missing a sock."

"Then you lost it, lady, before I got here."

At first I thought he might be a cowpuncher on the rodeo circuit since they sometimes came in and out of town in the summer when the season was on, but there was something too neat about him, too clean, and he had that look that I'd seen in the eyes of the college kids, a look like he had some place to go and it wasn't here. And then when I walked by him, dragging my basket in a huff, there wasn't any smell to him at all and his hands looked soft so I knew he'd never held a rope and that he was just passing through on his way somewhere else.

He's the kind of guy they have over at the college—clean-cut and trim, everything just right—and I would've thought he was from there, if the college was in session. Then it occurred to me he's too old to be a student. There was something a little knowing about his eyes like someone who's already been out in the world. But he's got that wired look so I decide he's the new track-and-field coach, the one they were advertising for last year.

I've got my own plans to travel. I have a Maxwell House coffee can in the kitchen where I keep the money I've saved, not much, but enough to get me to San Diego someday, maybe Disneyland. I have this longing to see the sea. I've always been on Mountain Time. I've only heard about this place where the water meets the land or seen the way the surf comes crashing into the shore at the start of *One Life to Live*. I'll be lucky to make it to Montrose or Grand Junction, but I'm saving to get to San Diego and see the sea.

That night Scott comes home and does what he always does. Gives me a kiss on the cheek and a pat on the rear. His mustache tickles my ear and I pull a little bit away. Then he pops a beer and takes the kids out to the corral for a pony ride. I'm left standing at the sink, snipping the stems off the beans, and then I stop.

From the sink I can see out to the corral, out toward the mountains across Blue Mesa. I look out across this place where I've lived my entire life, and I see the mountains and the sky. I see my husband who I've been with since I was fifteen years old, and my three children, going around on the spotted pony. Scott takes a sip from his Coors but he is careful not to let Stephanie fall. Stephanie is the baby, the one who didn't come out right, and we have to watch her all the time. The other two are all right, except Scott Junior doesn't always go to school. And Nicole is going to drive herself crazy, always trying to do everything right. I watch this scene, the same one I see every night, and try to think about what will happen after the children are grown. What will I see from this window?

I close my eyes, trying to imagine, and what I see is the blond man from the laundromat. This surprises me because all my life I've been with Scott and I've never even thought of myself with another man. But suddenly I see this long drink of water, skinny blond guy and our clothes all neat and folded by the side of a bed, sweet smelling, and I think of his soft hands and his doeskin flesh. I close my eyes and for an instant shut out what I've known all my life.

When I open them, everyone is there and they want dinner on the table. Stephanie talks as best she can and tries to tell me what she'd like, her body bobbing back and forth as she stammers, and Scott Junior takes a Coke, even though I tell him not to, while Nicole, the only one who really helps me so it's hard to fault her, sets the table, but I can see she's not happy about having pot roast again. Then, just before dinner, Patti calls. She says Ross isn't home yet and she's locking him out. She says that any man who isn't home by seven o'clock doesn't deserve to eat. She's going to put his dinner on the porch and put the bolt across the door. She says, "Do you think my husband is seeing another woman? Do you think there's someone else in his life?"

The rodeo was opening at the fairgrounds Friday night, and on Sunday I went to watch the carnival being set up. It's something I always like to do each year. I like watching it get set up and taken down. I like thinking about where it's been and where it's going, how it never stays in any place too long. It makes me think about faraway places. Places I've read about but probably won't ever get to see.

It always takes them so long to set up, a week maybe or more, and so before the carnival even opens, I've got a week when I go and just watch. Usually I take the girls because what else am I going to do with them. We go and sit in the car and watch the lights being set up or the ferris wheel get put together. I make them all kinds of promises I can actually keep like that I'll buy them cotton candy or let them jump until they drop on the Kiddie Kastle. Or if Scott Junior comes along I tease him about the last time he went on the Tilt-A-Whirl. But mostly I like to just sit and watch the men as they raise the canvas and the poles, or the bright lights of the ferris wheel as it begins to spin.

Another thing I love about the carnival is how Scott will watch the kids while I go on every ride. It's almost the only time I'm ever really alone and I get to just be with myself. Scott won't go on the big rides because he gets sick, but he'll watch me from the wings as I ride the Sizzlers, the Salt and Pepper Shakers, and the Around the World. I like Around the World best because it doesn't tip you or spin you or make you twirl. It just hurls you out with its arms and you feel as if you can just keep going and going; how if it released you, nothing would keep you down.

I sit until dusk with the girls in the backseat, as the concessions go up, the lights turning on, all shimmering against the pale pink Colorado sky even though Nicole keeps saying, "Mommy, can't we go home" and I have to shush her. I just sit and stare until finally it gets dark and I have to take everybody home.

Scott and Ross are watching a game, drinking beer, as we walk in. The phone's ringing off the hook. I know it's Patti, ready to skin Ross alive. Any minute her car will swing in the drive, and I'll have to stand between the two of them. Suddenly I feel tired and wish I could just go to bed. I think of the carnival lights. How beautiful they are against the sky.

I know a methodical person when I meet one and I think this guy's that way so if he's still in town, he'll be doing his wash on Tuesday. On Tuesday I go back to the laundromat, same time. Patti doesn't want to take the kids, but I say it's something I just have to do. Then I put on a tight pair of jeans and some lipstick and go just at the time I think he'll show up, but he's not there. I start to do my wash, separating the clothes very slowly. I think how noisy this place is with all the machines going around. I'm starting my spin cycle when he arrives, dragging a big brown laundry bag behind him. He speaks to me first. He says, "Did you find your sock?"

"Yes, it was caught up in the leg of a pair of jeans."

"I told you," he says, "I don't leave anything behind."

We do our wash in machines across from each other. I watch as he puts fabric softener in, measuring out just the right amount. Later I see him put a Bounce in his dryer and I'm impressed. I think to myself maybe I don't need to separate my whites and colors in the dryer. Maybe he knows something I don't know. "You're not from around here," I say.

And he smiles and says, "No, I'm sure not. I'm from California." He says it in such a way I can tell he's proud. I think how he's someone who comes from the place where I want to be.

"What's it like there?" I ask.

"Oh, you know, the ocean, the beach, the freeways, same old stuff."

"Yeah," I say, "I know." I'm afraid he'll ask me what I know, so I turn back to the work I have to do.

"And you?"

"I'm from around here."

He's starting to fold. "Seems like a nice place to be from."

"You going to be here long?"

He shakes his head. "I travel for business," he says.

"Rodeo?" I ask. Scott used to do the circuit before Scott Junior was born. He did cattle roping and rode broncos until one day a horse tossed him twenty feet, then stomped on his ribs. In the hospital I told him he had to stop. I said it was rodeo or me. But the blond man just laughs, shaking his head. "Now, do I look like that kind of a guy?" When he says this, he leans against the folding table in my direction, his elbows resting on his warm T-shirts and towels. His face is only inches from mine. I feel his breath against my face, hot and steamy like the air from the machines.

Even though I promised Patti I'd be back by five, I stop at the carnival on the way home and see that it's mostly up now. They've got their lights on and the music is playing. The ferris wheel is already going around and around. I stand there until the sky darkens and the lights are bright against the sky. Patti's in a huff when I pick up the kids. She looks me up and down, clicking her tongue inside her mouth. "I've never known you to have that much wash to do."

When I get home, Scott's sitting in front of the baseball game, beer in hand. "The carnival's up," I say. "Maybe we can go later."

"We'll go Friday," Scott says. "I wanta watch the game."

"So, Friday," I say.

Even as I say it, I think of the man from the laundromat. I think how Friday is three days away and he does his wash on Tuesday, and how that means another week until I see him again, but I've got the carnival to look forward to on Friday. I've already made up my mind what I'm going to do when I see him again. I'm going to ask him for his address. I'm going to tell him that I expect to be visiting California soon and I'd like to look him up. I'll tell him how I don't know anyone there and how it would be nice to have someone to call. I think how that won't seem forward or out of place. Maybe he'll give me a business card with his home number scribbled on the back. And I'm sure I can call him at home. But I'll ask politely, "Would your wife mind if I call?" but of course there's no wife because why would he be on the road so much, doing his laundry on his own.

That night in bed Scott lies beside me and I think how he has been with me for fifteen years, been my husband for the last ten. And I don't know what he thinks about as he lies in bed. I have no idea what's on his mind. I decide to ask him. I say, "Honey, what are you thinking about? What is on your mind?" And he replies, "I'm thinking about the cattle I have to move off the mountain next week." What more can I say? After a man says something like that to a woman, what is there to say?

The kids are ready at six sharp on Friday, but Scott hasn't walked in the door. Stephanie is already starting to bawl and bob back and forth and Scott Junior says to hell with it, he isn't going, but then Scott comes in with no time to shower. I say, "Aren't you going to change at least? Aren't you going to wear other clothes," but the kids are all fighting by this time, so we get in the van and leave.

When we get to the carnival, it is all lit up, a bright pink and green and yellow against a purple sky. It is as if a spaceship had landed right in the middle of Blue Mesa where we live. The minute the kids see it, they scream with delight. Stephanie bobs as fast as I've ever seen her, and Nicole has to put her hands on her sister to hold her back. Scott Junior is out of the car in a flash, heading for the baseball throw. Nicole takes Stephanie by the hand, and Scott puts his arm around me as together we walk among the concessions and rides.

Stephanie wants to go jumping on Kiddie Kastle, and Nicole takes her there while Scott and Scott Junior go off to toss some rings and balls. Then I take the girls to the merry-go-round and watch them go around, Stephanie with her head thrust back, laughing all the way, and Nicole, holding on to her, sweet as can be. I stand there, watching them, holding on to one another, and I know how I could never leave them really, but if I could just go away for a little while, just step out of my life into someone else's, I'd be better; I'd be fine.

When Scott comes back, he's won a picture of Elvis in a wooden frame and a giant roadrunner stuffed animal. He scoops Stephanie into his arm and says I could go on some rides and he'll watch the kids. First I do the Tilt-A-Whirl with Scott Junior, but then I want to go on the bigger rides, the ones I know he doesn't like because he is a tough kid with a weak stomach and with him it's all show. He wouldn't set foot on the Sizzler or the Hot Tamale. So I do those rides first.

Then I look at the Around the World. The ride just sits

there, like a wilted plant, but I know what will happen when it starts up soon. I pay my ticket and get into my little cab. As the ride starts up its arms begin to extend like the tentacles of an octopus. My cab begins to rise from the ground. I see my family on the ground. Scott with the portrait of Elvis in one hand and Stephanie in the other. In his cowboy boots and hat, I can't see his face and he reminds me of one of those faceless guys they used to have in the Dick Tracy comics.

The ride starts up, slowly at first, then faster and faster, gathering speed. I see them beneath me, waving as the ride spins me away. Soon I am parallel to the ground and can't see them anymore. All I see is mountains, mere shadows in the distance, as I rise above the carnival lights and press my head back, gazing into the night sky. I imagine myself on a mission hurtling through space. I go around and around and feel as if I could just keep on going. Then the ride begins to slow down. I feel it losing momentum, feel myself dropping back to earth. As it begins to slow, I feel as if my stomach has been left behind me. Slowly my family comes into view and they are waving, as if I have been away for a long time, and I wave back, as if I have.

Scott helps me down, and Nicole and Stephanie cling to my arms. I am wobbly as a newborn calf. The night sky overhead is beautiful, and the Milky Way runs overhead as if painted in yellow Day-Glo. Scott takes me by the arm, seeing I am breathless, and puts his hand to my forehead. "You're red. Are you all right?"

I feel as if I can breathe again after having my face in a plastic bag. "I'm fine," I say. "I'm all right." Scott wants to play darts. He puts his arm around me and says there's a nice concession with velvet paintings, the kind he knows I like to put over the mantel or hang in the kids' rooms. He promises he'll win one for me. I think how sweet it is of Scott to think of me, how he is good for remembering the little things of life.

As we cross the Arcade, Patti and Ross are walking just

ahead of us. They've got their arms around each other like sweethearts, and the kids are nowhere in sight. He keeps slipping his hand into her back pocket and she keeps taking it out, putting it around her waist. They turn off the side of the Arcade onto the darkened fairgrounds. I think how Patti's always complaining to me, how her life is a roller coaster, but I think how maybe she's lucky it's not like mine, flat like the mesa where we live.

We head in the direction of the dart concession. Barkers call. They offer us their giant stuffed animals, their velvet paintings, their Kewpie dolls. "Here," one shouts, "make this basket and make my day." Another throws a softball, "Easy as pie." From the distance I can see the barker at the dart concession where Scott is leading me. He hurls darts backwards over his shoulder, popping balloons behind him, and calling out to passersby.

I recognize him, not by his face, but by his clean pressed look, by the way everything fits so smooth around his skin. At first I don't think he recognizes me, but slowly it seems to come to him and he smiles a crooked smile. "Here," he says, looking Scott up and down, "win one for the lady."

"Let's go," I say, "I don't want any of those," pointing at the velvet paintings. But Scott knows I do because I'm always asking for more paintings to put on the walls and make our house look more like a home.

Scott takes the darts and puts his dollar down. He bites his mustache, takes careful aim. He misses the first, then the second. He puts another dollar down, then misses again. Scott Junior wants to play, and Scott puts money down for him. I wish I hadn't eaten the cotton candy and the popcorn with the kids and I'm wishing I hadn't gone on any of the big rides at all because my stomach is starting to feel shaky, the way Scott Junior always says his does.

I think Scott is ready to stop playing, but the blond man keeps saying, "Come on. Win one for the lady." I feel his eyes on me as if he knows something about me I don't even know. Scott tries again. He pulls in his breath and throws the dart with all his force, but the balloon just seems to move out of his way. So now the blond man jumps down.

"Here," he says, "Let me help you." He takes the darts and tosses them one, two, three over his head. The balloons all pop. "Take your pick," he says to me, "Which one will it be?" Scott, looking dejected now with the Elvis picture in his hand, doesn't say a word. I think how I've only seen him look this way once before, the time the bronco kicked in his ribs.

I look over his prizes. The velvet paintings of mountain streams and wild beasts, Mexican villages and beautiful girls. "No thank you," I say.

But the blond man says take it, so I pick the lions—big yellow, ferocious lions—from halfway around the world against a blue velvet background to hang above Stephanie's bed. Stephanie bobs beside me, rubbing the velvet with her hand. "Thank you," I say. "Our daughter will like this."

The blond man from the laundromat smiles as if we are partners in a scam. "See you," he says.

As we start to leave, a toothless lady barker beckons to me with tobacco-stained fingers. The children still want to play, but I look at the prizes—giant stuffed animals that look gray and frayed as if they've seen too many carnivals where nobody has won. I clutch the girls by the hands, leading them away, and tell Scott Junior to walk straight ahead. It is late as we get to the car. I turn and look back to see the carnival for the last time, shimmering against the sky, and I think how I can see all the pieces and joints where it is assembled. How it looks as if it could crumble, all come tumbling down.

That night when we get home, everything smells. Everything feels dirty, and I can't seem to get the odor of the carnival off my skin. The kids' clothes are covered with dust and grime. Stephanie's pants have a syrupy goo on the leg and Scott Junior's shirt is covered with grime. Even Nicole, who is normally so neat, has gum on her socks. So I think I'll do the wash tomorrow, even though it's Saturday. I'll do it even though the laundromat will be full and it's not my washing day.

Dwight Yates

Painted Pony

The truth was that Harry Blackwing counted as a full-blood of the Agua Caliente, the richest tribe in the nation, become so through land sales to Palm Springs developers and revenue earned from the land retained. And it was true that in 1956 a parcel of property Harry once called his own was purchased by a consortium of movie stars and eventually became part of a golf course. He spent much of that settlement check memorably, in Las Vegas. And to the friendly women and fellow gamblers who wanted to know where and how he had come by such a sum of cash, he told the truth. But in a later, equally memorable and comparably dissolute decade, he began to fudge it. He told an Italian count that the Blackwing were a tribe unto themselves, not to be confused with the Blackfeet, their mortal enemies. To the count's perpetually confused wife he confided that he was actually Mohican, the very last one.

The countess and the count and Harry hunted mushrooms in a wood north of Siena (Harry nearly killed the three of them by claiming medicine-man knowledge of edible fungi; they were saved by the noble couple's truly knowledgeable chef). That was the summer of 1975, the year Harry's celebrity as a painter reached its zenith, the year he was suddenly wealthy again and drinking like a trout. It was the summer he wore ridiculous clothes without a second thought and convinced himself that he was finally comfortable with the name Blackwing, the *nom d'artiste* forced on him years before by a gallery owner in San Juan Capistrano. It was, in another assessing of it, the summer he turned sixty and began to wallow in his own destiny, the summer his personal myth came to be more than he could juggle.

Through June and July he had done what his hosts and the friends of his hosts expected of him. He went sailing and ballooning and alping. He took to calling the count and countess by their first names (frequently, he could not remember their last names). But the more he was with his European friends, so attractive, so thoroughly old money—moving through their world as innocently and boorishly as tourists—the worse Harry felt about whatever unexamined motive it was that kept him there in the crowd of first names. Even the pictures he painted were mere imitations of himself, and recognizing that was always, for Harry, the end of the current illusion.

Finally, one night in August, or thereabouts, following an afternoon party taken from somewhere to somewhere else and finally to someone's yacht—in Portofino, probably—Harry spun a long, elaborate tale about riding his painted pony through the grasslands of the Great American Prairie and coming upon a vast herd of wild buffalo, "mocha brown and pungent and stretching from here to Sunday." He went into exquisite detail about preparing to hunt, then hunting, and when he finished his narrative, the purple-saged plain littered with dead, arrow-pierced bison and the odd calvary man skewered, Dieter, the German archaeologist and race car driver, raised his glass and toasted Harry as a truly charming liar.

There was a moment then, while Harry stood stunned, when everyone else seemed to think the German's remark very amusing, as if the whole telling of the story had been to serve as its prologue. Then Harry responded by trying to action-paint Dieter's white shirt with a whole bottle of Campari. Failing at that, he tried wrestling the Teutonic cur to the deck. Soon both of them were overboard, flailing at each other in the Ligurian Sea, or whatever it was the first names were calling that patch of the Mediterranean. Count and Countess were upset but not as upset as Harry. To hell with them, he said. To hell with it all, and he returned to Santa Fe.

In the next ten years he made steady big money, lending his name to all manner of junk, including designer moccasins. He married again, divorced again, and drank each evening, always feeling well in the morning, but never, as they say, feeling good. In 1985 he turned seventy and thought about salvaging what was left of his life. He did not know yet how he might do this, but he decided that, to begin with, there was much he would renounce, starting with Santa Fe.

"I am no longer a professional," he told his business manager, now executor. "It is in your capable hands."

They were lunching on blue corn tamales with guava sauce and drinking some very decent chardonnay. Fresh roses sat between them. Harry had tired of such restaurants.

"You'll never stop painting, Harry. Daily bread for you."

"I do not intend to stop painting. I am no longer a professional Indian." There was, they both agreed, much to get settled.

Driving north, Harry thought about refining his soul, an undertaking whose worthlessness rather appealed to him. Introspection had never brought him close to revelation, and as he drove toward Taos, then beyond, past the spare grasses of a late spring, it was once again a bust. Maybe he had too much belly for the spiritual life. Abstractions seemed uncomfortable in his company and quickly moved on. Was he up to this? He didn't think he was pointedly unhealthy. All the organs he could inventory were functional, even his abused liver. The thumb of one hand was crooked, had been so from youth, the result of working cattle and missing his dally, the accelerating rope cinching his thumb against the saddle horn. Two fingers of his other hand had been broken in a street brawl when he was nineteen. Like the thumb, the fingers had not healed well, but he didn't mind. The crooked fingers were his sacrifice for socialism, because it was a political brawl, even though Harry had only entered the fray to impress a girl, and she had disappeared when he came to consciousness again, supported in the arms of strangers singing IWW songs. Harry had sustained head injuries as well as broken fingers, but his head had probably healed. During World War II, many enemy rounds had come close, but none had touched him.

At the Four Corners Monument, he stopped, not knowing if he wanted Arizona, Utah, or Colorado. He had too many credit cards to feel like a pilgrim, but the thought was there. A Navajo woman selling necklaces from the back of a covered truck spoke to Blackwing in her language and he smiled, not understanding a damn thing. He had ruled out returning to New Mexico or Palm Springs, but he hadn't ruled any place in. Sometimes, he thought, where you are is a long way from the place you need to discover. It was windy and cold just standing there. He bought a heishi necklace from the old woman and started driving again.

The necklace made him think about painting and thinking about painting made him feel rueful and want a drink. He decided then not to think about anything and simply regard the country. He chose roads that looked inviting and then had to stop in the middle of the night because he had no idea where the hell he was, and the nowhere he had arrived at didn't seem near anything, so he pulled off the road and shut down the truck. In a few minutes he could hear coyotes. "Sing, you mangy dogs," he said and stretched out across the seat in his old down bag.

"What do you call this place?" he asked the woman behind the counter.

"A general store. What would you call it?"

He smiled at her. "I mean the town."

"Mentira. Isn't there a sign? Which way'd you drive in from?"

"East. I think east."

"There's a sign on both ends come to think."

He had been looking at the light along the river and missed the sign, but now this woman could answer all his questions and seemed to have all the time in the world for him. She was middle-aged with blunt but appealing features, red hair going sandy. She was running the store, the gas pump, and the cabins out back, one of which he had decided to take, his bones sore from a night in the truck.

"Utah, right?"

She smiled as she picked a key from a plywood board with lots of keys left hanging. "Now you're getting a fix on it. It's twenty-two for the one night."

He liked the smell of the cabin and the looks of it, the blue-checked plastic tablecloth and the knotty pine walls. He liked the bed that slept him well, and he had especially liked the light along the river to the east. The town was otherwise of little consequence to him or, apparently, to nearly everyone else. The woman explained that the freeway had left Mentira to its own devices. That was fifteen years ago, and those devices only attracted some tourists in season, station-wagon families coming to or from Bryce Canyon and Zion. In the morning he paid for a month in advance. Her name was Wanda, and she owned it all, with only a girl to help her stock shelves and maid the cabins.

She told Harry she was widowed and thought the place would be impossible, but it turned out to be surprisingly easy to manage, mainly because there was never any business. She told him all this and he hardly knew her. It was a very small town.

"Did you hear the train last night?" she asked.

"I did."

"The rooster this morning."

"Him, too."

"That's what's to hear. And there's even less to see."

"Would there be a cafe where they fry eggs and overwhelm you with coffee, preferably a horseshoe counter where people talk about the weather and it is OK to smoke, that sort of place?"

"You are a connoisseur," she said and gave him directions.

Blackwing figured that what he could count on in a place like this was light and deprivation. If his ex-wives and children wished to visit him, it would be because they wanted to see him, and he did not expect to be so flattered. He had his eye on the big room above the store. Knock in a skylight and maybe a swamp cooler for summer months and he'd have a studio. He couldn't ask the woman about that now, not on his second day in town, but he would have breakfast and sketch it all out on the napkin. But what if she used the room? He was getting ahead of himself, feeling good. He walked the streets of Mentira under spring sunshine, the sun-dusted streets of the West. He felt so naturally good that he had no need of a drink, unless it would be just one drink to celebrate feeling so naturally good.

In the beginning, when the men he hired were getting it ready, Wanda visited the studio frequently. Then she left him alone to paint until curiosity brought her up the stairs again.

"Did your children get you all this? Looks like the whole kit."

He allowed that he had sufficient equipment.

"Harry, is a suggestion out of place?" She was looking at the canvas on the easel. It was mid-August and he had been painting for two weeks, early and late to avoid the heat.

"Please," he said.

"You might consider drawing out your trees and your horizon line first. Get your lines down firm and then start filling in with your color. It might look less tentative then."

"I must try that," he said.

She ceased to visit when she failed to see much improvement in his paintings, yet she always inquired about his progress.

"Well, it certainly gives you enjoyment, doesn't it?"

"Some days not so much enjoyment," he said.

"But you do stick to it."

"It doesn't always let me go," he said.

They were drinking vodka from wide-mouth mason jars in the back of the store, but in earshot of the bell on the front door. Wanda drank hers with orange soda and Blackwing took his straight. After arriving in Mentira, he was sober for twenty-seven days. Then he drove his truck to Las Vegas, bought a case of Absolut vodka, and drove directly back, not a bottle opened. He unloaded the entire case in the back room of the store. "Hide it," he told Wanda and instructed her not to tell him where, but to keep a bottle accessible, and if he requested it, then she was to give him one drink in the evening not more than four times a week, not a skimpy drink, but eight full ounces, and she was to sit with him if she would please, and they were to start that very evening if she did not mind.

"Why do you put that stuff in it?" he asked her.

"It tastes better."

"I thought you were Polish."

"This is Swedish vodka."

"Next time I will get Russian."

"Don't bring anything Russian in here."

"You are Polish after all," he said and smiled.

She asked him about his tribe, and when he told her he was

one of the hot water Indians from Palm Springs, she laughed and said no, seriously, she wanted to know.

"My father was Cherokee and my mother a Seminole maiden. They met because my father's family used to winter in Miami Beach. Of course that was before it was all built up and ruined."

Wanda liked that explanation, perhaps because it vaguely paralleled her own experience, a Pole who had married a Mormon. Her husband, she told Harry, had not enjoyed the longevity of Mormons.

"America is amazing," she said, and he agreed.

She directed a family of Japanese tourists to Harry's studio one morning. Father, mother, and a small daughter climbed the stairs, bobbed and bowed and asked his assistance. They were on a side trip from the Grand Canyon, striking out on their own in search of Indians. They pointed out the window to their rental car, and the father showed Harry the small red teepees on the road map, teepees that they had expected to mark Indian villages. The family had stopped at three village sites, the Japanese man told Harry, but had yet to see an Indian or an actual village, although white people in recreational vehicles were gathered in these places, also apparently awaiting the Indians. Now the family was running out of time. They had to return to California and see Disneyland. What would he, an Indian himself, suggest? Harry assured them that Disneyland supplied Indians, that they would not be disappointed. The family all wanted pictures of themselves with Harry, and then the woman gave him a small samurai sword, probably a letter opener, a trinket. "And you may have the Island of Manhattan," he said to her, but it was to the little girl that he gave the heishi necklace.

In the summer he could not find the light he had liked in the spring, but it returned in late September, and for a succession of days at the end of the month, Blackwing was drawn to the loony sadness in the trees that the light revealed. It was the damnedest thing, an animation, a hovering emotion, and he began to feel proprietary about it, even doubting that white people or Japanese people could sense it—the first time in his life he had had such stupid sentiments. Professional Indian bullshit, he labeled that. The sadness in the trees, nonetheless, was a lovely thing. It seemed to sit in certain cottonwoods along the river and circle about the junipers rising from the cut channels in the hills across the river, on the northern slopes of the hills that turned blue on summer evenings but in September had lost the blue and turned the amber and rust of the season. He could not find it in the tall cypress surrounding the cemetery of the small town. The Italian Cypress is too thin to carry emotion, he thought. Like a damn fashion model. He knew that in *quattrocento* Italy such trees were planted in cemeteries as signs of the resurrection, and the practice, if not the association, persisted here and there. The cypress were sleek, like deployed missiles, and he disliked them for that similarity, even while forgiving them. "It's not your fault," he said, an old man talking to trees.

Alone, he talked aloud increasingly, and told Wanda not to be alarmed.

"It's all right," she said. "Doubles the number of guests."

"So you have heard me?"

"No," she said. "Maybe you only think you are speaking aloud."

He considered that likelihood. "Either way, I'm *un poco loco.*"

"That you can say so proves you are in fine shape."

She was good at this back-and-forth, and he enjoyed her company. She was the only woman he remembered feeling strong friendship for, unclouded by desire, yet his memory had grown fitful. There must have been others.

He began then to spend every evening along the river, watching the light until it fell from the trees and entered the water, watching it sashay the riffle of the gravel bar. He often removed his shoes, rolled his trousers, and waded over the smooth stones. With difficulty he had trained his eyes to see light and movement across water for themselves and not as a fisherman sees them—to see simply as a student of light, and this discipline had nearly displaced his first memory of water-shine on a stream he fished as a young man, one that ran into a river that eventually joined the Pacific. His grandfather had taught him to fish and also to paint and had told Harry stories of the old people dipping their hands in red dye and stamping their palm prints on their horses' necks and then drawing lines of yellow and blue on the horses' flanks. When his grandfather died, Harry fished alone and remembered the stories as he waded the rivers of summer evenings, mindful of his connection to all waters. Once, unless he was mistaken, he had seen figurations in the pools, heard animal voices in the riffles. It was a wonderful experience—expansive—and laced with a scent of death.

But here in Mentira, as he stood in the water, what he wanted was a drink. If the light held, perhaps he could settle for that and not have the vodka unless Wanda suggested it, which she might, although he would not encourage her to suggest it, at least not intentionally.

She was occupied with local people when he returned, people there to visit as much as shop. He found the bottle and poured three fingers' worth in a jar to take up to his studio. It was almost enough to have it in his hand. He sat with his drink and looked at his canvas. Painting, he told himself, has only to do with something out there that you want to make part of you and with something a part of you that you must bring out there. It is that simple and that impossible, he thought. "You have been my assistant," he said to the vodka. "Not honest company, but not bad company." In a moment he had to turn on the electric light, and very soon he turned it off again and went out to his cabin.

"Have you eaten?" she asked.

"A great deal, somewhat earlier."

"Do you wish a drink?"

"I think not tonight."

"You are being a good scout."

"Perhaps. Perhaps not."

"Let's have coffee later, after I close."

"I would like that."

"I'll fetch you."

"Do you think," he asked, "we should go to Las Vegas and get in trouble?"

"This winter we could do that," she said.

"Not big trouble," he said.

"Sufficient trouble," she said. "I'll come for you when the coffee is ready."

"Good."

She went out then turned right back. "Harry, I hear you are a famous artist."

"Who says?"

"Miriam at that flower shop."

He looked at Wanda framed in the doorway. She was so handsome and open to the world. He often compared her to a first edition of a good book, seemingly unread, discovered by chance in a little shop. Not a woman who aroused lust, but a woman who drew a man to her with her constant warmth. Maybe lust could get into it after all, if he had any left.

"Miriam at that flower shop is mistaken," he said.

Wanda smiled. "I'll pry it out of you later," she said and left him sitting at his table.

His grandfather and an attraction to light had started him painting, and he had begun in a way that seemed natural to him, using an unschooled technique all his own. Later he looked at reproductions of Cezanne and Matisse, Miro and Klee, Kokoschka. He studied these and others whom he liked as a young man. He studied until he understood them thoroughly and could no longer paint as he had in the beginning or in any way that made him happy, although he could paint in many styles that began to make him money. In the sixties he read the mythology of the plains Indians and tried to paint in that tradition. He was attracted to the symbolic shields of the Northern Cheyenne, and he fashioned these in the style of Tibetan mandalas, which they almost resembled. Pretentious gallery notes spoke of *Heamavihiio*, of breath of wisdom, and of *Miaheyyun*, the universal understanding. The paintings sold quickly, and Blackwing kept cranking them out, giving them more psychedelic zap than was honest. They became embarrassing. He had been close to something of value, and he had let it become money. All he wanted to do now, with what remained of his life, was to paint the sweet sadness of the trees.

They joked that Wanda came to his bed only after she learned of his renown.

"I've become an artist's groupie," she said.

"And my celebrity is the only thing I seem able to give," he said. She kissed his cheek then and brought her chin back to the declivity above his collarbone, which is where she liked to keep it as they lay in the dark and talked. "The warmth of this," she said. "Just the warmth of this is better than anything."

"My ex-wives have all my money; otherwise I would buy you something."

"What would you buy me?"

"I don't know. What do you want?"

"Nothing. Maybe one of your paintings."

"I can't afford my paintings."

"You are making new ones."

"But they are no good."

"Were the old ones so much better?"

"The others are all worse."

She squeezed him and lay across his chest, her ear to his heart. "I want your sense of it all," she said. "Give me some of that."

"What I know," he said, "is that when I was young I had heroes, but then I grew too proud for that, and suddenly I was old, and all I had were ex-wives and hateful children."

"Who were your heroes?" she asked.

"Painters, baseball players, rodeo clowns."

"And the children?"

"Painters, baseball players, rodeo clowns," he said.

Wanda took four days to visit her daughters in Phoenix. Blackwing painted for the first two days and grew discouraged on the morning of the third. He had come back from the cafe with a thermos of coffee, October wind chewing the streets. He let himself into the back of the store with the key she had given him, climbed to the studio, and knew at a glance it was not working. He had tried various undercoats to allow some luminosity to bleed through—a mix of zinc white with one of the yellows, then, in another attempt, titanium white. That was the problem, he thought, the undercoat, but maybe the problem was major, a stubborn disparity between vision and capacity for execution. "The hell you say," he said aloud, or so it seemed. He struggled with it anyway, until noon, but it resisted, so he rummaged about in the back of the store for the vodka, had a long lunch of it and kept painting. It was so stupid. He was trying to be bold but it only looked undisciplined. Had she been here this wouldn't have happened. A goddamn nurse is what I need, he thought.

After an hour, he picked up the small samurai sword from his work table. It lay across a letter from the Japanese girl who had written of wearing her heishi to a Shinto shrine. He stuck the sword in his coat pocket along with the vodka bottle and filled his other pocket with paints and headed for the river. One way to paint the trees, he had just concluded, was to paint the goddamn trees. Cold, bright air stung his face as he cut through the fields. He tried to imitate the rasping song of the blackbirds in the reeds, and then shouted to them: "Redwing, I am Blackwing!" By God, he could become a performance artist, take a Japanese name, paint whole forests!

He began with a tube of cerulean blue, squirted on the trunk of a large cottonwood and rubbed in with the palms of both hands. A nice effect, except where the bark peeled off from the force of his smearing. He picked up those chips of blue and wedged them back in higher up, then let fly with the cadmium red, then a tube of alazarian crimson, others, his whole pocket's worth, before climbing the bank to get a look at it. His breathing was labored, some constriction through his left shoulder. Clearly, this project was going to take a lot of paint. Gallons of it. A compressor and spray gun. It was going to take easily as much vodka. He threw the empty bottle skyward and out over the river, then threw the flattened and rolled tubes of paint. He envisioned throwing himself, if he could only get out and beside his body, if he could do that, somehow get a purchase in the up there and reach down for himself. It was just a minor engineering problem that kept him from flying. The hard part, the willingness to give himself over was *fait accompli*. "*Fait accompli!*" he yelled into the wind and riverhush. He would have to settle for crawling to the water's edge, use this opportunity to really learn the territory, nose to the ground. Only about ten yards of bleached river rock and bunch grass to negotiate, but on his stomach it would be a real safari. Blackwing kneeled, brought his color-smeared hands to his face and applied the war paint of blue and crimson. He placed the small samurai sword in his teeth and started out. It was astonishingly easy, pushing with alternate elbows as he had in the infantry years ago. And as he began, the first stones that stabbed his belly triggered memories of places and friends and paintings he had loved, and as he continued, he willed the remaining stones to do the same. In no time he was at the river bank, drinking the fetid water that tasted of flesh.

Harry heard the buffalo first. It was difficult to raise his head enough to watch them clamber out of the river, water draining from their backs and glistening on their flanks. A large herd,

cantering up the bank and turning north in a jerky column movement, but soon, and without even moving, he was aware of the
animals from many points of view. He could see the lot of them
from on high and simultaneously regard the indignant eyes of
every bull and cow and calf, their wet and matted manes quickly
drying, and the scent of that giving way to something more as-
tringent. Prairie sage, he decided, as his heartbeat began to merge
with the drumming hooves. It was more difficult to raise his head
when the paint-streaked pony appeared at his side, tapping one
hoof like a show horse. In a minute, Harry said. But the pony
began to nuzzle and snort, its hot horse breath blowing sand into
the old man's face. A fresh mount, a fair wind, a summons. He
should have left a note for Wanda—to explain about all this—
but he couldn't worry about that now. It was going to be enough
just to hang on.

Annick Smith

It's Come to This

No horses. That's how it always starts. I am coming down the meadow, the first snow of September whipping around my boots, and there are no horses to greet me. The first thing I did after Caleb died was get rid of the horses.

"I don't care how much," I told the auctioneer at the Missoula Livestock Company. He looked at me slant-eyed from under his Stetson. "Just don't let the canneries take them." Then I walked away.

What I did not tell him was I couldn't stand the sight of those horses on our meadow, so heedless, grown fat and untended. They reminded me of days when Montana seemed open as the sky.

Now that the horses are gone I am more desolate than ever. If you add one loss to another, what you have is double zip. I am wet to the waist, water sloshing ankle-deep inside my irrigating boots. My toes are numb, my chapped hands are burning from the cold, and down by the gate my dogs are barking at a strange man in a red log truck.

That's how I meet Frank. He is hauling logs down from the Champion timberlands above my place, across the right-of-way I sold to the company after my husband's death. The taxes were piling up. I sold the right-of-way because I would not sell my land. Kids will grow up and leave you, but land is something a woman can hold on to.

I don't like those log trucks rumbling by my house, scattering chickens, tempting my dogs to chase behind their wheels, kicking clouds of dust so thick the grass looks brown and dead. There's nothing I like about logging. It breaks my heart to walk among newly cut limbs, to be enveloped in the sharp odor of sap running like blood. After twenty years on this place, I still cringe at the snap and crash of five-hundred-year-old pines and the far-off screaming of saws.

Anyway, Frank pulls his gyppo logging rig to a stop just past my house in order to open the blue metal gate that separates our outbuildings from the pasture, and while he is at it, he adjusts the chains holding his load. My three mutts take after him as if they are real watchdogs and he stands at the door of the battered red cab holding his hands to his face and pretending to be scared.

"I would surely appreciate it if you'd call off them dogs," says Frank, as if those puppies weren't wagging their tails and jumping up to be patted.

He can see I am shivering and soaked. And I am mad. If I had a gun, I might shoot him.

"You ought to be ashamed . . . a man like you."

"Frank Bowman," he says, grinning and holding out his large thick hand. "From Bowman Corners." Bowman Corners is just down the road.

"What happened to you?" He grins. "Take a shower in your boots?"

How can you stay mad at that man? A man who looks at you and makes you look at yourself. I should have known better. I should have waited for my boys to come home from football practice and help me lift the heavy wet boards in our diversion dam. But my old wooden flume was running full and I was determined to do what had to be done before dark, to be a true country woman like the pioneers I read about as a daydreaming child in Chicago, so long ago it seems another person's life.

"I had to shut off the water," I say. "Before it freezes." Frank nods, as if this explanation explains everything.

Months later I would tell him about Caleb. How he took care of the wooden flume, which was built almost one hundred years ago by his Swedish ancestors. The snaking plank trough crawls up and around a steep slope of igneous rock. It has been patched and rebuilt by generations of hard-handed, blue-eyed Petersons until it reached its present state of tenuous mortality. We open the floodgate in June when Bear Creek is high with snow melt, and the flume runs full all summer, irrigating our hay meadow of timothy and wild mountain grasses. Each fall, before the first hard freeze, we close the diversion gates and the creek flows in its natural bed down to the Big Blackfoot River.

That's why I'd been standing in the icy creek, hefting six-foot two-by-twelves into the slotted brace that forms the dam. The bottom board was waterlogged and coated with green slime. It slipped in my bare hands and I sat down with a splash, the plank in my lap and the creek surging around me.

"Goddamn it to fucking hell!" I yelled. I was astonished to find tears streaming down my face, for I have always prided myself on my ability to bear hardship. Here is a lesson I've learned. There is no glory in pure backbreaking labor.

Frank would agree. He is wide like his log truck and thick-skinned as a yellow pine, and believes neighbors should be friendly. At five o'clock sharp each workday, on his last run, he would stop at my blue gate and yell, "Call off your beasts," and I would stop whatever I was doing and go down for our friendly chat.

"How can you stand it?" I'd say, referring to the cutting of trees.

"It's a pinprick on the skin of the earth," replies Frank. "God doesn't know the difference."

"Well, I'm not God," I say. "Not on my place. Never."

So Frank would switch to safer topics such as new people moving in like knapweed, or where to find morels, or how the junior-high basketball team was doing. One day in October, when red-tails screamed and hoarfrost tipped the meadow grass, the world gone crystal and glowing, he asked could I use some firewood.

"A person can always use firewood," I snapped.

The next day, when I came home from teaching, there was a pickup load by the woodshed—larch and fir, cut to stove size and split.

"Taking care of the widow," Frank grinned when I tried to thank him. I laughed, but that is exactly what he was up to. In this part of the country, a man still takes pains.

When I first came to Montana I was slim as a fashion model and my hair was black and curly. I had met my husband, Caleb, at the University of Chicago, where a city girl and a raw ranch boy could be equally enthralled by Gothic halls, the great libraries, and gray old Nobel laureates who gathered in the Faculty Club, where no student dared enter.

But after our first two sons were born, after the disillusionments of Vietnam and the cloistered grind of academic life, we decided to break away from Chicago and a life of mind preeminent, and we came to live on the quarter section of land Caleb had inherited from his Swedish grandmother. We would make a new start by raising purebred quarter horses.

For Caleb it was coming home. He had grown up in Sunset, forty miles northeast of Missoula, on his family's homestead ranch. For me it was romance. Caleb had carried the romance of the West for me in the way he walked on high-heeled cowboy boots, and the world he told stories about. It was a world I had imagined from books and movies, a paradise of the shining mountains, clean rivers, and running horses.

I loved the idea of horses. In grade school, I sketched black stallions, white mares, rainbow-spotted appaloosas. My bedroom was hung with horses running, horses jumping, horses rolling in clover. At thirteen I hung around the stables in Lincoln Park and flirted with the stable boys, hoping to charm them into riding lessons my mother could not afford. Sometimes it worked, and I would bounce down the bridle path, free as a princess, never thinking of the payoff that would come at dusk. Pimply-faced boys. Groping and French kisses behind the dark barn that reeked of manure.

For Caleb horses meant honorable outdoor work and a way to make money, work being the prime factor. Horses were history to be reclaimed, identity. It was my turn to bring in the monthly check, so I began teaching at the Sunset school as a stopgap measure to keep our family solvent until the horse-business dream paid off. I am still filling that gap.

We rebuilt the log barn and the corrals, and cross-fenced our one-hundred acres of cleared meadowland. I loved my upland meadow from the first day. As I walked through tall grasses heavy with seed, they moved to the wind, and the undulations were not like water. Now, when I look down from our cliffs, I see the meadow as a handmade thing—a rolling swatch of green hemmed with a stitchery of rocks and trees. The old Swedes who were Caleb's ancestors cleared that meadow with axes and crosscut saws, and I still trip over sawed-off stumps of virgin larch, sawed level to the ground, too large to pull out with a team of horses—decaying, but not yet dirt.

We knew land was a way to save your life. Leave the city and city ambitions, and get back to basics. Roots and dirt and horse pucky (Caleb's word for horseshit). Bob Dylan and the rest were all singing about the land, and every stoned, long-haired mother's child was heading for country.

My poor mother, with her Hungarian dreams and Hebrew upbringing, would turn in her grave to know I'm still teaching in a three-room school with no library or gymnasium, Caleb ten years dead, our youngest boy packed off to the state university, the ranch not even paying its taxes, and me, her only child, keeping company with a two-hundred-and-thirty-pound logger who lives in a trailer.

"Marry a doctor," she used to say, "or better, a concert pianist," and she was not joking. She invented middle-class stories for me from our walk-up flat on the South Side of Chicago: I would live in a white house in the suburbs like the one she had always wanted; my neighbors would be rich and cultured; the air itself, fragrant with lilacs in May and heady with burning oak leaves in October, could lift us out of the city's grime right into her American dream. My mother would smile with secret intentions. "You will send your children to Harvard."

Frank's been married twice. "Twice-burned" is how he names it, and there are Bowman kids scattered up and down the Blackfoot Valley. Some of them are his. I met his first wife, Fay Dell, before I ever met Frank. That was eighteen years ago. It was Easter vacation, and I had taken two hundred dollars out of our meager savings to buy a horse for our brand-new herd. I remember the day clear as any picture. I remember mud and Blackfoot clay.

Fay Dell is standing in a pasture above Monture Creek. She wears faded brown Carhartt coveralls, as they do up here in the winters, and her irrigating boots are crusted with yellow mud. March runoff has every patch of bare ground spitting streams, trickles, and puddles of brackish water. Two dozen horses circle around her. Their ears are laid back and they eye me, ready for flight. She calls them by name, her voice low, sugary as the carrots she holds in her rough hands.

"Take your pick," she says.

I stroke the velvet muzzle of a two-year-old sorrel, a purebred quarter horse with a white blaze on her forehead.

"Sweet Baby," she says. "You got an eye for the good ones."

"How much?"

"Sorry. That baby is promised."

I walk over to a long-legged bay. There's a smile on Fay Dell's lips, but her eyes give another message.

"Marigold," she says, rubbing the mare's swollen belly. "She's in foal. Can't sell my brood mare."

So I try my luck on a pint-sized roan with a high-flying tail. A good kids' horse. A dandy.

"You can't have Lollipop neither. I'm breaking her for my own little gal."

I can see we're not getting anywhere when she heads me in the direction of a pair of wild-eyed geldings.

"Twins," says Fay Dell proudly. "Ruckus and Buckus."

You can tell by the name of a thing if it's any good. These two were out of the question, coming four and never halter broke.

"Come on back in May." We walk toward the ranch house and a hot cup of coffee. "I'll have 'em tamed good as any sheepdog. Two for the price of one. Can't say that ain't a bargain!"

Her two-story frame house sat high above the creek, some Iowa farmer's dream of the West. The ground, brown with stubble of last year's grass, was littered with old tennis shoes, broken windshields, rusting cars, shards of aluminum siding. Cast-iron tractor parts emerged like mushrooms from soot-crusted heaps of melting snow. I wondered why Fay Dell had posted that ad on the Sunset school bulletin board: "Good horses for sale. Real cheap." Why did she bother with such make-believe?

Eighteen years later I am sleeping with her ex-husband, and the question is answered.

"All my wages gone for hay," says Frank. "The kids in hand-me-downs . . . the house a goddamn mess. I'll tell you I had a bellyful!"

Frank had issued an ultimatum on Easter Sunday, determined never to be ashamed again of his bedraggled wife and children among the slicked-up families in the Blackfoot Community Church.

"Get rid of them two-year-olds," he warned, "or . . ."

No wonder it took Fay Dell so long to tell me no. What she was doing that runoff afternoon, seesawing back and forth, was making a choice between her horses and her husband. If Fay Dell had confessed to me that day, I would not have believed such choices are possible. Horses, no matter how well you loved them, seemed mere animal possessions to be bought and sold. I was so young then, a city girl with no roots at all, and I had grown up Jewish, where family seemed the only choice.

"Horse poor," Frank says. "That woman wouldn't get rid of her horses. Not for God, Himself."

March in Montana is a desperate season. You have to know what you want, and hang on.

Frank's second wife was tall, blond, and young. He won't talk about her much, just shakes his head when her name comes up and says, "Guess she couldn't stand the winters." I heard she ran away to San Luis Obispo with a long-haired carpenter named Ralph.

"Cleaned me out," Frank says, referring to his brand-new stereo and the golden retriever. She left the double-wide empty, and the only evidence she had been there at all was the white picket fence Frank built to make her feel safe. And a heap of green tomatoes in the weed thicket he calls a garden.

"I told her," he says with a wistful look, "I told that woman you can't grow red tomatoes in this climate."

As for me, I love winter. Maybe that's why Frank and I can stand each other. Maybe that's how come we've been keeping company for five years and marriage is a subject that has never crossed our lips except once. He's got his place near the highway, and I've got mine at the end of the dirt road, where the sign reads, 'County maintenance ends here.' To all eyes but our own, we have always been a queer, mismatched pair.

After we began neighboring, I would ask Frank in for a cup of coffee. Before long, it was a beer or two. Soon, my boys were taking the old McCulloch chain saw to Frank's to be sharpened, or he was teaching them how to tune up Caleb's ancient Case tractor. We kept our distance until one thirty-below evening in January when my Blazer wouldn't start, even though its oil-pan heater was plugged in. Frank came up to jump it.

The index finger on my right hand was frostbit from trying to turn the metal ignition key bare-handed. Frostbite is like getting burned, extreme cold acting like fire, and my finger was swollen along the third joint, just below its tip, growing the biggest blister I had ever seen.

"Dumb," Frank says, holding my hand between his large mitts and blowing on the blister. "Don't you have gloves?"

"Couldn't feel the key to turn it with gloves on."

He lifts my egg-size finger to his face and bows down, like a chevalier, to kiss it. I learn the meaning of dumbfounded. I feel the warmth of his lips tracing from my hand down through my privates. I like it. A widow begins to forget how good a man's warmth can be.

"I would like to take you dancing," says Frank.

"It's too damn cold."

"Tomorrow," he says, "the Big Sky Boys are playing at the Awful Burger Bar."

I suck at my finger.

"You're a fine dancer."

"How in God's name would you know?"

"Easy," Frank smiles. "I been watching your moves."

I admit I was scared. I felt like the little girl I had been so long ago. A thumb sucker. If I said yes, I knew there would be no saying no.

The Awful Burger Bar is like the Red Cross, you can go there for first aid. It is as great an institution as the Sunset school. The white bungalow sits alone just off the two-lane on a jack-pine flat facing south across irrigated hay meadows to where what's left of the town of Sunset clusters around the school. Friday evenings after Caleb passed away, when I felt too weary to cook and too jumpy to stand the silence of another Blackfoot night, I'd haul the boys up those five miles of asphalt and we'd eat Molly Fry's awful burgers, stacked high with Bermuda onions, lettuce and tomato, hot jo-jos on the side, Millers for me, root beer for them. That's how those kids came to be experts at shooting pool.

The ranching and logging families in this valley had no difficulty understanding why their schoolteacher hung out in a bar and passed the time with hired hands and old-timers. We were all alike in this one thing. Each was drawn from starvation farms in the rock and clay foothills or grassland ranches on the flood-plain, down some winding dirt road to the red neon and yellow lights glowing at the dark edge of chance. You could call it home, as they do in the country-and-western songs on the jukebox.

I came to know those songs like a second language. Most, it seemed, written just for me. I longed to sing them out loud, but God or genes or whatever determines what you can be never gave me a singing voice. In my second life I will be a white Billie Holiday with a gardenia stuck behind my ear, belting out songs to make you dance and cry at the same time.

My husband, Caleb, could sing like the choir boy he had been before he went off to Chicago on a scholarship and lost his religion. He taught himself to play harmonica and wrote songs about lost lives. There's one I can't forget:

> *Scattered pieces, scattered pieces,*
> *Come apart for all the world to see.*
> *Scattered pieces, lonely pieces,*
> *That's how yours truly came to be.*

When he sang that song, my eyes filled with tears.

"How can you feel that way, and never tell me except in a song?"

"There's lots I don't tell you," he said.

We didn't go to bars much, Caleb and me. First of all we were poor. Then too busy building our log house, taking care of the boys, tending horses. And finally, when the angina pains struck, and the shortness of breath, and we knew that at the age of thirty-seven Caleb had come down with an inherited disease that would choke his arteries and starve his heart, it was too sad, you know, having to sit out the jitterbugs and dance only to slow music. But even then, in those worst of bad times, when the Big Sky Boys came through, we'd hire a sitter and put on our good boots and head for the Awful Burger.

There was one Fourth of July. All the regulars were there, and families from the valley. Frank says he was there, but I didn't know him. Kids were running in and out like they do in Montana, where a country bar is your local community center. Firecrackers exploded in the gravel parking lot. Show-off college students from town were dancing cowboy boogie as if they knew what they were doing, and sunburned tourists exuding auras of campfires and native cutthroat trout kept coming in from motor homes. This was a far way from Connecticut.

We were sitting up close to the band. Caleb was showing our

Lyrics from "Scattered Pieces" by David J. Smith, 1973.

boys how he could juggle peanuts in time to the music. The boys tried to copy him, and peanuts fell like confetti to be crunched under the boots of sweating dancers. The sun streamed in through open doors and windows, even though it was nine at night, and we were flushed from too many beers, too much sun and music.

"Stand up, Caleb. Stand up so's the rest of us can see."

That was our neighbor, Melvin Godfrey, calling from the next table. Then his wife, Stella, takes up the chant.

"Come on, Caleb. Give us the old one-two-three."

The next thing, Molly Fry is passing lemons from the kitchen where she cooks the awful burgers, and Caleb is standing in front of the Big Sky Boys, the dancers all stopped and watching. Caleb is juggling those lemons to the tune of "Mommas Don't Let Your Babies Grow Up to Be Cowboys," and he does not miss a beat.

It is a picture in my mind—framed in gold leaf—Caleb on that bandstand, legs straddled, deep-set eyes looking out at no one or nothing, the tip of his tongue between clenched teeth in some kind of frozen smile, his faded blue shirt stained in half-moons under the arms, and three bright yellow lemons rising and falling in perfect synchronicity. I see the picture in stop-action, like the end of a movie. Two shiny lemons in midair, the third in his palm. Caleb juggling.

It's been a long time coming, the crying. You think there's no pity left, but the sadness is waiting, like a barrel gathering rain, until one sunny day, out of the blue, it just boils over and you've got a flood on your hands. That's what happened one Saturday last January, when Frank took me to celebrate the fifth anniversary of our first night together. The Big Sky Boys were back, and we were at the Awful Burger Bar.

"Look," I say, first thing. "The lead guitar has lost his hair. Those boys are boys no longer."

Frank laughs and points to the bass man. Damned if he isn't wearing a corset to hold his beer belly inside those slick red-satin cowboy shirts the boys have worn all these years.

And Indian Willie is gone. He played steel guitar so blue it broke your heart. Gone back to Oklahoma.

"Heard Willie found Jesus in Tulsa," says Melvin Godfrey, who has joined us at the bar.

"They've replaced him with a child," I say, referring to the pimply, long-legged kid who must be someone's son. "He hits all the right keys, but he'll never break your heart."

We're sitting on high stools, and I'm all dressed up in the long burgundy skirt Frank gave me for Christmas. My frizzy gray hair is swept back in a chignon, and Mother's amethyst earrings catch the light from the revolving Budweiser clock. It is a new me, matronly and going to fat, a stranger I turn away from in the mirror above the bar.

When the band played "Waltz Across Texas" early in the night, Frank led me to the dance floor and we waltzed through to the end, swaying and dipping, laughing in each others' ears. But now he is downing his third Beam ditch and pays no attention to my tapping feet.

I watch the young people boogie. A plain fat girl with long red hair is dressed in worn denim overalls, but she moves like a queen among frogs. In the dim, multicolored light, she is delicate, delicious.

"Who is that girl?" I ask Frank.

"What girl?"

"The redhead."

"How should I know?" he says. "Besides, she's fat."

"Want to dance?"

Frank looks at me as if I was crazy. "You know I can't dance to this fast stuff. I'm too old to jump around and make a fool of myself. You want to dance, you got to find yourself another cowboy."

The attractive men have girls of their own or are looking to nab some hot young dish. Melvin is dancing with Stella, "showing off" as Frank would say, but to me they are a fine-tuned duo who know each move before they make it, like a team of matched circus ponies, or those fancy ice skaters in the Olympics. They dance only with each other, and they dance all night long.

I'm getting bored, tired of whiskey and talk about cows and spotted owls and who's gone broke this week. I can hear all that on the five-o'clock news. I'm beginning to feel like a wallflower at a high-school sock hop (feelings I don't relish reliving). I'm making plans about going home when a tall, narrow-hipped old geezer in a flowered rayon cowboy shirt taps me on the shoulder.

"May I have this dance, ma'am?"

I look over to Frank, who is deep in conversation with Ed Snow, a logger from Seeley Lake.

"If your husband objects . . ."

"He's not my husband."

The old man is clearly drunk, but he has the courtly manner of an old-time cowboy, and he is a live and willing body.

"Sure," I say. As we head for the dance floor, I see Frank turn his head. He is watching me with a bemused and superior smile. "I'll show that bastard," I say to myself.

The loudspeaker crackles as the lead guitarist announces a medley—"A tribute to our old buddy, Ernest Tubb." The Big Sky Boys launch into "I'm Walking the Floor Over You," and the old man grabs me around the waist.

Our hands meet for the first time. I could die on the spot. If I hadn't been so mad, I would have run back to Frank because that old man's left hand was not a hand, but a claw—all shriveled up from a stroke or some birth defect, the bones dry and brittle, frozen half-shut, the skin white, flaky, and surprisingly soft, like a baby's.

His good right arm is around my waist, guiding me light but

firm, and I respond as if it doesn't matter who's in the saddle. But my mind is on that hand. It twirls me and pulls me. We glide. We swing. He draws me close, and I come willingly. His whiskey breath tickles at my ear in a gasping wheeze. We spin one last time, and dip. I wonder if he will die on the spot, like Caleb. Die in mid-motion, alive one minute, dead the next.

I see Caleb in the kitchen that sunstruck evening in May, come in from irrigating the east meadow and washing his hands at the kitchen sink. Stew simmers on the stove, the littlest boys play with English toy soldiers, Mozart on the stereo, a soft breeze blowing through open windows, Caleb turns to me. I will always see him turning. A shadow crosses his face. "Oh dear," he says. And Caleb falls to the maple floor, in one motion a tree cut down. He does not put out his hands to break his fall. Gone. Blood dribbles from his broken nose.

There is no going back now. We dance two numbers, the old cowboy and me, each step smoother and more carefree. We are breathing hard, beginning to sweat. The claw-hand holds me in fear and love. This high-stepping old boy is surely alive. He asks my name.

"Mady."

"Bob," he says. "Bob Beamer. They call me Old Beam." He laughs like this is a good joke. "Never knowed a Mady before. That's a new one on me."

"Hungarian," I say, wishing the subject had not come up, not mentioning the Jewish part for fear of complications. And I talk to Mother, as I do when feelings get too deep.

"Are you watching me now?" I say to the ghost of her. "It's come to this, Momushka. Are you watching me now?"

It's odd how you can talk to the ghost of someone more casually and honestly than you ever communicated when they were alive. When I talk to Caleb's ghost it is usually about work or the boys or a glimpse of beauty in nature or books. I'll spot a bluebird hovering, or young elk playing tag where our meadow joins the woods, or horses running (I always talk to Caleb about any experience I have with horses), and the words leap from my mouth, simple as pie. But when I think of my deep ecology, as the environmentalists describe it, I speak only to Mother.

I never converse with my father. He is a faded memory of heavy eyebrows, Chesterfield straights, whiskery kisses. He was a sculptor and died when I was six. Mother was five-feet-one, compact and full of energy as a firecracker. Every morning, in our Chicago apartment lined with books, she wove my tangled bush of black hair into French braids that pulled so tight my eyes seemed slanted. Every morning she tried to yank me into shape, and every morning I screamed so loud Mother was embarrassed to look our downstairs neighbors in the eyes.

"Be quiet," she commanded. "They will think I am a Nazi."

And there was Grandma, who lived with us and wouldn't learn English because it was a barbaric language. She would pol-ish our upright Steinway until the piano shone like ebony. I remember endless piano lessons, Bach and Liszt. "A woman of culture," Mother said, sure of this one thing. "You will have everything."

"You sure dance American," the old cowboy says, and we are waltzing to the last dance, a song even older than my memories.

"I was in that war," he says. "Old Tubb must of been on the same troopship. We was steaming into New York and it was raining in front of us and full moon behind and I saw a rainbow at midnight like the song says, 'Out on the ocean blue!' "

Frank has moved to the edge of the floor. I see him out of the corner of my eye. We should be dancing this last one, I think, me and Frank and Old Beam. I close my eyes and all of us are dancing, like in the end of a Fellini movie—Stella and Marvin, the slick young men and blue-eyed girls, the fat redhead in her overalls, Mother, Caleb. Like Indians in a circle. Like Swede farmers, Hungarian gypsies.

Tears gather behind my closed lids. I open my eyes and rain is falling. The song goes on, sentimental and pointless. But the tears don't stop.

"It's not your fault," I say, trying to smile, choking and sputtering, laughing at the confounded way both these men are looking at me. "Thank you for a very nice dance."

I cried for months, off and on. The school board made me take sick leave and see a psychiatrist in Missoula. He gave me drugs. The pills put me to sleep and I could not think straight, just walked around like a zombie. I told the shrink I'd rather cry. "It's good for you," I said. "Cleans out the system."

I would think the spell was done and over, and then I'd see the first red-winged blackbird in February or snow melting off the meadow, or a silly tulip coming up before its time, and the water level in my head would rise, and I'd be at it again.

"Runoff fever" is what Frank calls it. The junk of your life is laid bare, locked in ice and muck, just where you left it before the first blizzard buried the whole damned mess under three feet of pure white. I can't tell you why the crying ended, but I can tell you precisely when. Perhaps one grief replaces another and the second grief is something you can fix. Or maybe it's just a change of internal weather.

Frank and I are walking along Bear Creek on a fine breezy day in April, grass coming green and thousands of the yellow glacier lilies we call dog-tooth violets lighting the woods. I am picking a bouquet and bend to smell the flowers. Their scent is elusive, not sweet as roses or rank as marigolds, but a fine freshness you might want to drink. I breathe in the pleasure and suddenly I am weeping. A flash flood of tears.

Frank looks at me bewildered. He reaches for my hand. I pull away blindly, walking as fast as I can. He grabs my elbow.

"What the hell?" he says. I don't look at him.

"Would you like to get married?" He is almost shouting. "Is that what you want? Would that cure this goddamned crying?"

What can I say? I am amazed. Unaccountably frightened. "No," I blurt out, shaking free of his grasp and preparing to run. "It's not you." I am sobbing now, gasping for breath.

Then he has hold of both my arms and is shaking me—a good-sized woman—as if I were a child. And that is how I feel, like a naughty girl. The yellow lilies fly from my hands.

"Stop it!" he yells. "Stop that damned bawling!"

Frank's eyes are wild. This is no proposal. I see my fear in his eyes and I am ashamed. Shame always makes me angry. I try to slap his face. He catches my hand and pulls me to his belly. It is warm. Big enough for the both of us. The anger has stopped my tears. The warmth has stopped my anger. When I raise my head to kiss Frank's mouth, I see his eyes brimming with salt.

I don't know why, but I am beginning to laugh through my tears. Laughing at last at myself.

"Will you marry me?" I stutter. "Will that cure you?"

Frank lets go of my arms. He is breathing hard and his face is flushed a deep red. He sits down on a log and wipes his eyes with the back of his sleeve. I rub at my arms.

"They're going to be black and blue."

"Sorry," he says.

I go over to Frank's log and sit at his feet, my head against his knees. He strokes my undone hair. "What about you?" he replies, question for question. "Do you want to do it?"

We are back to a form of discourse we both understand.

"I'm not sure."

"Me neither."

May has come to Montana with a high-intensity green so rich you can't believe it is natural. I've burned the trash pile and I am done with crying. I'm back with my fifth-graders and struggling through aerobics classes three nights a week. I stand in the locker room naked and exhausted, my hips splayed wide and belly sagging as if to proclaim, Yes, I've borne four children.

A pubescent girl, thin as a knife, studies me as if I were a creature from another planet, but I don't care because one of these winters Frank and I are going to Hawaii. When I step out on those white beaches I want to look good in my bathing suit.

Fay Dell still lives up on Monture Creek. I see her out in her horse pasture winter and summer as I drive over the pass to Great Falls for a teachers' meeting or ride the school bus to basketball games in the one-room school in Ovando. Her ranch house is gone to hell, unpainted, weathered gray, patched with tar paper. Her second husband left her, and the daughter she broke horses for is a beauty operator in Spokane. Still, there's over a dozen horses in the meadow and Fay Dell gone thin and unkempt in coveralls, tossing hay in February or fixing fence in May or just standing in the herd.

I imagine her low, sugary voice as if I were standing right by her. She is calling those horses by name. Names a child might invent.

"Sweet Baby."

"Marigold."

"Lollipop."

I want my meadow to be running with horses, as it was in the beginning—horses rolling in new grass, tails swatting at summer flies, huddled into a blizzard. I don't have to ride them. I just want their pea-brained beauty around me. I'm in the market for a quarter horse stallion and a couple of mares. I'll need to repair my fences and build a new corral with poles cut from the woods.

My stallion will be named Rainbow at Midnight. Frank laughs and says I should name him Beam, after my cowboy. For a minute I don't know what he's talking about, and then I remember the old man in the Awful Burger Bar. I think of Fay Dell and say, "Maybe I'll name him Frank."

Frank thinks Fay Dell is crazy as a loon. But Fay Dell knows our lives are delicate. Grief will come. Fay Dell knows you don't have to give in. Life is motion. Choose love. A person can fall in love with horses.

Kent Nelson

Ditch Rider

Earlier that evening Scott had gone up the ditch to check the weirs and to make certain water was coming down. He had a date with Vicky afterwards, so he'd put on a clean pair of bluejeans and a plaid shirt, and instead of the rubber boots for irrigating, he'd worn his blue-and-red leather cowboy boots, hand stitched. He'd even combed his hair. Then he'd taken my dirt bike up the county road with a shovel across the handlebars.

That had been at six-thirty and still light. I hadn't noticed whether there was water until after dinner when I went out to take a piss and to settle the calves. It was dark then, and the wind had stopped. A few thin clouds rolled above the dry pinyon mesas to the west. Chimney Peak and Courthouse, two granite blocks to the east, were slick with moonlight, and it was so bright I didn't need the flashlight. The ditch was empty. You could hear it was empty. But there had been water earlier, because a sheen of mud reflected moonlight, and water stood in the low spots.

One of the calves had pneumonia, and by the time I finished doctoring and got back inside, it was after ten. I called up Vicky to see whether Scott was there and what he'd done up the ditch.

Vicky's mother answered. "I haven't seen him," she said. "They all went to the movies."

"Did Scott go?"

"I don't know," she said. "Who's Scott?"

She sounded drunk. "This is Jack Lindstrom," I said. "Scott's uncle."

"Well, I'll tell Vicky you called." And she hung up.

The problem was the summer had been so dry. A chinook had blown most of June, and with the dry wind, the snowmelt had been too quick in the mountains. By July the creek that fed the ditch had lowered by half, and now, in August, it was barely a quarter of what it had been at high water. Even when clouds boiled up over the mesas, they spilled off without leaving any moisture.

Some days I got a foot of water on my field, some days nothing, then half a foot. It was Pie Reynolds and the Pollards stealing water. Scott or I had to spend a portion of every day walking the ditch to make our presence known, and even that didn't do any good.

As always I had a mind to call the sheriff, but I was peace loving. What we really needed was a ditch rider. In the old days a man on horseback could make himself a decent wage riding half a dozen to a dozen ditches keeping the water running. Water was scarce in that part of Colorado, valuable as gold, and the ditch rider was judge and enforcer. There was no court or monkey-suit lawyers or proof of damages. He made certain however he wanted to the people who paid him got the water they had a right to.

I'd talked to Pie Reynolds a number of times, and Pie was agreeable. Yes, he knew my property had the best priority on the ditch. Yes, there were three feet coming in at the creek. Yes, some of the water got out onto his alfalfa. It was an accident, he said, a mistake. His wife had done the irrigating. Or muskrats had undermined the ditch bank. He thought he'd closed the diversion. He was sorry, it wouldn't happen again. But the next day there'd be a foot of water running into his meadow.

Lute Pollard wasn't so friendly as Pie. When I phoned, Lute hung up, and if I knocked on the trailer door, he wouldn't come out. One day a couple of weeks earlier I'd found him and his son Harry out putting water on their pasture, and I asked what they thought they were doing.

"What's it look like we're doing?" Lute asked.

"Irrigating," I said, "with my water."

Harry stopped shoveling. "Get off our land."

"It's my water," I said. "I have a right to walk the ditch."

"So walk the ditch," Lute said. "We're borrowing the water for a while. Now go to hell. We ain't letting our crop burn."

I cut their water back at the places they were taking it out of the ditch, but as soon as I'd gone, they diverted it again. And the next time I came up the ditch there was a high barbed-wire fence at their property line.

I was thinking about this, lying in bed, halfway expecting to hear Scott drive in any minute on the bike. I didn't relish calling the sheriff. It would only make Reynolds and the Pollards angry.

When I took the job on Trinket McCormick's ranch, I hadn't known anything about cattle. My ex-wife and I had run a restaurant in Sedalia, Missouri, and after she left me for a man in St.

Louis, I'd come out to Colorado to fish for trout and figure out what I should do next. I'd known for a long time my wife was playing around. I told her if she didn't stop, I'd leave her, but she had given up one man and started behind my back with another. She was the kind of woman who liked turmoil. She kept me in limbo that way. I'd think one day she cared about me, and the next she'd throw a glass at me across the dinner table. I stayed down at the restaurant and made a pretty good business of it, except she got half when I sold.

That summer I slept in the camper on the back of my truck. With varying amounts of skill and luck I fished the Yampa and the Gunnison and the San Miguel, but the time on my hands made me nervous. In the fall I hired on with Trinket as a jack-of-all-trades, master-of-none.

Trinket was the last of the McCormicks in the valley. Over the years she'd sold off land piecemeal for cash to live on, each time deeding away water, but keeping the best priority for the homestead. I cooked her meals, did errands in town, the chores on the ranch—fed cattle, doctored, irrigated. Then in November she broke her hip in a fall and had to go to Denver to a home.

That winter I learned a lot about cattle. I learned about pneumonia and sulfa drugs and feed additives. I learned about the stress cattle suffered in the wind and cold, and which bulls did not get along in the same pen with which other bulls. I read about marketing and transport and the various strategies to build up a weak herd, which was what Trinket had left. I learned that cattle prices are cyclically low, ranging between low and lower, and raising cattle was more work than I wanted, because no matter how well you played the odds, there was no margin for error.

It was that winter I thought about Scott. My sister in Missouri had been having a rough time with her husband, and Scott was not the easiest kid to have around. He was in trouble at school, and maybe with the police—my sister never said exactly—and it occurred to me he might like the ranch as a change of scenery. Besides, having him come out would take some pressure off me.

"I don't know, Jack," my sister said on the phone. "He's unruly. I wouldn't wish him on anybody."

"You aren't wishing him on me. He can help."

"He won't be any help. I'll tell you that right now. I'm at the end of my rope with him. It isn't easy right now."

"Nothing is easy," I said.

"Scott used to be a good boy. But don't say I didn't warn you."

Scott wasn't so bad as my sister let on. He was more unmotivated than wild. He slept too much, didn't cut his hair, didn't eat right, and I admit he could be exasperating. Once I took him over to the San Miguel to teach him to cast flies, but he wasn't interested in fishing. He carried two cans of Coors in his creel, and after he'd drunk those, he'd gone back to the truck and listened to music on the radio.

I made him do chores, of course—mostly feeding the cattle and watching the calves. He was good with the calves. He had a gentleness that surprised me, but I wouldn't say he enjoyed even that. He minded tending the calves less than he minded other work. But he wasn't sour. He moped, but he didn't whine, and he got no pleasure from a job done well.

What he liked least was ditch work. He hated wearing the rubber boots and shoveling, checking the water, cutting back willows. He didn't like walking the ditch to see who was stealing water. But he liked to ride the dirt bike.

The phone rang. I had dozed off for a moment on the bed, and when I got my bearings I thought it must be Scott.

It was Vicky. "Is Scott there?" she asked.

"Not yet," I said. "I thought he was with you." I looked at the clock. It was a little past midnight.

"I just got back from the movies," Vicky said. "I'll bet he's with Donna. The bastard." She hung up like her mother.

I lay there for a moment with the phone in my hand. It was the kind of situation I dreaded—having to hope bad things weren't true. An accident was the first thing I thought of. The best that could happen was nothing.

Scott had been pretty good about his curfew, but not perfect. He'd missed one or two, always with some explanation or lie that I could usually live with in my own fashion. He hadn't mentioned Donna. But then Scott wasn't the kind who offered a lot of information.

I thought of calling the state patrol, but it was early for that. So what I did was I got up and put on my work boots and my dark windbreaker. There was no point in riding around the county looking for a motorcycle. I could use the time to check and see what was going on up the ditch.

There was a shovel by the door, and I got some wire cutters from the shed. Then on an impulse I went back to the house and got my .22 pistol.

It had been hot that afternoon, but at that altitude it was cold at night. I pulled the windbreaker to my throat and snapped the cuffs. The moon had risen higher, farther away it seemed, but still bright enough to see snakes on the road. I had the flashlight to read the weirs.

I went on foot and turned right on the county road. At the top of the hill I could see the arc lights of a handful of ranches up the valley. The ditch made a visible line across the contour of the land: above it was gray sage and yucca and black pinyon pine and below it were the fields of alfalfa and timothy. Farther up were the billowy cottonwoods along the creek at Pie Reynolds's house and beyond that was the arc light at the Pollards' trailer.

About a half mile up the road angled sharply higher toward the mesa, and at that point I ducked under a loose strand of barbed wire and made my way along the uphill side of the ditch.

Scott would have ridden the dirt bike farther up the road to the headgate beyond Pollards' place because it made sense to check the headgate first. Sometimes a log got jammed in the weir or someone downstream cut us all off for the sake of his own ditch. But if there was water coming in the headgate, then you had to walk down the ditch to see who was taking what. I was doing it the opposite way.

Night was the most efficient time to irrigate. It was cooler and surface water didn't evaporate so readily as when the sun was out. The wind usually slacked off. And, then, too, it was easier to steal water when everyone else was asleep.

There was no water on McCormick's property or on the adjacent land to the west. The next two lots belonged to an investor from back East who was going to build an A-frame and drink gin on his deck till his liver gave out. He didn't care about water. I walked his property, crossed a break of willows, and then came to the edge of Pie Reynolds's forty acres. There were bike tracks there, but I couldn't tell when they'd been made or who made them. Reynolds sometimes used a three-wheeler to do chores.

I listened for a minute. A semi moaned in the distance on the highway toward Montrose. The Pollards' dog barked. Then it was quiet again. I heard water trickling onto Pie Reynolds's field.

I slipped through the barbed-wire fence and walked up farther. There wasn't much water in the ditch for Reynolds to steal, but he was taking it all. I filled the holes he'd dug through the bank.

Magnussen's was next. He had second priority and usually was honest about what he took. But I felt my anger getting to me, and I shut him down, too. At the line of Magnussen's field I shined the flashlight on the weir. One foot and a fraction was coming through the cement box. There should have been three.

Just above the weir was where the Pollards had erected the new barbed-wire fence. It was six feet high and hard to climb, and strung so tightly you couldn't squeeze through. Scott bitched about the fence every time he came up the ditch, and I didn't blame him.

I cut four strands of wire and leaned through.

The Pollards had an elaborate array of underwater hoses to siphon water down under the ditch bank. I plugged the hoses with wedges of grass, tore out a board that shunted water through a cut, dammed up another diversion with dirt. I did all this quietly, trying to keep the dog from barking.

The farther I worked up the ditch, though, the madder I got. What was going to stop Pollard? I closed another hose with grass.

Finally I came over a slight rise and in sight of the trailer. Pollard's dog heard me or got my scent and started barking from the porch. It was some kind of shepherd mix, big and broad chested. It braced its legs on the top step, and its breath steamed in the air.

I circled down into the alfalfa field at the edge of the ring the arc light made and waited in the dark. I figured if I were that far away, the dog would not leave the porch. But Pollard would come out to see what the ruckus was.

And I was right. The light came on in the trailer, and then the porch light. The door opened, and Lute peered out. His dark hair and dark beard made him look, in an undershirt and loose pajama bottoms, like a crazed man blinded by light. He scanned for a moment, didn't see anything, and finally swore at the dog. The dog stopped barking. Pollard closed the door, and the light went out.

I waited another five minutes, but the light did not come on again. The dog lay down against the door where I couldn't see him. I could feel underfoot the wet earth, the mud. Water was running everywhere around me.

There was something about the way Pollard had looked, about the dog's barking that worked into me. Or maybe it was my own sneaking down into the field. I couldn't explain it exactly. Maybe it was not knowing where Scott was, or that what he'd done that afternoon had been for nothing. What we both did was for nothing. But I had to do what I'd come for.

Pollard had cut a diversion right in front of the trailer, and the moment my shovel sucked wet ground, the dog began barking again. He leaped down the steps this time into the bare yard. He could see me now, and his bark was more savage. He came on toward me, stopped, and I raised the shovel to fend him off. All the time he kept barking and snapping. I knew Pollard would be up again. I drew the pistol, and from almost point-blank range I shot the dog between the eyes. My ears rang. The dog yelped once and crumpled into the ditch where he shuddered in the water and then lay still.

Then I did something I didn't expect. Instead of running, I jumped the ditch and scrabbled up through the yard to the dark side of the trailer.

The door opened and the barrel of a shotgun protruded from behind the screen door. It was quiet now in the yard. No barking, no sounds of trucks, no airplanes. The only sound was the murmur of water flowing in the ditch.

Pollard came out slowly, barefooted, still in his undershirt and pajama bottoms. He lifted the shotgun to his shoulder. I waited until he was in the middle of the porch, a little way from the door.

"Leave it, Lute," I said. "Point the gun at the ground. Don't even look around."

"That's my dog," Lute said. He gestured with the shotgun toward the ditch.

"Was," I said. "Put the shotgun down."

He hesitated, then bent over and laid the shotgun on the wooden deck.

"Now step over toward the stairs."

He took three or four steps, turned, and shielded his eyes to look back at me. "Is that you, Lindstrom?"

I stayed in the shadow of the trailer. "Anyone else in the house?"

"No."

"Harry in there?" I aimed above his head and squeezed off a shot. "Tell him to come out."

Lute glanced at the door. "Come on out," he said.

A woman opened the door and came out in a black slip.

"Tell Harry to come out, too."

Harry followed the woman onto the porch. Harry had a dark swirl across his cheek and a gut that ballooned under a white T-shirt. He had on a pair of jockey shorts. "What're you going to do?" Harry asked me.

I didn't know what I was going to do. Nothing so far as I knew. I was going to scare them. But seeing Lute and Harry on the porch made me think these were people you couldn't scare. "I'm going to kill your daddy," I said.

"Bullshit," Harry said.

"I'm the ditch rider," I said. "You're stealing water, and I'm going to see you don't."

Harry laughed. "So who's going to stop us?"

I came out from the corner of the trailer and into the light. "The punishment is what I say it is." I held the pistol straight out with two hands. "Now I want you to step down from there."

I motioned them forward, and they all went down the steps into the dirt yard. I picked up the shotgun. There were four shells in the magazine and one in the barrel. We went down toward the ditch where Lute's dog was lying in the water.

Water had backed up behind the body and was flowing through the diversion and onto the field. I touched the woman's shoulder with the shotgun. "Get the dog out of there," I said. Then I leveled the shotgun at Harry. "Harry, I want you to go down into the field."

"What for?"

"You walk thirty yards down into the alfalfa and lie down.

You hear me? Lie down on that ground and start talking real loud so I can hear. Say 'I ain't going to steal water no more.' Say it.''

"I ain't going to steal water no more," Harry said.

"If you stop saying it, I'm going to shoot your daddy like I shot the dog."

The woman dragged the dog up onto the bank and sat down, breathing hard. She was shivering.

"Get going, Harry," I said.

Harry walked down into the alfalfa where I had been. "It's cold."

"You haven't felt cold yet," I said. "Lie down and start talking."

I held the pistol to Lute's head. That's what it took to be believed. Harry, at least, believed me. He eased himself down into the mud and started talking.

I turned to Lute. "Now pick up that shovel, Lute, and close off the water."

Lute drove the shovel into the earth, lifted out a heavy load of sod, and tamped it down into the opening. All the while the woman was muttering to herself and rubbing her arms to keep warm. Harry was yelling and moaning down in the field.

When Lute finished, I took the shovel and pushed him up the ditch toward the headgate. He walked in the water because he didn't have on shoes.

"My nephew was up here this afternoon," I said. "You see him?"

"I ain't seen him," Lute said.

"He was here."

"Maybe he was," Lute said. "So?"

Just then Harry stopped jabbering. He was crawling backwards down into the grass.

I fired a shotgun blast into the air and Lute ducked. "Keep talking, Harry," I said. "Louder."

Harry started yelling.

"What's the truth, Lute? You see him or didn't you?"

"He was up here on the motorcycle," Lute said.

"And?"

"Nothing. He cut us back."

Ahead of us the creek got louder, and I shined the light across into the willows. There was still a fair flow in the stream, and the ditch was clear. We stopped at the weir.

"How much water, Lute?" I aimed the light at the gauge just past where Lute was standing.

"Three feet," he said.

"You understand arithmetic, Lute? There's three feet coming through, and I'm supposed to get two feet at the end."

Lute didn't say anything.

"You understand that?"

"I get it," Lute said.

I knew he didn't. He got the arithmetic part, the *words* part, but not the rest of it. I wanted to explain the other part to him, but I wasn't sure how.

"I want you to kneel down," I said.

"What?"

"You heard me. I want you to kneel down right there in the water."

"You ain't going to do nothing," he said. But there was some doubt in his voice, maybe a bit of fear.

"I'm thinking of it," I said. "Kneel."

He knelt in the water. His pajama bottoms were already wet and dragging low around his waist, and when he got onto his knees they dropped lower over his ass. The water ran fast around his thighs.

"I want you to pray," I said. "I want you to pray that my nephew is safe, which he better be. And I want you to pray you're going to change yourself so I won't have to come up here another time."

Lute closed his eyes. I could see his lips moving, but he might have been swearing at me and probably was.

I turned away and walked back down the ditch. I passed the dead dog and the woman sitting numbly on the bank rubbing her shoulders and Harry who was still out in the field jabbering in the darkness. I cut the Pollards' fence down, and Pie Reynolds's fence, and I left the Pollards' shotgun stuck barrel down in one of the mounds of earth at Reynolds's property line.

Scott was at the house when I got back. The dirt bike was parked out back by the shed, its chrome fenders gleaming in the moon-light. I put the shovel and the wire cutters away. Then I stood in the yard for a few minutes and watched the moon float above the mesa. The clouds had dissipated in the cold air, and stars were everywhere around me. Music thumped from Scott's room, strong and hard against the quiet. His windowpane rattled.

I guess I felt a little crazy then. I didn't expect things would be better with Pie Reynolds or the Pollards, but they wouldn't be the same either. I felt good about that. We'd have to wait and see what happened next.

And it would not be the same for Scott. The dirt bike was easy: I'd keep the key. The curfew, the lies—those were harder. I had heard enough lies in my life, and I'd be damned if I'd hear any more from him.

The music stopped, and the light in Scott's room went out. Suddenly I could hear the cars on the highway, a hum that was not engines but tires. And from the mesa, somewhere in the trees, a coyote sang a yap and a howl that never failed to thrill me. It was as if the night had a voice. I yapped and howled back to it, grinned at myself, and went over and sat on the leather seat of the dirt bike to wait for the water to come down the ditch.

David Long

Lightning

"Ivan, he won't do it," Gretchen said from the daybed. "Believe me, he won't. He's going to let the damn place freeze. You go on up there. While he's gone."

Now that she was like this—plainly crippled, no longer solely identifiable as his mother—Ivan didn't feel the fight no much, the natural, chemical urge to dig his feet in. Ivan's wife, Phoebe, sat in the rocker by the east window, one of her fingers stuck in the massive library book she'd been reading to Gretchen. She straightened her neck and gave him a look: *Do what she's asking. How much can that hurt?*

It was mid-November. Ivan and Phoebe had been at the ranch a week by this time. No one had begged them to come, but they'd come anyway—Phoebe had talked to Gretchen on the phone, and gotten the sense, she told Ivan, that things were *this close* to coming apart. So they'd driven up, and were quartered in the log-walled room off the porch—it smelled of chinking and forgotten chenille and a desiccated Air Wick hanging from the curtain rod. Ivan had been getting up in the sharp cold each morning and going out to work alongside his father. The tools felt remote in his hands. *What am I doing here?* he kept thinking—open to evidence that his father was gratified by his company. But Perry didn't oblige. A film, a gray mood, had settled on everything. This had been the year of the fires, dry smoky winds, two thin cuttings of hay. A few dozen Angus dotted the middle pasture, as animated as glacial till. Perry had sold the herd down, Ivan saw—there'd be scarcely fifty calves in the spring.

Perry had been cooking the meals himself, and then he'd hired a woman from up the road to come in, a Mrs. Ankli whom Ivan distantly remembered, but this arrangement hadn't worked out any better. Now Phoebe had taken over the kitchen. "I'm sorry all this is getting dumped on you," Ivan said. Phoebe shrugged it off. "You sure?" he asked her. But she looked rather at peace. She threw on sweats, grabbed her hair back in a pony-tail, swamped out the worst of it, chewing on sunflower seeds, giving off bursts of tuneless humming. After lunch she tended Gretchen in the bathroom, guided her into the dayroom, fixed the flotilla of pillows. Gretchen had lost interest in the stacks of novels spilling from the shelves. "All I want is true stuff," she demanded. Phoebe drove to town the second afternoon, re-turned with boxes of groceries and a book called *Shackleton*. Gretchen inspected it and lay back. Heroism in the Antarctic, feats of lunatic endurance—it would do. She listened fiercely, not hectoring in the old way. She stared out past the blowing yard, past the fences. Across the river the lodgepole rose up, green-black and prickly, disappearing into the weather.

Which thought had led her back to John Andrew? Ivan wondered from the doorway—he'd been stopped, on his way outside, by the cadences of Phoebe's reading voice.

Gretchen's eyes bore in on him. She pressed him again,
"Take care of it, Ivan."

So Ivan took Perry's Jeep up to the hill cabin, banging over
the ruts and shale. The Jeep, too, had deteriorated. The gas pedal
had been replaced by a barn spike that caught in his boot sole.
The roof crinkled, lacquered over with duct tape. Ivan had
watched the day go from pearly to raw; a sleeting wind whipped
at the grass. The one wiper made a wan, jiggling pass across the
windshield. No one, Ivan guessed—least of all, Perry—had gone
near the hill cabin since Ivan's brother, John Andrew, had for-
saken it. Gretchen (she'd explained to Phoebe, but never directly
to Ivan) had been the only witness to his leaving. She'd been
awake one night in July, late, watching the northern lights while
Perry snored and twisted the bedclothes. Sleep came flukily,
grudgingly—she was stir-crazy, only her thoughts fatigued. So
she'd seen John Andrew's truck barrel down from the hill cabin,
headlights out, a careening, denser patch of dark, cheating across
the curve of damp lawn, clipping a corner post without stopping—and only a tap of the brake lights at the cattle guard. "That
was it," she'd told Phoebe. "That was his grand farewell. Not so
much as a horn toot."

John Andrew's own family—Gala and their two girls—had
departed early in May, as the greasy buds of the cottonwood
were finally snapping open, the low spots in the hay fields drying
and spiking green. After that, the hill cabin became a hermitage,
a welter of bad spirits. Ivan knew that in Perry's world you let a
grown man alone with his hurt, that he'd stubbornly stayed away
each morning, electing to wait for John Andrew down below,
then taking in the puffy face, the jerky drifting eyes, and not
saying any more than "You ought to not be hitting it so hard,
John." *Weren't they a pair*, Ivan thought. But Perry would shun

the place itself, as well, Ivan knew. They'd left a taint on it, Gala and John Andrew.

Ivan nudged through the back door and regarded his brother's leavings. A congealed rancid smell rose off the shredded paper trash fouling the linoleum. A windowpane was smashed out above the sink; porkies had climbed the woodpile and scraped through the hole, ransacked the counters, chewed the rubber stripping off the icebox door—it hung open, the bulb blackened.

On the Hide-A-Bed in the front room lay a sleeping bag, shucked inside out—a child's bag, grimy flannel depicting pheasants and hunters. The bedroom door was pocked with bootheel-shaped gouges. Ivan toed it open, thinking *Here will be the mother lode.* But the room was empty and unremarkable, except for dents in the carpet where bureau and bedposts had rested, and a scattering of thin cloth strips. Kneeling, Ivan found these to be the scissored remnants of a summer dress. He should run a stream of gasoline through these rooms, he thought. He should stand out in the crushed shale and feel the front of his clothes bake.

Wouldn't a little joyful noise cut loose in his soul then?

But why be that way? You don't hate John Andrew, he reminded himself. It was actually Phoebe he heard. He drew a breath. He pulled the gloves from his vest pocket, thrust his hands in, wiggled down into the crawl space and crawled. He got vise grips on the valve and shut the water off. Upstairs again, he bled the pipes, filled the toilet tank and traps with Zerex. He taped a square of masonite over the sink window, swept the miscellany into a box and carried it outside, dragged the dead fir limb from the yard, and, bending, blowing, made a fire of that much.

Standing over it, the black smoke batted by the wind, he thought, *If a story can ruin you, can a story save you?*

His brother's unwound from this exact spot, this one chunk

of sanctified earth: a grassy bench along the northwestern fence line, where Perry had gone as a ten-year-old to rain artillery down on a bend in the West Fork, where he escaped to as a young married buck, so he could smoke and ruminate and still be within eyeshot of the clamorous, red-roofed house down among the cottonwood. Perry would never have explained this in straight language. But had he not led John Andrew and his bride Gala up here one day in April, pointed out the white-flagged stakes driven into the soft grass, had he not announced that he'd decided to build them a place of their own and this was where? Ivan could see Gala drinking in this news, sparkling—she would touch Perry on his bare forearm, lightly, offering surprise, though she wouldn't be surprised, because all things flowed to Gala. And John Andrew would have his usual nothing to say, his big square face projecting a bashful, manly satisfaction—Perry's number-one son caught in a shower of blessings.

In decent weather, you could see it all from here. Zig-zagging, shaped like a child's drawing of lightning, Gretchen had once observed. (Like *which* child's? Ivan wondered.) It was river and foothills and bare-faced mountain on one side, road and government land on the other. Four old skinny homesteads wired together by Ivan's grandfather, worked since the 1950s by Perry and a succession of hands, men like Arch McPheeter—stocky, grousing old Albertan, dead of a stroke long ago now—then by the team of Perry and John Andrew, with various McKee and Santa boys at branding and haying. But the lower piece, sometimes called The Point—where the hypothetical lightning would come scorching down, a sweet caché of twenty-odd acres, out of the wind, thick with red willow and a few old cedars (Ivan had loved it dearly as a boy, felt it peculiarly his)—had become, lately, the property of an orthodontist from Buena Vista, California. He'd strung electric fence around it, erected an unseemly stone and timber gate at the road, hung a sign reading El Rancho Suzette in corny wood-burnt script. Yet no one had consulted

Ivan about this transaction. No one had explained why his father would suddenly divest himself of this parcel. Ivan had simply gone to the mail and discovered a check with a note from Perry stapled to it: *This is your part of what I got for the lower piece. I don't care what you do with it. P. W. C.*

In a proper world Perry and Gretchen would have retired to the hill cabin, settling into what Perry called "his dotage," which only meant he would sleep an hour later and pretend to take orders from John Andrew. Gretchen would spoil her grand-daughters at the Sperry Mall, now and then, and otherwise take to the cabin's sliver of loft and read herself into a state of grace. She'd be Perry's college girl again, his unexpected treasure. John Andrew and family, meantime, would assume the main house. Gala would insinuate her ownership, gradually, like a medicine time-released into the bloodstream—first the filigreed curtains would go; one by one, new avocado appliances would appear; Gretchen's words of wisdom *(If you want to cry, go in the bathroom and run the water.—E. Roosevelt)* would vanish from inside the cupboard doors, the yellowed Scotch tape effaced with a razor blade.

None of that would come to be.

In a slot in the hutch, Ivan had found the letters, addressed merely *Cook Ranch* in Gala's childish hand. *You realize there's still items John and I have to deal with, like it or not. Really, I just don't see how you can expect me to believe you don't know where he is . . .* pages of it. Ivan had folded them away, wishing he hadn't looked, wishing to remember Gala in her better days, sleek and smart mouthed, trailing a fragrance that left him in a condition of heated wonderment. Hadn't they all taken to her, even Gretchen—especially, somehow, Gretchen?

Ivan had never known precisely whose idea that union had been—John Andrew's (because Gala was the shining daughter of a surgeon in Sperry, emblem of everything he felt lesser than, having been raised out, away), or Gala's (because John Andrew was as handsome as she was, and had no nonsense in him, no waffling, and because marrying him was a rebellion, yes, but one of the right dimension and heft). Maybe they'd loved each other. Early on, at least, before it had begun to cost.

But then, what did any of this matter? Gretchen, by reason of her illness, was beyond living in the hill cabin, anyway. The tingling along her arms had become, over many months, a numbness; the numbness, a heavy dead wasting. Her shoulders curled in. Her calves were like slivers of almond.

Who could you point at, who could you blame for that?

Perry had gone to town after lunch—salve and staples to pick up at Equity, a little banking.

"Look," Ivan had offered, "let me go and do that—what do you say?"

Perry cast him a soured look. "Can't wait to kite out of here again, that it?"

"No, look, Dad—" Ivan started in, felt a hot surge of embarrassment, and let it go.

Sometime after the stock sale, before Ivan and Phoebe arrived, Perry'd taken a fall. Ivan guessed that his father had looked down through his glasses wrong and missed the step on the Farmall. But Perry refused to say. Barklike scab graced his cheekbone, and something was wrong with his hip. It surprised no one that Perry declined to have it looked at. All week, Ivan had watched him try not to gimp, seen him squeeze away the stab of pain with his left eye.

"How about stopping at the doctor's?" Ivan said.

Perry stood drinking his coffee, a sheen on his temples, his free hand balled under his arm. "No thanks," he said.

Now lights veered up the West Fork road. Ivan thought that the last thing he wanted was for his father to find him there in John Andrew's mess. But it was the Forest Service truck, not Perry's old brown LeSabre. It rumbled by, vanishing into the road cut.

The wind had dropped and the sleet had become a fine listless snow. Ivan mushed his boot around in the ashes, scattered them. Up on the pole above the turnaround, the yard light clicked on and began glowing a deep salmon. Ivan went back to the kitchen, reached in and switched it off. He climbed into the Jeep, fired the engine, and pulled eagerly on the heater knob, which gave a quarter inch, but no more.

If his brother's story spooled out from this one point, so too, did his. Picture the older boy groomed to be Perry, his fingertips dull with grease, his knuckles nicked and infected, the meat of his shoulders hard packed from bucking bales, his lips as chapped and straight lined as Perry's. Then picture the other boy, Gretchen's by unspoken default, grilled on spelling words and quadratic equations, asked to scratch thirty lines a day in a private ledger, given Peterson's bird book in his stocking, where John Andrew found shells for his Mossberg Special . . . All of that, so that Ivan would wow them in the world-at-large. When he chafed under this program enough times, Gretchen grabbed him aside, stood him back against the coat hooks in the mud-room. "I'm going to tell you something I shouldn't be telling you," she said. "Look at me." Ivan looked, chilled. "I love both of you to pieces, but you're my smart one. You've got something he won't ever have. Choices, Ivan."

Yes, a feast of choices.

The fall John Andrew married Gala, Ivan inaugurated his five-year carom shot through the university. He took Business and Society, he took Introduction to Major Religious Texts, he took Civil War Battles, Contemporary Social Problems, Soils. He ignored Perry's threats, assured Gretchen again and again that he was only a handful of credits from graduating. He thinned down, grew his hair. He tended bar, worked on a road crew out of Drummond one summer, sold fireworks, went door to door for the city directory. He missed a Thanksgiving, a Christmas. Then came four or five years when he wasn't home at all. He trailed a barmaid to Fort Collins, drifted east in the aftermath, Omaha,

Milwaukee, then up through the hardwood country along Lake Superior, taking work when he found it, quitting without rancor a few weeks or months later. He would just not go in one morning—there would be nothing special about that day, no gripe or grinding hangover or anything to glorify as wanderlust. He'd just feel vaguely, sickeningly, lost—as though he'd worn out his welcome.

The first time he saw Phoebe, she was at a round formica table in the rear of the Ashland, Wisconsin, public library. She was teaching an older man in blue coveralls to read. Ivan couldn't say why he waited, why he followed her out onto Vaughn Avenue and down to the Finnish bakery, and stood watching her clutch the white sack of limpa bread to her chest—except that he'd already fallen in love. Compared to Gala, she was big and plain. Her hair hung. She had thick wrists and skin that blotched at the slightest irritation. It was idiotic. Yet, as near as he could pinpoint such a thing, his attraction had begun the moment he'd seen the man in coveralls shut his book, push his chair back, and say, with a shy bow, "Thank you again, miss."

And what words had rushed from Ivan's mouth so that Phoebe seated herself with him, in one of the booths across from the glass counters, accepting the first cup of coffee? How was it he'd managed to be right about her? "You were dazzled by my inner beauty," Phoebe kidded him whenever the subject arose.

"Uh huh," Ivan answered. "That's what it was." But the memory terrified him. How can you trust yourself? How do you know to leap?

Lights came on outside the main house. Ivan ground the tires in the pea gravel and let the engine die. No, he did not hate his brother. They were too different for hatred, too ignorant of each other. John Andrew had been almost heedless of Ivan, hell-bent on becoming the man he was supposed to become. Nothing of Ivan's could speed that along, so nothing was worth coveting. Ivan, for his part, had fixed his eyes on John Andrew, year after year—he knew how his brother looked with a milk glass tipped to his mouth, or what he'd say when he stabbed his feet into cold boots. Ivan could see as little as one wrist, fly casting, and know it was John Andrew's. But that was all he knew—he'd simply memorized John Andrew, the way he'd memorized the lay of the mountains, the quirks of the river.

How weird it was, Ivan thought, climbing out, that John Andrew should take his place as the absent son.

Perry still wasn't back. Nonetheless it was dinner time, and Gretchen was seated at the big table. Sara Dog, the asthmatic setter John Andrew had left behind, was working a path between the kitchen and the buffet, her nails clitter-clattering on the linoleum, then muffling disconcertingly when she hit the rug. Phoebe had tried a curry recipe—the pot had bubbled on low heat all afternoon. She'd put out glass dishes of coconut and peanuts and chopped eggs. She sat, finally, her ears flushed, a fine mist on her cheeks.

Having waited, Gretchen lifted a forkful to her lips, winced, but found it blander than she'd expected.

"What were you burning?" she asked Ivan.

How did she miss nothing, even now? He looked across at her—her hair was cut like a helmet, the color of galvanized nails. Though she'd been out of the sun for months her skin stayed olivy, buffed-looking. Rills of eerie green vein branched across the backs of her hands.

"I just took care of it," Ivan said. "Isn't that what you wanted?"

His mother frowned, paused. "He was gone before he left," she said finally. "One night the two of them were outside at the table after supper, taking coffee, your father and John Andrew. Your brother had the white mug with the broken handle."

Despite himself, Ivan pictured it: the plank boards gone mealy with weather, the green-gold light splashing through the cottonwood leaves.

"They wouldn't look at each other. John Andrew had his hat off. He kept dragging his fingers over his scalp. Your father sat there rubbing his calluses."

She wasn't so much talking as reciting; Ivan knew enough not to interfere. "Your father got up and started for the Quonset, but then he stopped and came over behind John Andrew and talked straight into his back. Then he left, and John Andrew didn't so much as take a breath until your father was out of sight, then . . ."

She turned her head in that way she had now, squeezing a cough from her throat. "Then looked after him—it was an awful, raw look, Ivan. Like the earth had been cut into. Then he dragged himself back up to the hill cabin again and there was only the mug sitting there on the table."

Another cough, two fingers pressed to her mouth. "It's still there. Right outside the window, Ivan. For a while, I couldn't look at it without thinking, John Andrew took that cup down from his lips."

"Oh now, Gretchen . . ." Phoebe said.

"But you detach yourself," Gretchen went on. "You see things as they are. A cup sits out in the rain, it catches water. That's what you see."

She looked sharply out toward the kitchen where Sara Dog was wheezing and circling. "Lord, will you put her out," she told Ivan.

Ivan rose.

At the door, the dog swept through his legs, skidded on the glazed incline of Gretchen's ramp, and was gone. Ivan took a few steps out into the empty drive. He found himself breathing a downdraft of wood smoke, staring up toward the bench where the hill cabin no longer floated in its pool of chemical light.

Back at the table, he saw Phoebe glance over at Gretchen's mostly untouched plate.

"How'd you like some egg custard, Gretchen?" she asked. "I

thawed out some raspberries. You don't mind, I hope."

Gretchen gave her daughter-in-law a puzzled, shaken look. Which, in turn, shook Ivan. When the two women were off in the dayroom, he thought, they seemed intimate—traffickers in state secrets. Now Gretchen looked as though she couldn't quite place this woman who'd been rummaging in her freezer.

"But we didn't pick this year," she said, and was quiet.

Ivan didn't know what to say.

Phoebe, finally, asked: "Do you think we ought to see about Perry?"

Gretchen raised herself, imperial again. "He'll take care of himself," she said. "He's perfectly capable."

Ivan felt a slipping, a little crackle of fear. "Has he been going out like this? Has . . ."

Gretchen stared.

OK, *then*, Ivan thought. *What do I know about any of this?*

He shoved his chair back, feeling Gretchen's eyes still trained on him, as if he were an object to study with an empty mind. A cup with a broken handle, collecting rain.

But an hour elapsed, and another. Sometime in the recent past, a satellite dish had been installed—it stood out in the grass by the pumphouse, aimed up toward the mouth of the valley. (Ivan and John Andrew had been raised on the one weak signal that straggled in from Sperry. Ivan had felt perennially out of it at school—"We don't get that," he was always saying.) Now Gretchen was tucked under her afghan, watching a show about the Amazon. A toothy native man was showing off an eighty-pound nugget of gold that God had allowed him to dig from the ground. Gretchen sat steely eyed, her lips like rinds. But every minute or so her gaze veered up to the mantel clock.

Ivan couldn't bear it finally. He grabbed a coat from the mudroom and bolted out to the car—once outdoors, he realized, rooting madly in his pockets, that he only had keys for the Jeep.

But rather than go back, he slid in and pumped the nail sticking up through the floorboard. He backed around by the nine-bark, rattled out through the main gate, and followed the river in the direction of town. The headlights were caked with gumbo and issued barely more than a glow. He kept it floored anyway, hammering over the washboard, through puddles of wet flattened leaves. Wasn't this asinine, to be out like this, his heart stuttering? What did he expect to find, ominous tracks shooting off the embankment? His fingers were freezing, the rims of his ears. He knew this place, knew it the way he knew every old thought in his head. But it felt immensely foreign and chastening tonight, and Perry seemed the most inscrutable thing in it.

He slowed to a crawl, bumped onto a stretch of crumbled blacktop that announced the little settlement of Mullan's Crossing. The mercantile sat tall-fronted at the end of the road, flanked by cabins—dark as slabs of granite. Next door, at Reuben's chimney, smoke bent off toward the clouds.

Perry's car was nowhere in sight, but Ivan walked up onto the flat porch and squinted through the fogged glass anyway. He saw, as he'd let himself hope, that Terri McKee was behind the bar. She was lost in a tattered paperback—one customer was asleep on his forearms, two others were throwing darts in back. No one he knew, he thought—and why should he anymore?

He let himself in.

Terri's head lifted—she recognized him instantly, came and flung her arms around his neck. "Ivan!"

Her hair was red, voluminously frizzed, but going to gray, seized up in two beaded barrettes. But she was still a skinny Minnie, Ivan saw— if he looked any longer, he might decide she couldn't keep any weight on. She and Ivan were old allies, fellow sufferers of the endless bus ride down the West Fork road. One spring they'd stolen a day to run the river, and their raft had dumped them into the roiling water at a narrowing called Sculley's Bend. Freezing, his chest heaving, Ivan found himself on the silted rocks, hugging Terri, kissing her face and eyes, her cold, freckled neck, holding her fiercely. It was their joke later, this sudden passion of Ivan's. It was their one kiss. "It's OK," Terri had told him. "You were just amazed you were alive."

Like John Andrew she'd married straight out of high school—eighteen months later, her husband had tripped a wire, walking patrol near An Loc.

Ivan pulled away. "You haven't seen my father?" he asked her.

"He was in here," Terri said. "You didn't pass him?"

Ivan felt a punch of relief, which immediately churned over into resentment.

"What'd he do to himself?" she asked.

"That?" Ivan said. "Fell."

"I mean he looked kind of . . ."

"I know."

Ivan unsnapped the jacket, which, he realized, was an old one of John Andrew's. It even smelled like him, like solvent or smoke.

"My dad didn't say I was home?" Ivan said.

Terri shook her head. "Not a word. You're the sweetest surprise."

Ivan looked at her. *Imagine being a sweet surprise*, he thought.

"Ivan," Terri said. "Sit, huh?" She gave his hand a pat. "I can't believe I almost missed you. We don't stay open winters anymore." She'd married Leo Leveque a few years ago, Ivan remembered, and he remembered this Leo, last son of the original Reuben—jowly, sad-looking, barely younger than Perry.

One of the men called from the back, but Terri ignored him. "We go down to see his daughters," she told Ivan. "I don't miss it up here. But then I do. Can't wait to get out, then I go kind of crazy."

She reached around to pour him a shot, hesitated. "Oh, hon, what was it you liked?" she said.

"Anything's fine," Ivan said.

She leaned in. "How's your girl. You still in love—?"

Ivan flushed, sat finally, letting the relief he felt come ahead. "Lucky boy."

Ivan raced past the orthodontist's padlocked gate, drew alongside Perry's fence. Off in the dark, higher up, a stab of yellow caught his eye, then was gone.

Ivan braked and swung onto the property, drove through the turnaround by the main house, and took the hill, his lights bouncing, dinging off the rocks and blowing weeds. He found his father's car, angled into the firs with its door open. Ivan shut it gently, and called out—"Dad?"

Off in back, by John Andrew's shed, he heard a plastic tarp crackling. He walked clear around the cabin, looking, and finally went inside, through the same door he'd locked that afternoon. He found Perry sitting on the Hide-A-Bed, smoking, his back to the doorway.

"It's me," Ivan said.

Perry made the springs creak, getting the weight off his bad hip. "Leave the lights out," he said.

"What's going on?" Ivan asked.

"She send you out prowling?"

Ivan didn't answer, but approached, waiting for the logic of this business to dawn on him. He could hear Perry's gravelly breathing, but not quite see how his eyes were.

"Why'd you sell that piece?" Ivan heard himself ask. It had not been on his mind to get into that, but there it was.

"What do you care?" Perry said.

Ivan would not say *Jesus, I care.* You did not have to say things like that.

Perry rolled his shoulders heavily, shifting the weight again, stifling a grunt.

"You taking anything for that?" Ivan said.

Perry mashed the cigarette into the jar lid in his other hand. He appeared to nod.

"That a yes or no?"

"Ivan," Perry said. "You want something to drink?"

"There's nothing."

But Perry said: "The deep freeze."

So Ivan returned to the kitchen, smelling the Pine Sol he'd used on the countertops, and found a half-full bottle of vodka among the bags of shredded zucchini and freezer-burnt chicken parts Gala had left behind. He popped a paper cup from the dispenser by the sink, then another.

Perry drank off the inch or so Ivan gave him and thrust out his cup for a refill. Ivan balked, but went ahead. He squatted to set the icy bottle on the floor. Perry lunged and grabbed a handful of sleeve, jerking Ivan's face down next to his own. "Where's he gone to?" Perry demanded. "Try and tell me you don't know."

"You're crazy," Ivan said, shaking free. "You think I've been sitting on that all week?" He felt himself careening. "You think he'd ever tell me anything? He didn't tell me a shitting thing."

"Don't talk that way," Perry said, but his heart wasn't in it.

Ivan went on, a notch softer. "I'm just stating a fact. I'm the last one he'd come to."

Perry made a move to stand—without thinking, Ivan reached in to help, but Perry was past him and into the kitchen, rocking on the sides of his heels.

"I ought to burn all this," his father said.

Ivan had to laugh. "That was my thought," he said.

"It was you been in here?"

"I just picked it up some."

"I guess to Christ you must have."

"Let's just close it up again and go down," Ivan offered.

But Perry cleared his throat violently and spat into the sink.

"You don't know what a black day it was he laid eyes on that girl," he said.

Ivan fished around in the shadow, found the back of a chair, and sat. Perry's voice came at him through the dark—he pictured, for a moment, that scene his mother had described—Perry talking at the flat of John Andrew's back. "She got all she wanted," Perry said, "then she didn't want it. What kind of way is that? I don't blame her for getting itchy. You feel what you feel. You think your mother never got an itch. For God's sake, think how she feels now . . . can't hardly stand up. No, Ivan, I blame her for spoiling all this for him. She made him hate it. After that everything he laid his eyes on was dead for him."

Overhead, fir boughs scraped on the ribs of the tin roof. Ivan thought of John Andrew drinking in the kitchen here and wondering who in hell he was anymore, every noise acute as a needle shaft—and then the shame and panic that must have come as he understood that despite its buildup of history, his life hadn't ever begun, not really. And Gala, too, before that, killing time in her own fashion, watching the girls, resigned, waiting for something, which turned out to be nothing more momentous than the onset of fair weather. None of it was a mystery, just what happens.

Ivan let the dog in. The TV was off, the fire reduced to dull coals. The dog sniffed along the sofa, curled, and settled on her grungy pad by the wood box, wheezing. Ivan opened the icebox and stared into it, wondering if he was hungry, then let the door drift closed. What he wanted was to be with Phoebe, lying down with his clothes off, rescued from thought. Still he stopped and detoured up the stairs.

He tapped at his mother's door, leaned in. She was in a flannel gown, a dense plaid, buoyed by pillows.

"Don't run off," she said.

Ivan edged in. He'd not been in their bedroom in years. He

got as far as the foot of the bed, stood palming the bedpost, old walnut scored like a pineapple.

"He's sitting up there at the hill cabin in the pitch dark," Ivan said.

Gretchen nodded without surprise.

Ivan wanted to say *I know how you miss John Andrew*, but feared her face would snap to life: *No, you don't, how could you possibly know . . . ?*

But she said, softly, "Ivan, could you rub my feet?"

He didn't want to touch her. Yet, he pulled up the quilt—her feet were encased in pale pink socks specked with shamrocks. He sank gingerly to the edge of the comforter and began to knead, his thumbs on the soles, which seemed to radiate cold, even through the fabric.

In a moment his mother said: "I thought, at first, maybe he'll call Ivan."

"John Andrew? You honestly thought . . ."

"No, no. I know he didn't."

"He never let loose of anything," Ivan said.

Gretchen seemed to smile. "That's so," she said. "Let me tell you what he did," she went on, after a while. "Your father, I mean. He saw how it was all going wrong up there. He thought if John Andrew's money wasn't all tied up with ours, if he didn't have to wait for it. He thought if Gala had a place in town she'd be all right again—she could have that life and John Andrew could still do what he had to do, you see. Then that dentist had been pestering everyone up the road to sell him something on the river. So your father surveyed off that lower piece and cashed it out. I thought it would kill him. I thought it was the last thing on this earth he'd do."

Ivan stared at her.

"But then it didn't change a thing. It didn't make the slightest difference." She moistened her lips. "He thought he could stop the bleeding—that's how he talked about it. But you can't. I told him."

Ivan let his hands relax for a second. But she was right there: "No, Ivan, keep doing that. *Please.*"

"I feel so . . ." Ivan started to say, but let it go, and began rubbing again. Soon Gretchen's eyes fell closed.

Wind rattled the glass. His father had salvaged this bank of windows from a schoolhouse up the draw. Ivan remembered lifting them off the back of the truck, Perry on one side, himself and John Andrew on the other—hoisting them up to the new gabled room with ropes. Perry was smiling, clenching his ciga-rette in his teeth. Gretchen was up here, where the bed was now, watching, looking down at them, one summer's day.

"They come back on their own sometimes," Ivan said, but she was asleep.

Ivan woke before dawn. Phoebe lay on her back, one hand cupped at her throat. Ivan touched the place on the flannel where her breast was and felt the nipple work its miracle. He found her ear in the muss of hair and whispered into it: "I love you, love you." Her hand slid down his cheek. Ivan swung his feet onto the rag rug and dressed.

The house was quiet. Lacing his boots, out in the kitchen, he saw that the brown Buick had been parked behind the Jeep—so Perry would be upstairs, consigned to sleep, with Gretchen tak-ing up her little space beside him.

He set up the coffee maker, located an old sweater and jacket on a peg in the mudroom, and went outside.

A sheen lay on the fence rails, a wrinkle of ice on the stock pond, broken by a pair of gliding mallards. Ivan walked down to the hay barn and flipped on the floodlight. He found gloves that Perry had wedged in the crotch of the timbers and shook them out.

If there was an off-season, this was it. In a month they'd be kicking bales off the trailer, auguring holes in the ponds. And, in another eight weeks, calves.

Ivan noticed that Perry had cut down the rope he and John

Andrew had swung on, but a shiny groove still showed on the rafter. He smiled, and let the memory fall away.

An orange cat appeared between the bales. It jumped down and circled Ivan, rubbing hard against his legs.

ABOUT THE AUTHORS

LEE K. ABBOTT is the author of five collections of stories, the most recent of which is *Living After Midnight* (Putnam, 1991). His work has appeared in *The Best American Short Stories*, the *Pushcart Prize* anthology, the *O. Henry Prize Stories*, and *Editor's Choice*. Twice a recipient of fellowships in fiction from the National Endowment for the Arts, he is Professor of English at Ohio State University.

CATHRYN ALPERT's fiction has appeared in anthologies and magazines, including the 1989 and 1991 volumes of *The O. Henry Festival Stories*, *Zyzzyva*, *The Amaranth Review*, and *Puerto del Sol*. Formerly a professor of theater at Centre College in Kentucky, she now lives in northern California with her husband and two sons and devotes herself to writing fiction. "Alamogordo" is the first story in her novel-in-progress, *Rocket City*, set in New Mexico.

ALISON BAKER's short stories have appeared in *The Atlantic Monthly*, *The Ontario Review*, *The Threepenny Review*, *Ascent*, *The Kenyon Review*, and other magazines. Raised a Hoosier on the banks of Sugar Creek, in recent years she's been drawn ever westward by an irresistible force—from Seal Cove, Maine, to Salt Lake City, Utah, and at last to the edge of the Rogue River, in southwestern Oregon, which is about as far as she's willing to go.

RON CARLSON's most recent collection of stories, *Plan B for the Middle Class*, was published this year by W. W. Norton. He is also the author of *The News of the World* (stories) and two novels.

His fiction has appeared in *The New Yorker*, *Playboy*, *GQ*, and *Story*, and his story "Phenomena" was included in the first volume of *The Best of the West* (1988). He lives with his family in Tempe, Arizona, where he is the director of the creative writing program at Arizona State University.

SUSAN GAINES's stories have appeared in *The North American Review* and *The Missouri Review*, and she has completed a novel entitled *The Buffalo Farm*. She is at work on a second novel in which use is made of her long-forsaken graduate studies in chemistry and oceanography. She lives in northern California and works on a small farm and fruit-tree nursery.

FRANCES STOKES HOEKSTRA is an assistant professor of French at Haverford College in Haverford, Pennsylvania. Her stories have been published in *The Virginia Quarterly Review*, *The Southern Review*, and *The Black Warrior Review*. Of this story she writes, "The sentence '*Your mother is my kind of woman*' was said to me by a cowboy when I was twelve and I was astonished for days. Not always can one pinpoint with such precision the exact moment your mother ceases to be 'just' your mother."

WILLIAM KITTREDGE is a Westerner both by birth and by inclination. His most recent book, *Hole in the Sky*, a memoir, was published in 1992 by Alfred A. Knopf. A collection of his essays, *Owning it All*, was published in 1987. His two volumes of short stories are *We Are Not in This Together* and *The Van Gogh Fields*. He lives in Missoula where he teaches fiction writing at the University of Montana.

DAVID LONG was raised in rural Massachusetts and migrated to Montana in the fall of 1972. He is the author of two collections, *Home Fires* and *The Flood of '64*. His most recent stories have appeared in *The New Yorker* and *Story*; "Blue Spruce," from his collection-in-progress, is included in the 1992 O. *Henry Prize Stories.* "Home Fires" was featured in the first volume of *The Best of the West* (1988). He lives in Kalispell with his longtime companion and their two sons, Montana and Jackson.

TOM MCNEAL has published fiction in *The Atlantic, Carolina Quarterly, Epoch, Playboy, Quarterly West, Redbook,* and several anthologies. He has taught English in Hay Springs High School in northwest Nebraska and creative writing at Stanford University. He presently works as a partner in a construction firm in California and lives near Lake Arrowhead with his dogs, Dougal and Willie.

MARY MORRIS is the author of six books—two novels, two collections of short stories, and two travel memoirs. Her first story collection, *Vanishing Animals & Other Stories,* was awarded the Rome Prize in Literature from the American Academy and Institute of Arts & Letters. Her second collection, *The Bus of Dreams,* was awarded the Friends of American Writers' Award for midwestern writing. She has been the recipient of Guggenheim and National Endowment for the Arts fellowships and a Creative Arts Public Service Award. Her short story "Slice of Life" was a winner in the PEN Syndicated Fiction Project and presented at the Library of Congress. She teaches in the creative-writing program at Princeton University.

KENT NELSON grew up in Colorado and for three years was the city judge in Ouray, a small town in the San Juan Mountains. He has worked as a reporter, travel agent, squash coach, college professor, and ranch hand. His awards include two National Endowment for the Arts grants and an Ingram-Merrill fellowship. More than eighty of his stories have been published in literary magazines and anthologies. His most recent books are *Language in the Blood,* a novel, and *The Middle of Nowhere,* stories, published simultaneously in 1991 by Gibbs M. Smith, Peregrine Smith Books.

VINCE PASSARO's fiction, literary criticism, essays, and journalism have appeared in *Harper's Magazine, Esquire, The New York Times Magazine, 7 Days, Spy, Mirabella, Story*, and other places. He lives in New York City with his wife, three children, and pets, making an insufficient living as a regular book critic for *Newsday* and teaching English and creative writing at Hofstra University.

ANNICK SMITH is a writer and sometimes filmmaker who lives in the Blackfoot Valley of western Montana. She produced the feature film *Heartland* about pioneer life on the Great Plains and helped to develop Robert Redford's forthcoming film version of Norman Maclean's *A River Runs Through It*. Smith was coeditor with William Kittredge of the Montana anthology *The Last Best Place*, and her essays have appeared in *Outside* and other magazines. "It's Come to This" is her first published fiction.

THOM TAMMARO's chapbook *Minnesota Suite* was published by Spoon River Poetry Press in 1988. His poems have appeared in *South Dakota Review, Midwest Quarterly*, and *North Dakota Review*. He has edited several anthologies, including *Common Ground: A Gathering of Poems on Rural Life* (Dakota Territory Press, 1988). He teaches at Moorhead State College in Minnesota.

CHRISTOPHER TILGHMAN is the author of *In a Father's Place*, a collection of stories published by Farrar, Straus & Giroux in 1990. His fiction has been widely published and anthologized (including in *Best American Short Stories*), and his story "Hole in the Day" was included in *The Best of the West 3*. He lives in Massachusetts with his wife and two sons and sometimes teaches fiction writing at Emerson College.

EVAN WILLIAMS holds a bachelor's degree in history from Colorado College and an M.F.A. from the University of Montana. His stories have appeared in *Northwest Review, North Country, Kinnikinnik*, and other magazines. *The Woman Who Was Wakan*, a collection of stories set on the Crow Indian reservation, won the University of Montana's Merriam Frontier Award and is published as a chapbook. He lives in Portland, Oregon.

DWIGHT YATES, a native of Montana, has twice made the mistake of leaving that state. His stories have appeared in a number of literary magazines including *Northwest Review, Zyzzyva, Quarry West, Puerto del Sol, Sonora Review, Western Humanities Review*, and *Quarterly West*. He grows oranges and raises children in Redlands, California, and teaches at the University of California at Riverside.

OTHER NOTABLE
WESTERN STORIES OF 1991

Sherman Alexie
from "The Native American
Broadcasting Storm"
Zyzzyva, Summer

Phyllis Barber
"At the Talent Show"
The Missouri Review, XIV:1

Sara Burnaby
"Bear"
Story, Autumn

Sandra Cisneros
"My Lucy Friend Who Smells
Like Corn"
Story, Spring

L. D. Clark
"Ghost Town"
RE:AL, Spring

William deBuys
"Dreaming Geronimo"
Story, Summer

Catherine de Cuir
"The High Altitude
Cookbook"
Sun Dog, 10:2 1990

Rick DeMarinis
"Paraiso: An Elegy"
Georgia Review, Winter 1990

Rick DeMarinis
"Wilderness"
Epoch, 40:2

Annie Dillard
"A Trip to the Mountains"
Harper's Magazine, August

Pete Fromm
"Bone Yard"
Crosscurrents, 9:4

William Geyer
"Overburden"
High Plains Literary Review,
Winter

Dagoberto Gilb
"The Death Mask of Pancho
Villa"
American Short Fiction, Spring

Katharine Haake
"Willow, Split Willow"
Iowa Review, 21:2

Elizabeth Harris
"Hybrid Wolfdogs"
Kansas Quarterly, 22:1 and 2,
1990

Patricia Henley
"Same Old Big Magic"
Ploughshares, 16:4, 1990

Pam Houston
"Highwater"
The Gettysburg Review, Winter

Jerrie W. Hurd
"Sam Talkingbird"
Kansas Quarterly, 22:3

Jeff B. Jackson
"Sequoia"
American Short Fiction, Spring

Mary Farr Jordan
"Brownsville"
Crosscurrents, 9:4

Arthur Winfield Knight
"The Death of Doc Holliday"
The Pittsburgh Quarterly, 2

David Long
"Attraction"
The New Yorker, December 9

David Long
"Talons"
Cutbank, 36

Greg Luthi
"God's Country"
Writers' Forum, 17

William Matthews
"Doc Holliday's Grave"
Alaska Quarterly Review, Fall
and Winter

Kristen Meek
"An Arizona Town"
Alaska Quarterly Review, Fall
and Winter

Kent Meyers
"Rattlesnake"
Quarterly West, 32

Kent Meyers
"Recruiting the Dead"
New England Review, 13:1, Fall
1990

Elizabeth Moore
"Destination"
Puerto del Sol, Summer

Antonya Nelson
"Fair Hunt"
The Southern Review, Autumn

Antonya Nelson
"The Facts of Air"
North American Review,
September-October-
November

Kent Nelson
"The Back Yard"
Boulevard, Fall 1990

Blair Oliver
"An Easy Thing to
Remember"
Cutbank, 36

Melissa Pritchard
"El Ojito del Muerto, Eye of
the Dead One"
The Southern Review, Autumn

Clay Reynolds
"Etta's Pond"
Writers' Forum, 17

Miles Richardson
"There Ain't That Much
Difference"
American Literary Review, Fall

Nancy Roberts
"The Importance of Birds"
Alaska Quarterly Review,
Spring and Summer

Deborah Slosberg
"Desert Landscapes"
Calyx, Winter

Darrell Spencer
"Let Me Tell You What
Ward DiPino Tells Me at
Work"
Epoch, 40:1

Darrell Spencer
"The Glue that Binds Us"
Cimarron Review, 94

Darrell Spencer
"Union Business"
Prairie Schooner, Spring

Marly Swick
"The Shadow of the Cross"
Atlantic Monthly, January

Donley Watt
"The Man Who Talked to
Houses"
Cutbank, 35

Allen Wier
"Bastard"
*Contemporary Southern Short
Fiction: A Sampler, The Texas
Review*, Fall/Winter 1990

Nancy Van Winckel
"After My Heart"
Zyzzyva, Fall

Christopher Woods
"Chimayo"
Crosscurrents, 9:4

Marcia Wunsch
"The Deception"
TriQuarterly, 81

MAGAZINES CONSULTED

We regularly receive the following magazines, and consider the stories in them for *The Best of the West*.

Alaska Quarterly Review • Amelia • American Literary Review • American Short Fiction • The American Voice • Another Chicago Magazine • Antaeus • The Antioch Review • Artful Dodge • Ascent • The Atlantic • Aura Literary/Arts Review • Bellowing Ark • Black Warrior Review • Blue Mesa Review • Brown Journal of the Arts • Buffalo Spree • California Quarterly • Calyx • Canadian Fiction Magazine • The Capilano Review • Carolina Quarterly • The Charitan Review • Chicago Review • Chiron Review • Cimarron Review • City Lights Review • Clerestory • Clockwatch Review • Colorado Review • Columbia: A Magazine of Poetry and Prose • Conjunctions • Crazyhorse • The Crescent Review • Crosscurrents, a Quarterly • CutBank • Denver Quarterly • Descant • Epoch • Esquire • Event • The Fiction Review • The Florida Review • Four Quarters • Gambit • Gargoyle • Gentlemen's Quarterly • The Gettysburg Review • Grain • Grand Street • Gray's Sporting Journal • Great River Review • The Greensboro Review • Harper's • Hawaii Review • Hayden's Ferry Review • High Plains Literary Review • The Hudson Review • Indiana Review • The Iowa Review • The Journal • Kansas Quarterly • The Kenyon Review • The Literary Review • McCall's • The MacGuffin • Mademoiselle • The Madison Review • The Malahat Review • Manoa • The Massachusetts Review • Mid-American Review • The Minnesota Review • Mississippi Review • The Missouri Review • The Montana Review • The Nebraska Review • New England Review • New Letters • New Mexico Humanities Review • New Orleans Review • The New Quarterly • The New Yorker • Nexus • North American Review • North Dakota Quarterly • Northern Lights • The Northern Review • Northridge Review • Northwest Review • The Ohio Review • Old Hickory Review • Ontario Review • Other Voices • Oxford Review • The Paris Review • Partisan Review • Passages North • Playboy •

Ploughshares • Portland Review • Prairie Schooner • Prism International • Puerto del Sol • Quarry • Quarry West • The Quarterly • Quarterly West • RE:AL • Redbook • River's Edge • River Styx • Room of One's Own • The Seattle Review • The Sewanee Review • Shenandoah • Sonora Review • The South Carolina Review • South Dakota Review • The Southern Review • Southwest Review • Sou'w-ester • Special Report • Stories • Story • Storyquarterly • Sundog: the Southeast Review • Taos Review • The Texas Review • Threepenny Review • TriQuarterly • The Virginia Quarterly Review • Webster Review • West Branch • Western Humanities Review • Willow Springs • Wind • Witness • Writers' Forum • The Yale Review • Yellow Silk • Zyzzyva

ACKNOWLEDGMENTS

"Getting Even" © 1991 by Lee K. Abbott. First published in *Southwest Review*. Reprinted by permission of the author.

"Alamogordo" © 1991 by Cathryn Alpert. First published in *Puerto del Sol*. Reprinted by permission of the author.

"How I Came West, and Why I Stayed" © 1991 by Alison Baker. First published in *The Atlantic*. Reprinted by permission of the author.

"DeRay" © 1990, 1991 by Ron Carlson. First published in *Gentlemen's Quarterly*. Reprinted by permission of the author.

"The Mouse" © 1991 by Susan M. Gaines. First published in *The Missouri Review*. Reprinted by permission of the author.

"One-Eyed Jacks" © 1991 by Frances Stokes Hoekstra. First published in *Virginia Quarterly Review*. Reprinted by permission of the author.

"Lightning" © 1991 by David Long. First published in *The Sewanee Review*. Reprinted by permission of the author.

"What Happened to Tully" © 1991 by Tom McNeal. First published in *The Atlantic*. Reprinted by permission of the author.

"Around the World" © 1991 by Mary Morris. First published in *Crosscurrents*. Reprinted by permission of the author.

"The Ditch Rider" © 1991 by Kent Nelson. First published in "Shenandoah. Reprinted by permission of the author.

"Utah" © 1991 by Vince Passaro. First published in *Story*. Reprinted by permission of the author.

"It's Come to This" © 1991 by Annick Smith. First published in *Story*. Reprinted by permission of the author.

"The Way People Run" © 1991 by Christopher Tilghman. First published in *The New Yorker*. Reprinted by permission of the author.

"The Lake District" © 1991 by Evan Williams. First published in *Northwest Review*. Reprinted by permission of the author.

"Painted Pony" © 1991 by Dwight Yates. First published in *Quarterly West*. Reprinted by permission of the author.